A man

Some say he is ~~~~~~~~~~~~ others say he is mad. None of them know the truth about Marshall Ross, the Devil of Ambrose. He shuns proper society, sworn to let no one discover his terrible secret, including the beautiful woman he has chosen to be his wife.

A fallen woman

Only desperation could bring Davina McLaren to the legendary Edinburgh castle to become the bride of a man she has never met. Plagued by scandal, left with no choices, she has made her bargain with the devil. And now she must share his bed.

A fire unlike any they've ever known

From the moment they meet, Davina and Marshall are rocked by an unexpected desire that only leaves them yearning for more. But the pleasures of the marriage bed cannot protect them from the sins of the past. With an enemy of Marshall's drawing ever closer and everything they now cherish most at stake, he and Davina must fight to protect the passion they cannot deny.

THE DEVIL WEARS TARTAN

KAREN RANNEY

An Avon Romantic Treasure

AVON
An Imprint of HarperCollinsPublishers

AVON BOOKS
An Imprint of HarperCollins*Publishers*
10 East 53rd Street
New York, New York 10022-5299

Copyright © 2008 by Karen Ranney
ISBN 978-0-06-125242-6
www.avonromance.com

First Avon Books paperback printing: September 2008

Avon Trademark Reg. U.S. Pat. Off. and in Other Countries, Marca Registrada, Hecho en U.S.A.
HarperCollins® is a registered trademark of HarperCollins Publishers.

Printed in the U.S.A.

10 9 8 7 6 5 4 3 2 1

I've been privileged to have known—and worked with—some great women in publishing. To each one of you—and you know who you are—thank you for everything.

THE DEVIL WEARS TARTAN

Chapter 1

1870
Edinburgh, Scotland

The wedding day was fine and clear. A brilliant Scottish blue sky hovered over Edinburgh. The breeze was warm; the air carried the freshness of spring. There was silence in the square; no raucous noise disturbed the serenity of this most fortuitous of mornings. Even the sun shone brightly in approval for the nuptials of the Earl of Lorne and Miss Davina McLaren.

The bride stood at the window surveying the morning. Her predominant emotion was neither anticipation nor fear. Davina McLaren was supremely irritated.

Her aunt, the woman who'd orchestrated this fiasco of a marriage, had been absent for the last three days. Just when the furor of dressmakers was at its most unbearable, Theresa took a train to London. Just when Davina could have used some womanly advice, her aunt was unaccountably gone. Finally, Theresa had arrived home late last night, claiming exhaustion, and promising explanations in the morning.

But that was not the greatest source of Davina's annoyance. She'd not yet met her bridegroom. In this modern day, she was being treated with no more regard than a piece of furniture. *Would you like that chair, Your Lordship? We've had it in the family for a number of years, but it's yours if you like.*

How very annoying.

None of her female acquaintances had been married in a similar fashion. Every single one of them had known her husband, either because they'd been acquainted for years or the bride's parents had made an effort to involve the bride in decisions about her own future.

But then, most of her acquaintances had been forbidden to talk to her in the last year.

Had she been invited to any balls, dinners, or other entertainments, would she have been able to pick her soon-to-be-husband out of a crowded room? Or was it true that he was a hermit? What a pair they were. She, who had been forbidden society's company, and the Earl of Lorne, who shunned it willingly.

Should she look for a man with the devil's looks? What had he done to be labeled with such a nickname? The Devil of Ambrose. He'd have black hair, no doubt. And piercing black eyes, perhaps. Would he have an evil smile? A large nose and a pointed chin? His ears would probably stick out at an angle, and be pointed at the top.

She could only imagine what their children might look like. Children. Dear Lord, children. Tonight, her wedding night, she was supposed to undress in the presence of a stranger and allow him to do *that* to her.

Thanks to Alisdair and her own foolishness, she was only too aware of what was expected of her on the wedding night. Alisdair Cannemot, adventurer, connoisseur of women, and despoiler of innocents. Perhaps that was not entirely correct. If he'd despoiled her, it had been with her willing cooperation. She'd gone to her own downfall armed with curiosity and not a little anticipation. When they were discovered, she'd already lost her anticipation, and her curiosity was being rapidly supplanted by a rather startling reality.

She was wrong in assigning Theresa any of the blame for this marriage. While it was true that her aunt had accepted the offer from the earl's solicitor immediately, it was also true that Davina was completely, fully, and despicably ruined, and this was probably the only offer she'd ever receive.

The prospect of being a spinster was almost as disconcerting as that of being married to a man she didn't know, and had never met.

No, she alone bore the brunt of responsibility for this marriage.

Regret was a strange emotion to feel on her wedding day, but it was better, perhaps, to feel regret than fear.

Her aunt bustled into the room, uncharacteristically flustered. Theresa Rowle possessed blue eyes the color of Scotland's sky, hair as red as the blood it had shed, and the disposition of a clan chieftain trapped in the body of a voluptuous woman. The serene face she showed the world masked a will of iron, a fact to which Davina could attest.

"There you are, Davina," she said. "We must hurry."

Davina ignored the second part of that sentence in favor of the first. "Where did you expect me to be, Aunt? Did you think I would escape?"

Her aunt halted, and stared at her as if she'd never before seen Davina. "What are you going on about now, child? Time is passing, and your trunks need to be readied. I have had a message from the earl. It is his wish that we have the wedding at Ambrose."

She began to direct the three maids who had followed her into the room with a series of hand gestures, pursed lips, and headshaking, all the while ignoring Davina as if she were simply an ornament. A chair?

Davina folded her arms in front of her and wondered just how much rebellion her aunt might tolerate. It felt as if the entire world had marshaled against her, but in this circumstance, at least, shouldn't she have some say?

"Isn't that a bit precipitous, Aunt? The arrangements are made. The guests have been invited. Do you expect all of those people to travel to Ambrose with only a few hours' notice?"

Her aunt waved a hand in the maids' direction, and they instantly disappeared from the room.

"Did you think that you would be forgiven so easily, Davina?"

Was there pity in her aunt's eyes?

"Did no one agree to attend?" Davina asked.

Instead of answering her directly, Theresa only smiled. All the same, it was an expression with more grimness than amusement.

"It is a good thing we are summoned to Ambrose, Davina. It will spare us the shame of a ceremony in an empty church."

When Davina didn't speak, her aunt continued. "People love to hear stories, Davina, and you've provided them with one that is not only entertaining, but gives them lessons to teach their daughters."

What did she say to that? Unfortunately, her aunt had spoken the truth.

"You should congratulate yourself on this match, Davina, and on the fact that the Earl of Lorne is so anxious for a bride that he's willing to overlook your reputation."

Everyone knew the story of the Earl of Lorne. A diplomat with a brilliant future in front of him, they said. A genius in dealing with difficult issues, a man who'd been sent to China on an errand for the Crown. Something terrible had happened to him, and he'd been a hermit ever since.

"Have you not heard the rumors about him?"

Her aunt's face grew stern. "I don't listen to such things, Davina, and I caution you not to do so."

"Are you saying that it's not his fault he's earned such a horrible nickname?"

"And what would that be?" Theresa asked.

"Devil."

Theresa shrugged.

"Aunt, the man is a mystery, and he's not been seen in polite company since he returned from China. Does that not give you cause for concern?"

"Not concern, Davina, as much as gratitude. You've

created an impossible position for yourself. You do not have a fortune; there are no male relatives who might champion your cause. There is nothing for you but to grow old as a spinster, and forever be singled out by the mothers of Edinburgh. Unless, of course, you become the Countess of Lorne. A title and a fortune go a long way toward cleansing a reputation."

Theresa marched to the door, opened it, and summoned the maids inside.

"Will you, at least, be in attendance, Aunt? Or are you remaining behind for some reason?"

Her aunt looked startled at the question. Suddenly she began to smile.

"I understand what all of this is about, Davina. You have nerves, and it's to be expected. Perhaps it would benefit you if we had a talk about what to expect from marriage."

Davina began to shake her head, and then, borrowing one of her aunt's often used gestures, held up her hand. "Please, Aunt, that is not necessary. I have no nerves other than the ones any woman would feel about marrying a stranger. Why did he not come to Edinburgh to meet me? Why did he not at least invite us to Ambrose early, so that we might become acquainted?"

Her aunt planted her hands on her hips and frowned at Davina.

"You're marrying the Earl of Lorne, Davina. Not any person off the street. He was the attaché at Stuttgart, attaché at Lisbon, and attaché at Paris. He was secretary to Mr. Gladstone on his mission to the Ionian Islands in 1858. He gained the rank of lieutenant-colonel in the service of the Second Aberdeen R.V. He was invested as a Companion, Order of St. Michael and St. George, just three years ago. The man is a legend."

"Quite so, Aunt Theresa, and no one can cease talking about him."

Theresa frowned at her. "Then you're well matched. No one can cease talking about you, either."

Silence stretched between them, moments punctuated by the rustle of silk, the lid closing on a trunk, the click of a lock.

Davina finally nodded, knowing there was no sense arguing with her aunt. Her father had left her little but their house, and the proceeds from the sale of it had not lasted long. There was her future to consider, and she'd created the dismal nature of it herself, hadn't she?

Trapped on the horns of logic. If her father had been alive, he would have smiled and tapped his finger against his nose to indicate to Davina that Theresa had it right. Perhaps she was fortunate that someone, anyone, wanted to marry her.

There was a tight feeling in Davina's throat that almost prevented her from speaking. "So I am to be the Devil's bride, then?"

Her aunt laughed, a tinkling little bell of a laugh that had captivated her many admirers. "What a silly appellation. Not at all, my dear girl. You're to be the Countess of Lorne."

Chapter 2

Two hours later Davina, her aunt, her aunt's maid, and Nora, the young girl her aunt had selected to accompany Davina to Ambrose, were sitting in the carriage. Following them was a wagon heaped high with Davina's trunks. Nothing was to remain behind at Edinburgh. The whole of her life, it seemed, was destined for the Earl of Lorne's home.

"You will see, my dearest," her aunt said. "Everything will work out for the best."

Davina didn't bother to respond. She was simply a chair, and the quicker she remembered that fact, the quicker she would adapt to this union. How odd that her aunt didn't remind her of her duty as a McLaren.

From time to time, Davina stole looks at her aunt, but Theresa's attention was focused on the view outside the carriage, almost as if she were far away and not sitting beside her at all.

"How was London, Aunt?"

The question evidently startled Theresa, because she forgot to reprimand her once again for not remembering the presence of the servants.

To fill in the awkward silence, Davina spoke again, "I thought you went to London in order to procure something for my trousseau."

Her aunt's laughter sounded oddly brittle. "You mustn't spoil the surprise, my dearest girl. How did you know I didn't? Perhaps I'm waiting for the opportune moment to present you with my gift."

"Since you've already spent a fortune on gowns and hats and all manner of accessories, Aunt, I can assure you I don't need one single additional gift."

Her aunt wasn't frivolous all the time. Theresa could be very serious upon occasion if circumstances warranted it. Look how quickly she'd taken Davina into her home when Davina's father had died. Theresa had been a great source of comfort in those days.

Nearly a quarter hour passed in silence. Finally Davina spoke again.

"Will it be very different being a countess?" she asked. "I cannot think so. I don't feel any different knowing I'm about to marry an earl. Will I have to treat people with more reserve?"

The two maids looked at her with interest.

Her aunt glanced at them and then at Davina, an unspoken warning that she was being tactless. One never spoke of one's position in front of the servants, any more than one divulged the extent of one's wealth.

For the rest of the journey, Davina was silent. Not once did she look at her aunt again, and when it was clear that they were nearing their destination—Ambrose was less than an hour outside Edinburgh—she acquiesced to her aunt's various instructions to straighten her bonnet, don her gloves, pull down her skirt, and not fuss when Nora dusted off her shoes.

The chair was getting reupholstered and its limbs polished, the better to show itself to advantage. Perhaps she should also get her cushions restuffed. Davina bit back a smile at the thought of arriving at Ambrose with a plenteous bosom.

Her aunt, however, misinterpreted her humor. "There, Davina, that is the attitude. You must show a brave face, regardless of the circumstances. I can promise you this marriage will be an advantage."

There was nothing to say to that, was there? So she kept her smile in place and nodded her thanks to Nora, and sat back against the cushions.

Only she and God knew how much she'd like to open the door of the carriage and begin running.

"Ambrose is majestic," her aunt said. "Can you not imagine the balls you could have here? The entertainments?"

"I believe my husband has the personality of a hermit, Aunt. What does it matter to have a place to entertain if you do not have the temperament for it?"

Her aunt looked askance at her. "As you are of a similar temperament, Davina, it sounds as if you and His Lordship will suit quite well."

Davina sat back and stared out the window, refusing to engage her aunt in a debate. First of all, there were the maids to consider, and secondly, she doubted if she'd win any argument. Her aunt had it in her mind that Davina was about to make a happy marriage, and there was nothing Davina could say to alter Theresa's mind.

Yet Theresa had done what she thought was the best; the decisions she'd made had been with Davina's interest in mind, not because of a feeling of responsibility but out of love.

"I shall do the very best I can," Davina said suddenly. "I shall try, Aunt. I will be the most dutiful wife the Earl of Lorne could wish to have."

Her aunt looked startled at her declaration, but only for a moment. Her face softened into a smile as she reached over and grabbed one of Davina's hands.

"That is all I can ask for, my dearest girl. That you give this marriage a chance."

Davina didn't respond, and the two of them maintained an amenable silence for the next few minutes.

The closer they came to Ambrose, the more awe-inspiring it appeared. The castle was built in the valley just beneath Donleigh Hill. On the west side, a steep drop gave way to a spectacular view of Loch Moirdair and the ruins of Bowlin Abbey nestled on its banks.

The Nye flowed under the arch of Ambrose's south battlements, ensuring a steady water supply even when under siege. Two turrets flanked the outer courtyard, their curtain wall construction still boasting broken brick and chipped mortar where cannonball had been leveled against Ambrose during some battle in the past. Ambrose could serve as a history lesson, since there were mentions of the great house in numerous books she'd read.

The castle was a monument to the tenacity of the Scots, as well as their indomitable resilience.

Once she would have been curious about her new home, eager to learn more about Ambrose, delighted with the idea that she was to reside in one of the most splendid places in Scotland. Now, however, the only feeling she had was a dread so strong that it was almost another occupant in the carriage.

What on earth had she done?

Chapter 3

Marshall awoke from his doze, feeling sick. The voices swirled around in his mind, so real that he looked around his study to ensure he was alone.

His skin was clammy; perspiration dotted his forehand and clung to the nape of his neck. He reached for the glass on the table beside the wing chair and took a sip, hoping the wine would calm his stomach. He was going to be married in two hours. A quick look at the clock amended that thought. Only an hour.

Had his bride arrived?

He sat back against the chair. What the hell had he done?

The room in which he sat was directly off his bedroom, and was his sanctuary, his haven. This study was not used to transact business as much as it was a place to escape to his books or his thoughts. Of all the rooms at Ambrose, this was the one room he could call singularly his.

No one was allowed in here but his valet and the occasional maid. The other inhabitants of the room, real only to him, preferred to appear between midnight and dawn. Today, however, they'd made an appearance at dusk, as if to remind him of the stupidity of what he was about to do.

Marriage? What an imbecilic notion.

Poor Davina McLaren. Did she think herself fortunate to snare an earl? Poor stupid girl. Perhaps she was simply greedy, and the condition of her bridegroom made no difference.

The marriage must happen. His remaining life span might well be counted in weeks rather than decades. He didn't like the idea of being the last Ross, especially when nothing but disgrace would be listed beside his name.

But when he'd sent his solicitor in search of a worthy bride, he'd never expected the man to return so quickly with a recommendation.

"She is a bookish girl, Your Lordship, and one with a good reputation until last year. Then she and a young man were caught together at a garden party. I understand that the scandal has dimmed her prospects somewhat."

"So she might be amenable to marriage with me, is that it?"

His solicitor had hesitated. "I suggest her only because of the speed with which you wish to marry, Your Lordship."

Normally, the process of obtaining a bride would have entailed endless balls, dinners, and masques, as well as tedious conversations, all of which would be intended to convince Edinburgh's sweet young things that he wasn't as evil as he was portrayed to be by rumor and innuendo. The rest of the time would be

spent trying to assuage any maternal and paternal wor-
ries on that score, as well as ensuring the parents of a
bride-to-be that enough money could make up for any
of his eccentricities.

Being wealthy might solve a great many social ills,
including the fact that he was rumored to be the devil.
Or, closer to the mark, a madman. But did he really
want to go through all that, simply to find a bride? Especially in his current state?

The question was moot. His demons would not
allow him time to court a woman. They would snare
him each night, and pull him close to the abyss.

Perhaps he'd simply grow tired of his madness and
do himself in, thereby ridding himself of the problem
of producing an heir entirely. Marshall had weighed
that option for perhaps all of five minutes. Like it or
not, the will to live was strong in him. Hadn't he proven
that in China?

So if he wasn't to do himself in, and he couldn't venture to Edinburgh, and he wouldn't go to London, then
what was he to do? Ignore the issue. Wish that it would
go away. But he suspected that his condition was growing worse rather than better.

He might have only weeks left of sanity.

The solicitor had stood in front of him, patient. En-
duringly patient, as Marshall had never been.

"Would her family agree to my suit?" he'd finally
asked.

"She only has one aunt left in her family, Your Lordship. I do not see any reservations there."

"Then suggest the marriage," he'd said.

Had it been only weeks ago? In some respects, it seemed longer. In others, only hours. Insanity took away his concept of time.

Now he stood, grabbing for the edge of the chair. Something was wrong with his balance. Hell, something was wrong with his entire life. He strode through the connecting door and into his bedroom. His valet was already there, carefully laying out his wedding garments.

Jacobs had one of those round faces that appeared perennially cheerful; large, wide brown eyes; a bulbous nose ending in a tilt; a shortened chin; and a slight overlap of his teeth.

Marshall had often thought that the man resembled a rather earnest chipmunk. The fact that he was short and rotund only added to the impression.

"If I might say, Your Lordship," Jacobs began.

Marshall stopped him before Jacobs could continue. "You may not," he said.

However, Jacobs had been valet to his father, a position that had evidently imbued him with a certain amount of courage.

"About your attire, Your Lordship," Jacobs said. "You want to appear at your best. You have those embroidered vests from China, sir. Would you like to choose one of those to wear?"

Marshall knew exactly the garments he meant. Vests that were heavily embroidered in gold, silver, indigo, and green thread, depicting cranes so lifelike they appeared in mid-flight. The vests had been tailored for him during one of his first missions to China.

"Burn them," he said. "I thought you had."

"Your Lordship, they are exquisite examples of superior workmanship." Jacobs's fingers traced the outline of one fulsome chrysanthemum. "My grandson wrote me about such beauty."

"I didn't think Daniel was overly interested in embroidery."

Jacobs didn't speak, his concentration on the vest he held.

"Take them," Marshall said abruptly. "Just never wear them in my presence."

He'd already rid Ambrose of its carved ivory, netsuke figurines, and silk paintings—all reminding him of the Orient. He wanted nothing to recall those days. He needed nothing tangible. Each night his visions were there, vivid and real.

"But your attire, Your Lordship? Something less somber?" He pointed to a stack of fabric on the bed. "It's tradition, Your Lordship."

Jacobs had it correct. Until the kilt was outlawed more than a hundred years ago, it had been tradition. Since it had been returned to favor, there was no reason for him to refuse.

He'd held on to his identity with both hands in the last year. He'd come home to Ambrose with gratitude. Unless he wished it, there was no need to ever hear another English accent or see another English face. Ambrose offered him sanctuary and peace, along with constant reminders that he was a Scot.

He was a Ross, with the proud blood of long-ago Ross men flowing in his veins. Today, at least, he should look like one.

Jacobs didn't say anything in response, only unfurled the fabric and stood with it stretched between his hands.

Marshall removed his clothing, washed, and donned the white dress shirt before giving in to Jacobs's implacable patience. He stood at attention while Jacobs measured the pleats, pinned them in place, and then stitched Marshall into a replica of the kilt his forefathers had worn.

A jewel-encrusted sporran was next, topped by a short black coat with small gold buttons with diamonds in the center. Jacobs knelt and helped him on with knee-high stockings embroidered with the Ross crest. His shoes were the last part of his wedding attire, the shiny black leather adorned with diamond-encrusted buckles.

He stood silent, allowing Jacobs to flit around him like an earnest bee.

What sort of woman would marry a man she'd never seen? Miss Davina McLaren must be desperate indeed. The fault was Marshall's that he knew nothing about his bride. He'd deliberately cloaked her in secrecy so as not to provide himself with any reason to cancel the nuptials. If she had a long nose, or a grating manner, or an irritating laugh, let him learn all those things after they were wed and when it was too late to change his mind.

At least she wasn't insane.

He hoped she'd cultivated some interests since she'd left the schoolroom, some variety of talents that would serve her well and keep her away from him.

The last thing he wanted was a devoted wife.

"Mrs. Murray has delivered another decanter of wine, Your Lordship," Jacobs said.

He glanced in the man's direction. "Has she? I think, on this occasion, Jacobs, that I should remain as sober as possible."

His valet did not respond—wise man—but his expression smoothed until it resembled a stone effigy. A chipmunk gargoyle.

"Will you be wanting a timepiece, Your Lordship?" Jacobs asked now, extending a gold chain affixed to a diamond-encrusted watch.

Marshall shook his head. Time had no meaning for him. He didn't give a flying fig if it was day or night. Why should he measure it? Nor did the timing of this particular ceremony matter all that much. It was going to occur or it wasn't. He didn't much care, either way.

When the carriage arrived at Ambrose, there was no ceremony to welcome Davina, perhaps because they couldn't advance past the dozens of carriages blocking the drive.

"Oh dear, we are late."

Davina glanced at her aunt. "They cannot hold a wedding without us, Aunt."

Theresa didn't answer, but her censuring look was comment enough.

"We shall never get there on time. There's nothing to be done but walk the rest of the way."

Theresa descended from the carriage. Davina and the two maids had no choice but to follow her.

"At least someone will be in attendance," Davina offered as they navigated through the sea of carriages.

A few minutes later they climbed the soaring, curving steps leading up to Ambrose's west-facing edifice. Someone in the house's past had been enamored of classical architecture, so much so that this entrance resembled sketches she'd seen of the Parthenon in Athens. Imposing columns greeted the visitor, and the wide steps leading to a massive double door seemed designed more to impress than to welcome.

No one stood beside the curving stone steps and offered a greeting. Even the majordomo was absent. No doubt he was assisting all the other occupants of the dozens of carriages blocking the drive. She was neither escorted to the chamber she would occupy at Ambrose nor introduced to the staff. Instead, the four of them were left standing in the foyer.

"What do we do now?" Davina asked.

"You will take off those ugly spectacles," Theresa said. "Are you trying to make yourself unappealing?" She leaned close to Davina and whispered to her, "It is too late, Davina. This course is already set."

"I can't see without them, Aunt." But her fingers were already moving to the temples.

Her aunt frowned at her. "I thought your eyes were weak only for reading."

Davina nodded, removing the offending spectacles.

"Would it not harm you to wear them otherwise? You're quite a beautiful girl without them," Theresa said. "Besides, if you wear them, I know you'll seek out the nearest book."

Davina bit back a comment as she put her spectacles in her reticule. She loved her aunt, she truly did. But her aunt had dancing and balls and laughter and the approval of men always on her mind. Theresa was a girl who'd never quite grown up, and Davina often thought herself Theresa's elder, and not the other way around.

A moment later, the missing majordomo suddenly appeared.

"Please inform the earl that we've arrived," Theresa said. "I'm Mrs. Rowle, the bride's aunt, and she is Miss Davina McLaren."

The majordomo stared at Davina, his pinched features revealing his annoyance. Evidently he thought her responsible for his chaotic day. Well, perhaps she was. But she hadn't planned on being late to her own wedding.

He snapped his fingers, and a tall, liveried footman appeared from behind a column. "Fetch the trunks, man, and hurry!"

The majordomo fixed another irritated look at her and announced, "The ceremony is being held in fifteen minutes, miss."

"I can't be ready in fifteen minutes," Davina said.

"You'll find the earl's staff is ceaselessly punctual," the man said. From his expression, there was more the majordomo wanted to say, but his ire was evidently not as imperative as the ticking of the clock.

He carried on a rambling discourse as they walked, detailing the history of Ambrose. Davina would have much preferred that he speak about her husband-to-be, but a stern look from her aunt kept her silent and biddable.

This, then, was the true price of scandal: to be forced into doing something she didn't wish to do because of a few moments of ill-chosen behavior.

"This corridor was once part of the Great Hall," he intoned in a voice that rasped like a dry husk, "rumored to have been a meeting place for the clans before the '45."

She caught a glimpse of the fabled Great Hall as they passed. Claymores, broadswords, and dirks were mounted on the buttressed walls. The gray flagstones were worn in spots, the majority of them covered with a Persian rug of muted colors.

On the sideboard were a dozen pewter frames, each surrounding miniatures of those whose time had passed. Grandparents, cousins, uncles, and aunts, all bore witness to the strength of the familial link: the broad forehead, high cheekbones, and thin nose were echoed in each successive face.

The walls of the corridor were not covered in weapons but full-length portraits of the earl's ancestors, some in court garb, a few dressed for hunting, the requisite hound at the subject's feet and a brace of hares slung over an aristocratic shoulder.

She stopped and studied one, startled not only by the family resemblance between the portraits but by the overwhelming sense of command from all these long-dead ancestors. They looked as if they were comfortable with command, with the sense of themselves. Handsome men, and not a little autocratic. Scots, with more than their share of pride and stubbornness. No doubt imbued with a belief in the continuance of what had gone before, and a certain smug acceptance in the permanency of the Ross family.

"Miss," the majordomo said, impatience etched on his features.

She nodded and followed him, avoiding her aunt's look. All too soon they were escorted to the chapel and then whisked into an anteroom.

Was the earl such a hideous creature that everyone was worried she would bolt if she inadvertently saw him before the wedding? Despite all her thoughts of being brave on this most terrifying of days, she didn't have the courage to broach the question to her aunt.

What if the answer was yes?

Chapter 4

This chapel was an addition to the older part of Ambrose, added when his ancestors had unexpectedly become aware that there was a God and His name wasn't Ross. The room was small and slightly off-kilter. The wooden floorboards were warped, and tilted at an angle from the arched door to the stained glass windows on the outer wall. The ceiling and the walls had recently been repainted in a blinding white, but the pews dated back two centuries or more, their scarred wooden surfaces now covered in crimson velvet.

The ceiling sagged a bit in places; the gouge in the wooden floor had been made when a drunken laird had put a sword through the boards during the funeral of his son; the small hole under the window was caused by dry rot, repaired of course, but a bane to all five-hundred-year-old homes. Over the past twenty years, restoration efforts had prevented the further crumbling of bricks on the chapel's exterior.

Behind the altar was a stained glass window, depicting not a religious scene but a strange figure resembling a lizard. His mother had always likened the image to

St. George battling the dragon, but his father had countered that it was probably the Fuath, a legendary water spirit with yellow hair and a tail, attired in green and possessing an evil nature. The window was either a wordless challenge to God in His own house, or a message to all worshippers that God can even protect the Ross family from the unnatural.

Would God protect Davina McLaren from the Devil of Ambrose?

His bride was late, Marshall had been informed, a fact that, strangely enough, didn't seem to concern him overmuch.

He arranged himself beside the altar as was customary, in the secluded nave where the bridegrooms of two hundred years had waited. He wondered how many of them had begun to second-guess their unions as he was doing at this moment.

His uncle stood behind him, also following custom. A few hundred years ago, the man in that position would have held his sword at the ready, defender of the laird, protector from any rival, bloodthirsty, cattle-stealing clan who might send a member to rob him of his life or his bride on this day.

The Ross family had been civilized for so long that it was difficult for Marshall to conjure such a scene ever happening—although he knew for a fact that it had. His family history was replete with stories of his ancestors' great heroism and even greater audacity.

What would they say, these forebearers of his, if they looked either downward from heaven or upward from hell to witness this day? Would they fault him for his actions of the past? Or judge that today he was reaping the full measure of his punishment for what had happened in China?

Outside, the pipers began to play "The Rowan Tree." He stood at attention, preparing himself by forcing a diplomat's smile to his face. So must he have looked as they sailed into Canton Harbor. He clenched his left hand tightly.

His bride was walking down the aisle toward him, her white lace dress and elbow-length gloves much too elaborate for this small chapel.

Her gaze was on the front of the chapel, and he knew when she saw him. Her eyes widened ever so slightly, and her footsteps slowed.

His solicitor had said she was pretty.

She wasn't.

His bride was radiant. Glorious. Perfect. There was color to her face, a flush that lent her pearlized skin a soft glow. Her auburn hair was riotous around her shoulders, a mass of tendrils held back from her face with tortoise-shell combs. She looked like a Florentine Venus.

No, she was more than pretty. She was crafted of alabaster and porcelain, with delicate pink lips and finely arched brows. He'd never actually thought about a woman's nose before, but hers was perfect. That chin was remarkably firm, however, hinting at stubbornness.

What color were her eyes? Surely not brown. They had to be some magnificent color to match her face.

Dear God, they were bluish green, the color of Bahamian seas.

He took a step forward and then stopped himself. He

should remain here beside the altar and wait for her to travel to him. Wasn't that the way these ceremonies went? The bride walked slowly past friends and family, clad in her pristine white dress with its acres and acres of lace, demonstrating her courageous sacrifice to the monster.

He realized he didn't want to wait, and before his uncle could stop him, Marshall took the two steps down to the aisle and advanced on Davina McLaren.

She halted in the middle of the aisle, ten steps or so from the altar. She didn't flinch when he approached her. Nor did she look away.

Brave girl.

When he was close enough that their conversation couldn't be overheard, he spoke to her.

"You look terrified," he said.

Her brows drew together, but she didn't comment. Fascinated, he continued to stare at her. After a moment, he was surprised to see her blush. The faint color, oddly enough, detracted from her appearance rather than adding to it.

"You should never blush," he said.

She looked startled at his comment. "I normally do not. But then, I'm rarely married."

"Are you afraid?"

"A little," she admitted.

"Of me? Or marriage?"

She seemed to consider the question, and as she did, he came to her side, turned, and extended his arm.

"Have you noticed that the entire chapel is filled with people staring at us as if we've lost our minds?" he asked.

Davina smiled. "I suspect they're waiting for me to turn around and run down the aisle."

She placed her small bouquet of heather and white roses in her right hand, and placed her left hand on his arm.

"Are you often given to such displays?"

"As often as I am married," she said.

How very odd that he felt like smiling.

She turned her head and regarded him somberly. "Of you, I think," she said, answering his earlier question. "And marriage. But more you. You're called Devil, you know. Why?"

She *was* brave. No one else had ever come out and asked him that question, even though he was sure they thought it.

He wanted to reassure her, keep her with him somehow, which meant he wouldn't give her the whole truth.

"Why does anyone get a reputation? People are curious, and when they can't find anything to say, they invent stories."

In silence she considered him. He wondered what she thought, and then realized that such speculation was unwise. Did he really want to know what she thought of him?

Finally she spoke. "No one told me you were so handsome," she said. "They shouldn't call you Devil, unless you're like Lucifer. Are you as evil?"

Yes. That wasn't an answer he had any intention of giving her. Instead he only smiled and led her to the altar and to her fate.

Chapter 5

In moments, it was done. In moments, she'd gone from being Davina McLaren, slightly older spinster, to Davina McLaren Ross, the Countess of Lorne.

Shouldn't such a change have taken longer? Shouldn't there have been a symphony to accompany such a momentous undertaking—instead of a lone piper whose music accompanied their departure from the chapel and their arrival in this room?

The magnificent receiving room of Ambrose was reminiscent of a palace. The ceilings were frescoed with dancing nymph-like cupids painted in the Raphael style. Thick blue draperies hung in swags from gold cornice boards. A series of gilt-edged mirrors stretched the length and width of the room. In front of them sat a sideboard of marble and gold, topped with blue frosted glass. The wooden boards of the floor were polished to a high sheen, half covered with a magnificent carpet in shades of blue and green. The receiving chairs were upholstered in blue silk, the mahogany wood of the chair burnished with gold.

She and Marshall were seated together at the end

of the room like royalty, greeting the assembled guests who stretched in a line around the room.

No one had prepared her for this. But then, no one had told her about her new husband, either. No one had warned her how magnificent he would look attired in a kilt, a garment that left absolutely no doubt as to a man's masculinity. Or the shape of his legs.

"You're the most beautiful bride, my dearest girl," her aunt said, sweeping Davina up into a hug before she was led away.

Davina only nodded in response. The moments were going by too swiftly. The ceremony had been too brief, the circumstances too odd.

One by one people were introduced to her, names she'd never heard before, and faces she wouldn't remember. She hoped she was gracious and polite. She heard herself saying words, and felt her lips curved into a smile. How very odd to feel that she was here and was not at the same time.

After another hour she was whisked away to the dining hall, and found herself seated at a long table at the head of the room. Only two places had been set among the profusion of silver candelabra, silver salvers, and charger plates. Three crystal goblets in varying heights sat at the right of both porcelain plates bearing the Ross crest and surrounded by a dizzying array of silverware. Around them sparkled at least four dozen pale yellow beeswax candles, their delicate scent eclipsed beneath the roses and dahlias clustered in small vases all over the table.

The guests were seated at long tables in front of them, and from her vantage point, Davina could see her aunt and Marshall's uncle in pride of place at one of the first tables. Most of the other people were strangers, yet despite her ignorance of their names or why they were attending her wedding, it was all too obvious that she was a source of fascination for them. Perhaps some other time she would be concerned about all those interested eyes. Right at the moment, however, she could not help but concentrate on the man to her left.

Instead of speaking about his accomplishments or his title, her aunt should have mentioned that Marshall Ross, Earl of Lorne, had brown eyes so dark they appeared as black as his hair. Or that he was tall, easily towering over her, and that each of his features was perfect and arranged handsomely.

If she didn't stop herself, she'd spend the whole night in rapt silence, studying him. She finally fixed her gaze on her folded hands, forcing herself to listen to the minister. He was reading some kind of blessing. She should spend the time heeding his words rather than musing on how attractive Marshall was. Or wondering about what was to come.

Would the act be different if the man was handsome?

Dear heavens, was she blushing again? She rarely blushed. Yet the idea of being alone in a room with this man was occasion enough to incite a warm flush traveling through her body. The idea of being made a wife seemed, well, impossible. It could not happen. Not with him. She would die of embarrassment.

"Why are you blushing?" Marshall asked from beside her.

"Did you know that there are people who are afraid

of homilies?" she asked, glancing at the minister. "Do you think a sermon is frightening?"

"It depends on the subject matter. Are you afraid of them?"

"No," she said, forcing herself to look at him. He was smiling, and for a moment—barely more than a second, actually—she was struck dumb by how handsome he truly was. "I'm not afraid of very much. I quite like storms, for example. And winter. And roses."

"That's good to know," he said softly. His voice was very low, very seductive, and sounded oddly enough like the J. S. Fry & Sons chocolate her aunt occasionally brought her from London.

"I'm not afraid of you," Davina said, with more bravado than truth. "Or marriage. Truly. It's simply a different experience, and I'm not used to being married. I shall have to adjust. Did you know that in Africa it's tradition to pay for a bride with livestock?"

"Ambrose has quite a few cattle," Marshall said. "Sheep as well. We would not have been averse to paying your dowry."

She looked at him fully then, startled by two facts. He hadn't questioned her knowledge of obscure African tribes. And he was teasing her.

"I wear spectacles," she said in the silence. "'Honesty is best, don't you think? If I lose mine honor, I lose myself.'"

He looked a little bemused. "Shakespeare?"

She nodded.

"I can't read without them," she added. "You should know that now. I'm almost blind. Not normally, but

when I try to read, I mean. The words go all squiggly."
She blinked a few times. "Did you know that a frog has
four fingers?"

"I don't mind that you wear spectacles," he said, his
smile back in place. "And I did know about frog fingers. I was quite the adventurer as a boy."

When their meal arrived, she gratefully paid attention to it, eating slowly and with great deliberation, the
better to lengthen the meal.

Only to herself would she admit the degree of her
trepidation. Very well, fear.

How did he reassure her? Or was there anything
he could say? Were the moments between them to be
punctuated by this awkward, stilted silence? He sat
back, his appetite as poor as it had been for months, his
interest spurred instead by his new wife.

Perhaps he should simply retreat to his chamber and
recognize that he'd made a mistake. He glanced at her
to find her looking at him out of the corner of her eye.
Just as quickly, she stared down at her lap again.

He'd be an idiot to retreat to his chamber and a fool
to go to hers.

Still, awareness thrummed between them, something oddly arousing. He wanted her—he was not so
much of a fool that he would ignore that. He was a man,
after all, despite his past or his tormented present.

A footman stopped before him, bowed low, and prof-
fered a salver on which a wineglass and carafe rested.
He shook his head to the footman's obvious surprise.
The man hesitated, and then finally moved away.

"Thank you," he said, "for agreeing to be married at Ambrose."

She put down her fork and glanced at him. "I do not believe that I was given much choice in the matter, Your Lordship," she said.

"My name is Marshall," he said.

She didn't respond.

"Ambrose is a beautiful place," she said. "From the number of guests, however, you must have a great many friends. I'd heard that you were a recluse."

He smiled. What other rumors had she heard? Perhaps a wiser man would ask her, but he wasn't all that eager to hear her answer.

"I think there are fewer friends here than relatives. That is Lady Ethel," he said, nodding toward an aging matron dressed in ivory. "She is a second cousin and was once a maid of honor to Her Majesty. Unfortunately, she never lets anyone forget it. I don't recognize most of the guests myself. Probably some of them are related to my mother. She came from a family of six brothers and four sisters. Some of the guests are no doubt cousins or second cousins.

"As for the rest," he added, "I suspect that they are neighbors, people who live near Ambrose. Once we were known for our hospitality."

"Not anymore?"

"I crave my privacy more than a reputation for hospitality," he said. There was more he could tell her, but perhaps any further revelations should wait until they were married a few weeks. He would feed her the truth a sentence at a time. What would she do once she learned the whole of it? No doubt run screaming from Ambrose.

"You appear perfectly healthy, Your Lordship. Surely you were physically able to travel to Edinburgh."

Her comment was more a question than a statement, but he chose to discuss neither the reason for the change of location nor his physical condition. Instead Marshall only smiled in response and waved away the next footman with another decanter of wine. Had his servants become used to repeatedly filling his glass?

Poor Davina McLaren Ross. Wed to a sotted lunatic.

"You're remarkably lovely," he said. "Why have you never married?"

She looked surprised at the compliment. Or perhaps it was the question.

"My father died."

"My condolences."

She accepted his comment with a nod. "I was in mourning."

"But before that?" he asked.

"Is it necessary that you know? Is it not enough that we are married now?"

He allowed himself to smile at the edge in her voice. He'd evidently irritated his bride. Good. Perhaps if he annoyed her sufficiently, there would be a valid reason for him to remain in his own suite of rooms tonight. He wouldn't inflict himself on an innocent woman whose only sin had been to marry him. He clenched his hand, and then forced himself to relax.

"Why did you marry now? Why me?"

This time there was no doubt that it was the question that discomfited her. Was she going to speak of the scandal that made her willing to wed a stranger? Or was she simply greedy for his wealth?

"I didn't want to remain alone for the whole of my life. I want a family. Children," she said, her cheeks turning crimson. He'd never before seen anyone who blushed so unbecomingly.

He decided that he wouldn't continue with the questions. Not when it was only too obvious that his bride had her secrets, just as he had his.

The rest of their dinner passed quickly enough. Too quickly for his peace of mind. All too soon her aunt was there, with assorted women he thought he recognized. One of them, a young female with a particularly odd walk, led his bride away amid the chattering and giggling women.

"It's a custom, Davina," Theresa said. "Think of it as a good omen, a bit of luck for your bridal bed."

"Haven't we progressed beyond this, Aunt?" Davina asked, watching as a group of strangers prepared her chamber for the night ahead. The fact that one of them was heavily with child was supposed to bring fecundity. "It's a Scottish version of Lupercalia."

Her aunt eyed her, and Davina knew she was weighing whether to ask the question.

"Lupercalia was an ancient Roman ritual of fertility and purification," Davina said. "It involved the sacrifice of a goat and scourging."

As she'd anticipated, Theresa held up her hand to prevent any more revelations.

"The women are just making your bed, my dear. Not slinging entrails all over the room."

The chamber might benefit from a few entrails, but that was not a comment she'd make to her aunt. But it had been difficult to enter the countess's suite without gasping aloud.

The bed was high and wide, graced with four massive mahogany posts heavily carved with flowers, thistles, and leaves, and a headboard that was nearly as tall as the posts. The other furniture was mahogany as well, and polished so well that she could see the gleam of the lamps on the surfaces of the bureau, vanity, and bedside table. What distinguished the room from any other room she'd ever seen was the crimson Chinese silk on the walls. Not only was it a vibrant shade of red, but it was heavily embroidered with green vines and startlingly white chrysanthemums.

How was anyone expected to sleep in such a room?

"I shall never be able to close my eyes," she said in a whispered aside to her aunt. "It's so very, well, garish."

Theresa looked around the room with the practiced gaze of someone looking for the best in every situation.

"You know Marshall is a diplomat. A very learned man. I've heard that he can speak six languages with some fluidity." She took a deep breath. "It's to be expected that he has tastes that are somewhat different from most Scots. It'd up to you, Davina, to accept those differences. Indeed, to make the most of them."

She slapped her hands together as if finished with

a particularly troubling task, and turned with a determined smile toward the other five women.

"Are we nearly done? We must prepare the bride and
then give her a few moments to compose herself, don't
you think, ladies?"

With a minimum of fuss, the bedclothes were turned
down, her dress was removed, and Davina was attired
in a froth of white lace not unlike her wedding dress.
The difference being, of course, that she had no stays,
no undergarments at all. Even her garters were gone, as
were the delicate stockings knitted for her by nuns in
the south of France. Beneath the layers of lace Davina
was quite naked, feeling vulnerable and not unlike a
sacrifice.

Had women ever been sacrificed in Scotland? Davina
realized she didn't know, at the same time she realized
something else. She couldn't remember anything. Not
one Latin declination occurred to her. Nor was she able to
envision a map of the Empire in her mind. What was her
middle name? She shared it with her aunt. Aunt . . . ?

Dear God, she couldn't remember her aunt's name.

Why, exactly, was it so cold in here? Ambrose was
supposedly known for its comforts, but this room was
freezing. Was this a taste of what she was to endure in
winter?

Endurance. She'd been remarkably blessed in her
life. Granted, she'd lost her mother when she was four,
but the loss had faded. She'd always had her father's
love and affection, and Aunt Theresa's as well. Theresa, that was her aunt's name. Theresa Rowle. And her
own? Davina McLaren. Ross.

She arranged herself on the edge of the bed, fisted her hands on either side of her, and closed her eyes to spare them the sight of the Chinese red silk on the walls.

She'd simply have to endure this wedding night, that's all.

Garrow Ross surveyed himself in the mirror, pleased with his appearance. Growing older held no terrors for him. He'd disliked his youth, for the most part. Like all young men, he'd spent several years floundering, searching for a reason, a purpose in life.

From the moment he was conscious of his identity, he'd known that his older brother would be the heir to the title and would inherit Ambrose. That knowledge had ticked at him like an invisible clock hanging from his neck. That his brother would have been happier to be a scholar and not an earl was also something of an annoyance.

Garrow's path had been clear before he reached his twenties—he would need to do something, become something, or he would be a poor relation dependent on his brother Aidan's charity for the whole of his life.

Luckily, however, he'd stumbled upon a way to make money, and money, it had turned out, was the great equalizer.

He no longer spent any time regretting the fact that Ambrose had been entailed to his nephew. Nor did he care, overmuch, that he'd never be the Earl of Lorne. Oh, there were times when he thought about it, but almost immediately assuaged any envy with the thought of what he'd accomplished. He owned two beautiful homes, one in Edinburgh and one outside London. His clipper ships were renowned for their speed, and his warehouses were stocked with anything an avid and wealthy shopper could desire.

He slipped the leather straps of his brushes over each hand and vigorously brushed his silvery white hair. Like his brother, he had a full, thick head of hair. Unlike his brother, his health was excellent. But then he hadn't spent years in the Egyptian desert investigating tombs and crating up mummies to bring home to Ambrose. Poor Aidan. Had he died of the cough he'd brought back from the last season? Or had he felt a stirring of human emotion toward the last, and missed his wife?

Garrow spared a thought for dear Julianna. He missed his sister-in-law, but perhaps it was best that she was no longer alive. She wouldn't be witness to the wreck her son had become.

He leaned forward in the mirror and inspected his teeth. Finally he stood back and surveyed himself fully in the mirror, tucking a finger into his snug waistcoat. He was growing a little portly, and should take care to avoid his new cook's sauces. But food, like good wine, was a reward for dedication and diligence. He had no intention of sparing himself his rewards.

Perhaps he should give some thought to his own nuptials. For years he'd never considered marriage, being too occupied with his own future. But now that that was settled, and he was comfortably wealthy, perhaps he should begin to think seriously of sharing his remaining years with a wife.

He moved to the desk and opened the top right-hand drawer, extracting a file that had come to him that very night, the messenger being unobserved in the general merriment in the dining hall. He knew exactly what the letter and the papers within the file would contain, but he read them again, just to make certain. His smile broadened as he scrawled his name to the bottom of the letter and added a sentence of instructions. The *Hawthorne Rose* would sail within the week, and when her voyage was done, he'd be even wealthier than before.

He put the file in the desk, sealed the letter, and inserted it in the leather pouch. Tomorrow the same messenger, who was tucked away in one of the servants' rooms, no doubt with a bottle of wine and a willing maid, would return to Perth.

He was not a man who enjoyed irony. All the same, Garrow couldn't help but be amused at the incongruity of these circumstances. His fortune, immense as it was, had begun due to opium, looked upon in some circles as necessary and in others as morally corrupting. Yet that same substance was probably the cause of Marshall's insanity.

Night had fallen, softly draping Ambrose in shadows. Here and there pockets of light and bursts of laughter reminded Marshall that his home was filled with strangers. But while his guests were still entertaining themselves, they expected him to be with his bride.

Marshall stood in front of the door to the countess's suite. His fingers flexed once, twice, and then clenched into a fist. He stared at the gilt framing of the door, a creation of a carpenter employed more than a hundred years ago. Had the man known, when he crafted such a delicately carved frame, that an earl would stand motionless, staring at it in turmoil a hundred years later? Had he ever thought, this long-ago carpenter, that the door would come to represent a barrier greater than painted wood?

Beyond that door was temptation. Not simply a temptation of the flesh, although there was that. But Davina offered forgetfulness for a few hours. With her he wouldn't be the hermit lord, the Devil of Ambrose, the Earl of Lorne, his honor stained and shriveled by the actions of the past. With his bride he would simply be a bridegroom.

She knew nothing of him, and that was both disconcerting and a cause for rejoicing. He could be anyone he wished with her: kind and temperate, distant or caring. Or he could simply be the man he'd always known himself to be, only recently damaged and incapable of becoming himself again.

He should leave her alone. He should turn around and walk down the hall to his own suite. There he could forget about his bride by the judicious application of several glasses of wine. He could sleep, finally, and not require the touch of another human being. No one needed to hold him, or kiss him, or promise him any physical pleasure.

Wine would work well enough; it had before.

Ah, there was the temptation again. The world expected him to be with his bride. The world exonerated him for this night above others. Tonight he might be here to fulfill the obligations his rank and his birthright demanded. Never mind that he hated nightfall and dreaded his dreams. Never mind that he wondered if his bride might ease the transition from sanity to madness.

Perhaps he wasn't consumed by lust at all but simply melancholia, and was standing here in a misguided attempt to make amends for forcing her into marriage without being totally honest to her.

Forcing? He raised his right hand and placed his fingers in the middle of the gilded panel, stroking the delicate pattern of leaves and roses. Not quite forcing her, perhaps. But neither did he offer her honesty. Perhaps earlier, in the chapel, he could have halted the ceremony by simply holding out his hand. He could have taken her into the vestibule, and they would have spoken for a few moments, long enough for him to acquaint her with certain salient facts of their union.

"I'm known as the Devil because word has spread to Edinburgh of my screaming fits. When the madness is upon me, I see the very demons of hell. I have nightmares as well as visions that haunt my days. I am not entirely certain I'm of this world any longer, although I cannot quite dismiss the feeling that I am part of it. I am well on my way to becoming a madman, and yet I crave the touch of an innocent the way I crave my wine.

"Marry me and you'll have no lack of anything except for my company, perhaps. I'll use you when I will, and do so for as long as I'm strong enough to push aside my madness and perhaps my compassion."

She would have scurried back to Edinburgh as fast as her carriage could travel. She might have even regaled the whole of society with his strange confession so that no other woman would ever look at him with wide eyes and inquire about his soubriquet.

What a fool he was. As much, perhaps, as his bride. He allowed his hand to fall to his side.

The door suddenly opened, a sliver of light appearing first, and then her face.

"Are you lost, Your Lordship?" Davina inquired. But she didn't open the door further, and most definitely didn't welcome him inside. Instead she stared out at him, her face pinkened by her blush.

Perhaps she was as uncertain as he. Did she feel as if they tiptoed on shattered glass? Or on the thinnest ice after the first freeze of the season? Delicate, toe-first steps that measured the danger beneath them.

"Perhaps I am," he said, honesty restoring some of his equilibrium. Now to find the words to leave her. Sleep well? Would that be seemly in such a circumstance as a wedding night?

Perhaps he'd be better off saying something vulnerable, revealing the extent of his need. *Take me to your bed. Touch me.* No, that would be too revelatory.

He might promise to leave her alone as long as she offered him comfort of another sort. *Let me watch you sleep and marvel at the simple beauty of it. Or hear the sound of your breathing and coax the next breath with each inhalation of my lungs.*

For a few hours there would be nothing hideous about the night. Davina would not transform to another creature, would not become bloody and snarling. She'd remain just as she was, beautiful and sane.

"Are you lost?" she asked again, and this time she stood back and opened the door wider.

Another man might see this as an invitation, but he was somewhat wise in the ways of women and recognized it as a test. She would judge him in the next few minutes. If he placed his hand on the door and pushed it open, she'd label him a barbarian. Yet if he stood where he was and allowed her to dictate the pace, he'd be seen as weak. So he opted for a third course, one that suited his nature better and perhaps the circumstances as well. He simply spoke to her.

"I'm not lost, Davina, but I wondered if I've given you enough time to prepare."

"To become a wife and not simply a bride?"

At his smile, she continued. "My aunt says I am not tactful enough. My father would agree with her, I think. But I've never seen the virtue in hiding behind words, Your Lordship."

"Marshall," he corrected. "At this juncture, I think we should dispense with formality, don't you?"

"We do not know each other, Your Lordship. Would calling you by your Christian name delude you into thinking that we are friends? If so, I shall be glad to call you Marshall."

In that instant he capitulated to temptation. Raising his left hand, he pushed against the door gently. Davina stepped back, allowing him to enter her chamber, turn, and close the door.

Only then did Marshall allow himself to look at her completely. The furnishings of the room paled in drama and beauty to her.

She was attired in a white frothy material that swathed her from the throat to toe. She looked like a delicious French confection, the impression only strengthened by the fact that the fabric hinted at shadows, the darkness of her aureoles and the hair at the juncture of her thighs.

Someone had misjudged her and furnished her with a perfume that was too strong for her, hinting at spices from the Orient. Or perhaps the perfume was part of his madness, and she smelled only of her soap.

"You should have married long ago," he said. Was he blaming her for being here, for being his wife, for being vulnerable to his insanity? "You should have married and found love, either before the union or from it."

She blinked at him, and then frowned. "My father used to say that the past could not be changed, and the future may never come. I can only live in the present, Your Lordship."

This time he didn't correct her. Perhaps he wanted that extra bit of formality between them. But how formal was it when she stood half naked in front of him?

"Then shall we, too, begin to live in the present, lady wife?" He extended his hand to her, and she, looking bemused, took it with all the eagerness of a felon being led to the gallows.

Chapter 6

Instead of leading her to the bedchamber, he remained in the sitting room, selecting an overstuffed chair beside the fireplace.

She'd stood beside him in the chapel and sat with him at dinner. But in neither place had he looked quite so large. He seemed to dominate the sitting room, to the extent that she forced herself to stand erect, chin up, shoulders back. Her combative look, her aunt would have said.

Was she being combative? Or was she simply protecting herself? And what a horrid thought to have on her wedding night.

There was something about him that radiated power. Perhaps it was being an earl. Perhaps it was having been on so many diplomatic missions when he spoke for the Crown. Whatever quality it was, she felt it now, almost as if it traveled from him in waves. Or perhaps it wasn't power at all.

"Are you an evil man, Marshall?"

His small smile indicated approval of the use of his name.

"An interesting question," he said. "If I were evil I doubt I'd know it. Evil normally doesn't recognize itself. Shall I answer no, Davina? Would that reassure you?"

"Must we do this?" she asked abruptly, glancing toward the bedchamber. A single gas lamp was lit behind the closed door. Would he extinguish it before completing the act?

"I'm afraid we must," he said. "Otherwise it will be like being thrown from a horse. You'll never want to ride, and for the rest of your life you'll be curious and perhaps a little regretful."

She stared at him, incredulous. "Have you just equated bedding me to riding a horse?"

"There are those who say that the act is not dissimilar," he said.

There were tall blue and white porcelain urns at each corner of the fireplace, and a small mahogany table beside the chair where he sat. A green jade dragon with red ruby eyes sat on the mantel, its long tail undulating across the mahogany surface.

Marshall looked entirely too much at home in this very strange room.

She came and sat on the adjoining chair. She folded the nightgown around her legs modestly in an attempt to hide the fact that the material was diaphanous and too revealing.

He glanced at her and then away, and for that unconscious act of kindness, she felt a little warmth toward him. Not only was he handsome, but he possessed a sense of chivalry.

He clenched his hand repeatedly. Was he as nervous

as she? He turned his head and looked at her again as if he'd heard the question.

They stared at each other for several long moments.

"Then shall we do it?" she asked, standing. This act was going to happen; she might as well get it done. Without waiting for an answer, she crossed to the connecting door and opened it, revealing the bedchamber with its very large bed.

She didn't turn to see if he followed her as she walked to the three steps at the side of the bed. Only then did she take off the wrapper, tossing it to the foot of the mattress. The nightgown was a sheer and delicate column of snow-colored fabric that was gathered at the neck and left her shoulders bare. The garment clung to her breasts and the curve of her hips and buttocks before falling to swirl around her ankles.

There was not one degree of modesty left her, and for that reason, Davina covered herself up with the sheet. She lay back against the pillow, her gaze on the crimson silk above her.

"It's not truly like this," he said.

She turned her head to find him standing beside the bed, a look on his face that she'd not seen before. Was it kindness she saw in his eyes, or tenderness? Or did he simply pity her ignorance?

Perhaps she could tolerate kindness, and even welcome tenderness, but she would not be pitied, even by an earl.

She sat up, folding her arms in front of her, the better to hide her nearly bare breasts.

"You were lying there like a sacrifice," he said. "I can understand how you might think so, but it needn't be that way. I don't want you to fear me."

At her silence, he continued. "You've never harmed me, Davina. I shall not harm you."

From the moment she'd met him he had not done or said anything she expected. She didn't like feeling uncertain, and it made her irritated, but when she frowned at him, he only smiled in response.

"Who are you?" she asked. "Who is Marshall Ross, Earl of Lorne? I don't think I understand you."

"It's not an entirely bad thing to have a beautiful woman confused."

She tried to ignore the warmth she felt at his words, but it was impossible. He'd called her beautiful. Did he truly think she was, or was he only being the diplomat?

He suddenly leaned over the bed and kissed her, a gentle, sweet kiss on the lips. He straightened before she could draw away, and then climbed the three steps to sit beside her on the bed.

Outside, she could hear the wind whistling around the windows, fighting the building, roaring against the brick and mortar of Ambrose as if it were in a fierce winter battle. Inside, the room was so quiet, she could hear both of them breathing.

"I hadn't expected you to be innocent," he said, obviously picking his words with care. "Do you know what will happen?"

"I'm not innocent," she said. "I know quite well what will happen. You will put your member in me.

A moment or two later it will be over. You'll feel compelled to repeat the act periodically. Something about a man's dominant urges."

He glanced at her. "All that?"

"Have I amused you in some way?" she asked.

"Not at all, Davina."

"You're smiling."

"Am I?" he asked.

His eyes were crinkling at the corners, amusement seeming to color them even darker than normal.

"I don't think it's that entertaining, Your Lordship," she said. She couldn't decide if she was annoyed or hurt, and the very fact that she was vacillating between the two emotions irritated her even further.

"I didn't know you were so well versed, Davina," he said, still smiling.

Before she could comment, he leaned over her. Without warning her of what he was about to do, he pushed her down on the bed. "You'll have to forgive me," he said. "Consider it one of my dominant urges."

She lay there bared to his gaze, naked except for one very thin layer of fabric. The material clung to her body, leaving no doubt as to the contours beneath. She clenched her hands at her sides and closed her eyes and prayed for dignity, that she would not voice a whimper or a moan or a complaint. A Scotswoman was brave. A McLaren was valorous.

But he didn't plunder her body. Instead she felt a very gentle breath on her mouth just before he kissed her again. And this kiss was curious enough that she peered from beneath her lashes to look at him when it was finished.

He was smiling, but he did nothing more than reach out his hand to pull one of her curls free.

Instead of teasing her with words, or continuing their conversation, he pulled her to a sitting position and then kissed her again. He induced her to open her mouth to breathe into his, to allow his tongue to touch hers in the most intimate way. But the curious thing was the feeling such a touch evoked. Her face warmed, and her fingers tingled as well as her toes. Her heart began to beat rapidly, almost as if a kiss had some bearing on it.

Her mind darted from one topic to another, and then circled back to concentrate on the touch of his lips on her cheek, her nose, her closed lids, and then her chin.

He touched her breast with his hand, cupping the fabric around it. The effect was so startling that she gasped and opened her eyes simultaneously.

His smile had gone, and in its place was a sober gaze.

"I sent my solicitor to Edinburgh to pick a bride for me," he said conversationally. "He returned with news of you. He neglected to mention, however, that you were exquisite. Or that you had the tongue of an asp."

A laugh escaped her. "Surely you shouldn't say such things," she said. "Not on our wedding night."

He smiled. "Or that you had a mouth like a sorceress, one that tempts me to kiss you silent."

"Should I be flattered or shamed, Your Lordship?"

Or should she just close her eyes and pretend that this whole experience was over, done, and complete? Somehow, that didn't seem sensible at all. She'd always been curious, and this could be a very informative and interesting interlude.

This time, when he bent down to kiss her, she found herself turning toward him, and when he would have drawn away, she placed her palm against his cheek.

The look they shared was disturbingly intimate. As if he knew what she was feeling, and felt the same: confusion, pleasure, surprise, and a curious yearning. She wasn't hungry or thirsty, but she wanted something, some basic need that must be satisfied. The strangest feeling of all was that she knew he could satisfy it.

Her hands slid down to rest on his clothed arms, her gaze on his face. Somehow it didn't seem important anymore that she was nearly naked or that he was a stranger.

He drew away from her touch, and just when she thought he might leave her, he merely removed his jacket and began unbuttoning his shirt.

She wasn't prepared for him to undress in front of her. At first she didn't know where to look, but he didn't appear disturbed by her curiosity.

Before he removed his shirt he divested himself of his shoes, and then let his kilt drop to the floor. She concentrated on the tester above her for a few moments before she felt the mattress give, a sign that he'd returned to her side. Only then did she look in his direction again. His shoulders were bare.

Her glance raced down his chest.

Davina realized she'd never seen so much bare skin at one time. Certainly not masculine skin. Even when she'd bedded Alisdair, she'd done so with most of her clothes on. Nor had he undressed at all.

Marshall was naked. Dear God, he was naked.

Nor had he extinguished the lamp.

Oh my.

Perhaps she should have remained maidenly and reticent and kept her eyes closed, but curiosity kept them open. His shoulders were broad, his arms muscled in a way that hadn't been revealed by the shirt. His hips were narrow, but that was all she had a glimpse of before he kissed her again. Now there was no choice of keeping her eyes open or not. Her lashes fluttered down along with her senses. She went spiraling out of control, to a land of darkness and delight.

He touched her again, but this time she was naked. How very odd that she couldn't remember how her gown had been removed. Her arms were raised over her head and then placed around his neck, as if he somehow knew that she needed to hold on to him as a point of reference, an anchor.

Her breathing came faster, as if to keep up with the pounding of her heart. The world seemed to swirl around her in waves of color. He deepened the kiss, or she could have been the one who insisted upon touching his tongue with her own.

How deliciously he kissed. How utterly wonderful she felt.

When he kissed her throat, it felt as if it were right and proper. She arched her head back to give him room to trail a path of kisses from her ear down to her collarbone and across to her shoulders and then, blessedly, delightfully, wantonly, and wonderfully, to her breasts. When his mouth surrounded her nipple, she gasped.

His hands were everywhere, his fingers skimming across the flesh of her stomach, her thighs. His palm pressed against her left hip, and she wondered at the sensation. How could she feel so many things at once? He kissed her right breast and tongued the nipple, and then pulled at it gently.

Surely that sound didn't come from her?

He pulled back and looked at her. What other sight in this garish room was as beautiful as Marshall Ross? His brown eyes flashed with light; his mouth was smiling slightly; his cheeks were bronzed with color.

She reached out her hand and pressed her fingers against his lips. He responded by kissing them, and then smiling at her.

Words felt almost forbidden in those silent, enchanted moments. Her breath felt tight in her chest, and her blood felt as if it were beginning to boil, heating in her body and causing all manner of curious sensations. She wanted to smile. Then to lay her cheek against his and extend her arms around his shoulders, the better to hold on as this feeling buoyed her.

How did she explain what she felt to him? Or would he even care to know? Did he want her to share her thoughts? Or was a wedding night only for a bridegroom's pleasure?

Daringly she leaned forward and placed her lips on his. His mouth was shockingly warm. As she savored the sensation, his lips curved into a smile beneath hers.

Was he mocking her?

She tilted her head just slightly to the right and deepened the kiss. Without warning, his tongue touched her bottom lip, sending an intense spear of delight through her entire body. She drew back and looked at him.

His smile had faded, and there was not a hint of amusement in his expression. She bent forward and kissed him again, partly because she wanted to and partly because she didn't want to face that intense gaze any longer. There were too many questions in his eyes. Questions that he'd no doubt ask her soon, and in doing so break this spell.

He reached up with one hand and held her by the nape of her neck, pulling her forward. His other hand went to her throat, fingers splayed. A second later his fingers were on her face, his thumb at one corner of her lips. She made a sound at the back of her throat, a low protesting murmur. She wasn't in pain, but confusion mixed with delight swept through her body so strongly that it was like a fierce wind. Everything she thought she knew about passion had simply been wrong.

How wonderful that he could turn her warm with a kiss. How fascinating that her palms ached to smooth over his bare skin, feel the texture of it, measure his muscles, be heated with his warmth. What was that, unless it was passion?

Were wives supposed to feel passion?

This, then, was the answer to her earlier curiosity. This was what she'd thought to feel, this slightly wild sensation, this temptation of the flesh, this succumbing of the will and the sacrifice of self. She didn't care, right now, if he was her husband or her lover or if they were in public or in a bedroom lit only by a small lamp.

"Give me your hand," he said, his voice deep and dark.

She'd never been considered a biddable girl, but she did as he asked without question.

He placed her hand against his chest so that she could hear the booming beat of his heart. He said nothing further, only allowed the cadence of that organ to speak for him.

The night was suddenly silent. The wind had calmed, as if he'd decreed it. No birds called, no crickets chirped. No moths beat their wings against the silvery panes of glass. Even the moonlight was muted now, as if the disk of moon had disappeared behind a pocket of clouds.

"Davina." He only spoke her name, but she knew it was a question. How should she respond? With a yes? With a please?

He leaned over her again, tracing the line of her chin with one finger. Still he didn't speak, didn't attempt to convince her. Nor did he kiss her again when it was all she wanted.

In the silence, she nodded slightly. Marshall smiled and reached over to pull her to him.

She'd not thought that this night would be so different from her previous experience. But it was like comparing silver to pewter or silk to linen. The excitement she'd felt with Alisdair had been, no doubt, because of the daring of her acts. Never before had she felt this heady warmth, this delightful intoxication of the senses. Almost as if Marshall were a snifter of brandy and she was inhaling him.

Oh my.

He watched her, as still and silent as the air around them.

"What do you want me to do?" She'd never before felt so young or foolish, for that matter.

"What do you want to do?"

"End this," she said softly. "Finish it. Isn't that what you want to do?"

"Sometimes anticipation can be part of the pleasure."

Her anticipation was accompanied by a very real sense of dread. She knew what this act would entail. He'd enter her body. She'd feel the most incredible sense of discomfort, followed by an instant of something else, some indefinable sensation that might be pleasure if it lingered long enough. Then it would be gone, as simply as that. She'd no longer be an unmarried girl with foolishness in her past. She'd be a wife, a matron.

There was no reason to feel shame now. This act was sacrosanct and allowed. More than allowed, wasn't she to do it as often as her husband wished?

"Do you not want to have it simply done with and over? I thought men felt that way."

"Then shall we get to it?" His smile was soft, intriguing. "If you're impatient, that is."

She didn't say anything as he stretched out his hand and placed his fingers on her throat.

"What do you do all day that makes your hands so hard?" she asked, and knew again, by his sudden startled look, that she'd surprised him.

"I ride every day. The reins produce calluses."

"Every day?"

"Every day," he said.

"Even today?"

"Are you delaying the inevitable, Davina? Or have you suddenly decided that you aren't as impatient as you thought?"

"I'm not at all impatient," she said. "I'm simply attempting to be courteous."

Amusement danced in his eyes. "That is excessively sporting of you."

She smiled back at him. "It is, isn't it?"

Suddenly she was in the middle of the bed and he was leaning over her.

"I find that I'm impatient after all," he said.

"Truly?"

"Excessively."

"Oh."

The palms of his hands were warm, the tips of his fingers delicate as they trailed over her limbs. What she had once thought inviolate, he invaded, intrusive and gentle all at once. He held her chin as he kissed her, his fingertips stroking against her throat as he did so. The outline of one ear, the rounded curve of her shoulder, the angle of her elbow, each was a target for his touch.

When her hips arched he was suddenly there, sliding inside her with such gentleness and skill that she could only moan slightly in response and surrender.

He whispered instructions to her and she obeyed, wishing that she were more experienced. Shouldn't she hold something back of herself, be more circumspect or cautious? How could she? She'd never felt anything like what was happening to her, had never expected to. Her feet clung to his calves as he began to thrust rhythmically,

When she was a child, she'd seen a rainbow for the first time. It had stretched over Edinburgh in colors so brilliant that she'd been speechless in wonder. She felt the same now, awed by something she didn't quite understand.

This, then, was what the poets meant when they spoke of hearts wishing to weep, or a soul feeling as if it were entwined with another. She didn't know this man, but he knew her. When she sighed, his lips were there to capture the sound. When she placed her hand on his cheek in wonder, his hand pressed against the back of it as if to hold her spellbound.

In the next moment the world was gone, the night split by sunlight. She gasped, desperate for a breath. She wrapped her arms around Marshall's shoulders and held on to him as pleasure raced through her, colored gold and yellow-white.

"You weren't a virgin."

Her heart fluttered in her chest, a tiny bird encaged by her skin. Slowly Davina slipped her hands below the covers and clenched them into fists.

"You weren't a virgin," he repeated, raising himself up on one elbow to study her in the light from the lamp.

How very strange that he was more handsome at this moment than he'd been before. There was a ruddy color on his cheeks, and his brown eyes appeared almost black. His lips were curved into a smile. For a moment she was fixated on his mouth, wishing that she were brave enough to reach up and kiss him.

Perhaps it was his handsomeness that made her feel strangely shy. Or was it the sudden realization that intimacy had not made him less of a stranger? She knew the touch of his hands, the softness of his lips, the heat of his skin, but nothing truly important about his character. What made him happy? Sad? Was he kind to his servants or cruel? Was he arrogant or humble?

Who was the Earl of Lorne?

"Do you have nothing to say?" he asked.

She closed her eyes, praying for guidance. Would God be annoyed at her petition? Had God become tired of listening to her prayers?

Once more, God, and I shall trouble you no more. Or at least today. Give me the words to reply to him. Let me be wise and yet not offer myself up for more criticism.

Dear heavens, she was tired of being pilloried.

"No," she said firmly. "I wasn't a virgin."

Time stretched between them, measured in her slow and heavy breaths. She willed her heart to slow its frantic beat, pinned the corners of her mouth into the semblance of a smile.

"You have no explanation?" he asked.

"No," she said, forcing herself to look at him. "You knew there was scandal surrounding me, that I had shamed my family. Had you no idea I might not come to you as an innocent?"

He didn't speak. Neither did he look away.

"For what reason would I explain? For your approval?" She allowed the silence to stretch between them. "Is it necessary that you approve of me?"

"Have you always chosen your own path?"

She tried to bite back her smile, she truly did, but it was such an incongruous statement that she couldn't help but be amused.

"I am naked in a bed with a stranger I've just married. Hardly a decision I would have made myself. Or a path I would have chosen."

"You enjoyed yourself," he said. The statement was almost smug.

"I did," she admitted, looking away. "Should I be ashamed?"

"Do you feel shame?" he asked, moving to the edge of the bed and then standing.

A strange time to ask that question. Or was he simply calling attention to the fact that he was naked and nearly fully erect again. Had *he* no shame?

"Shame? It's a word that seems to have a variety of definitions," she said, "depending upon the person you ask. But it all comes down to behavior, does it not?"

"What do you decree as shameful behavior?" he asked.

Without thinking, she spoke. "Cruelty. Falsehoods."

"Not flashing your ankles or being too forward?" His smile was not taunting but kind. "Who was cruel to you, Davina?"

When she was silent, his smile faded. "Another confession that I'll not hear, I think," he said. "Never mind. I don't require that you share your mind with me. Just your body."

He moved to the door, grabbing his clothing as he went. Did he not intend to dress before leaving her?

"Will you not shock the servants?" she asked.

He only laughed as he walked through the doorway. A moment later, she heard the door of her suite close behind him.

Chapter 7

The morning sky was glowing richly pink and orange, bathing the world with celebratory colors. A tint of it touched the window, drifted shyly onto the sill, and brushed against Davina's hand as she sat on the vanity stool and watched Nora arrange her hair.

Nora didn't comment on her appearance, although she did smile occasionally as if attempting to stifle her amusement.

Davina stared at her reflection. Her eyes were different, sparkly somehow, and there was a pink mark on her chin. There were other places on her body that bore similar marks, but she'd powdered them and covered herself before allowing Nora into her room.

Nothing could lessen the heightened blush on her cheeks, however, and her lips appeared almost swollen. Anyone would know the extent of her experience if he looked hard enough.

Last night had been a revelation, but not simply a physical one. Somehow, Marshall had also invaded her mind, even occupying her dreams. As she sat patiently waiting for Nora to finish, she couldn't help but remember his touch. Without any difficulty at all, she could close her eyes and envision him beside her, wearing that strange half smile.

She opened her eyes, disappointed to find only Nora standing there.

Where was he? What was he doing? Were his thoughts as occupied with her as hers were with him?

Why had he left her after their first night together? Should she have been more circumspect in her response to him? Should she have been silent? Or should she have praised him in some way? Or should she have revealed the extent of her behavior to him, confessed her shame in detail?

This matter of being a bride was a great deal more complicated than it first appeared. Nor had she thought to ask her aunt such questions. Even now she didn't know if she could go to Theresa. Who, then, could she ask?

Dear heavens, what did she do now?

Should she be thinking so much of him? Or should she be dismissive of the entire experience, and treat her first night as a married woman with no more importance than the liaison with Alisdair? Except, of course, that it had been nothing like that afternoon with Alisdair. Nothing.

From this moment on, she'd never be the same. Her life would forever be labeled in two parts: before she was married, and afterward. Were there going to be other revelations in her marriage? Discoveries that would ultimately teach her as much about herself as about her husband?

Being bedded by the Earl of Lorne had been a fascinating experience, one that ranged from the tactile to the emotional. Davina had loved the touch of his fingers and his lips on her skin. His kisses had almost made her faint in delight, and she'd disappeared to another place when he'd brought her to pleasure. She'd never expected her wedding night to be so enjoyable. Nor had she anticipated being assaulted by so many feelings: fear, joy, and sadness.

"It's a fair day, Miss Davina," Nora said, interrupting her reverie. "Oh, Your Ladyship. You're the Countess of Lorne now."

How very odd. She was, wasn't she? How very strange that she'd not remembered until this moment. "Your Ladyship" didn't sound quite right, though. Perhaps she simply had to become used to it

"What about the peach gown, Your Ladyship?"

On any other day Davina wouldn't have cared about her attire. But she wanted to be dressed in her best today, to wear something that flattered her skin and brought out the color of her eyes. "I think the blue stripe, Nora."

Nora didn't comment, but her eyes twinkled as if she bit back a remark. Very well, let her maid think her foolish. What did it matter? What did it matter if the whole world saw her as silly and vain?

The fabric of her dress was a narrow greenish-blue stripe and fitted tightly in the bodice, a row of tiny black pearl buttons stretching from the neck to the waist. The pagoda sleeves were wide, ending in white cuffs at her wrists. The full shape of her dress was maintained by the balmoral skirt, comprised of a hoop topped by a woolen overskirt. All in all, it was heavier than a normal hoop cage, but at least it didn't require that she wear two petticoats to ensure that the outline of the hoop couldn't be seen.

The white collar and the dark blue bow at her throat gave her the appearance of a girl not far from the schoolroom. But there was a look in her eyes that belied that impression. Did passion linger in the expression? Or did her eyes reveal something more?

Nora had braided her hair, and the plaits were arranged in a coronet at the back of her head. With her pink cheeks and sparkling eyes, she looked quite acceptable. Pretty, perhaps. Thinking she was more than that would simply be vanity.

A moment later, Davina left the suite, holding her hand up when Nora would have accompanied her.

"I'm going to find my husband," she said. "I do not need a companion for that."

It was going to be difficult enough to view Marshall in the light of day; she didn't want any witnesses to their meeting.

Nora only nodded, but there was that look again, as if she knew quite well what Davina was thinking. Was her maid more experienced than she knew?

Eagerness propelled her down the corridor and to the very top of the stairs. The house was built in the shape of an H, with a more formal façade facing the curving drive. The area she faced now was the courtyard for the family, less structured and more informal, as if the plants had been left to grow as they would.

No one was in sight. No maid anywhere in view. Not a footman to be seen. She held herself still, listening for sound. Far away, she could hear laughter, but then it, too, faded. She might have been in an enchanted castle, so alone did she feel.

Windows stretched upward from the entrance to the family courtyard to the second floor. They were left unadorned by curtains, the view from the outside allowed to become part of the majesty of Ambrose. A deep blue Scottish sky, an emerald green lawn, and a garden ablaze in colorful blooms served as a backdrop for a perfect day. Not a cloud marred the sky, and a breeze ruffled the leaves of the trees that dotted the expanse before her. The scenery was almost like a painting, and Davina felt as if she were the only thing alive in the landscape.

Her attention was suddenly caught by something beyond the trees: a tall, pointed object that looked like a rooftop. Another building at Ambrose? The breeze wasn't as cooperative for the next few moments, and even though she waited, she couldn't see it again.

Davina finally descended the curving stairs slowly, kicking her skirt discreetly out of the way as she held on to the banister with her right hand. Even at the base of the stairs she was alone. No maid came up to her. Nor was there a male servant in sight. And Marshall? Where might she find him?

She probably should have sent him a note from her bedchamber and waited patiently for him to call upon her. Or sent for her aunt, to ask the proper behavior for the first morning as a countess. Theresa was steeped in propriety and would have known.

Instead, Davina faced the tall carved door leading to the courtyard.

The door looked, at first sight, to be so heavy that it would require two people to pull it ajar. But she found, when she turned the iron latch, that it opened without difficulty and closed easily.

Three shallow steps led to a courtyard of large gray slate tiles laid in a tight cobblestone pattern. Here and there were stone benches cunningly placed to take advantage of the shade of the mature trees. Stone urns were placed near the benches and filled to overflowing with flowering plants.

She might have been in Edinburgh, at The Meadows or any number of other public parks.

But it wasn't the sight of the courtyard that drew her onward, but the earlier vision she'd seen of something foreign to the landscape. She smoothed her forehead of its frown, ever conscious of her aunt's words: *A man does not like a woman who looks angry, my dear.* She wasn't angry; she was curious. Her father had once remarked that "curiosity is the bane of an intelligent mind, my child. It never ceases, nor lets up, but acts like a drug for the whole of your life."

She left the courtyard and picked her way across steppingstones set into the grass. Lifting her skirts to a modest height so they wouldn't become coated with dew, she concentrated on her footing. She passed the herb gardens, each row of plants neatly labeled, and what looked like a maze crafted of ornamental yews. Another garden filled with breeze-tossed blooms perfumed the air with the scent of flowers.

But there was another smell that was almost stronger than the summer morning. Something that hinted of dust and sun-baked earth.

At the top of a small rise, she hesitated, wondering if she was actually seeing what she was seeing. In the middle of a large clearing in the forest sat another building. Two stories tall, it was constructed of the same stone as Ambrose, and so similar that it might have been a fifth wing of the house that had strayed from the larger structure. In front of it lay another courtyard, this one composed of yellow stone hewn into large squares and set into the earth.

But it was the object in the middle of the courtyard that held her motionless in wonder and surprise. A massive obelisk was erected there, its pyramid-shaped top pointing toward the Scottish sky.

She continued to walk toward the building, uncaring about her footing, her gaze fixed on the obelisk. As she reached the courtyard, a breeze plunged beneath her skirts, danced around the lace of her pantaloons, and brushed against her ankles. Davina placed her hand down flat against her skirts to keep them from becoming airborne. A moment later, the air was still, the courtyard bright and sun-drenched, the glare such that Davina had to shield her eyes with her hand.

How could an obelisk be here? But there it was, standing proudly in the center of a stone courtyard as if she were in Egypt instead of Scotland. Approaching it carefully, she stopped some twenty feet from its base and followed the red granite pillar with her eyes all the way to the tip. Slowly she walked around the base, studying the pictographs incised in the stone.

"It's called Aidan's Needle."

She turned to find Marshall standing at the door to the building.

"It was carved at Aswan by order of Pharaoh Thotmes III in the fifteenth century B.C.," he said. "The Romans removed it to Alexandria."

"And you acquired it from there?"

"Actually, it was a gift to the Prince Regent from the Pasha of Egypt. The Prince Regent gave it to my father, who was happy to rescue it."

"And he brought it here." She placed her hand on the granite, surprised to find that it felt warm, almost alive. "It must have been a massive undertaking."

He nodded. "It was. It weighs more than two hundred tons. The journey to Scotland required three ships and took two years."

What a very strange place Ambrose was and how very odd that she'd no inkling of it before arriving here a day earlier. Yet in that short amount of time, her life had changed even more dramatically than she'd thought it would.

She looked around the courtyard. The obelisk was not the only strange ornament, although the other statuary certainly did not rival its height or dramatic impact. At the end of the courtyard were a pair of statues of men in stone chairs staring outward, their pose rigid, their pointed beards slightly curling at the end. On each head was a pointed hat with a serpent imposed on it, and both man and snake's stare were fixed for all eternity toward Ambrose.

"Did you know," she asked in the silence, "that Wadjet was considered to be the wife of Hapi in Lower Egypt? She was always depicted as a woman with a snake's head."

"How do you know that?"

"I read a great deal," she said. She turned toward him. "I've always been fascinated with Egypt, but I'd never thought to see something as strange as an obelisk in my new home."

He didn't respond.

Her bridegroom seemed a different man this morning. A stranger, rigid and arrogant. He was simply dressed in dark trousers and a white shirt open at the neck. His hair looked as if he'd run his fingers through it several times. His boots were well polished, the insides worn as if he also wore them for riding.

The look in his eyes, however, decreed him an earl. The distance in that gaze announced him a stranger.

She felt her face flush. What an utter fool she'd been to think that he might be eager to see her. But she didn't move away, or seek an excuse to leave him.

"Did I do anything wrong?" she asked, wondering if she was being too direct with him. If she was, then he'd simply have to become used to her idiosyncrasies. After all, that was part of marriage, was it not? To learn the foibles and flaws of another person and accept them? "Why did you leave me last night? Is it because I wouldn't tell you about my scandal?"

He looked startled at her question. "I would just as

soon leave the past where it is, Davina. I have no desire to unearth it."

"Are we to have separate bedrooms, then? I had assumed we would sleep together."

He turned away from her and walked to the edge of the courtyard. He stared toward Ambrose for so long, Davina wondered if he'd dismissed her from his mind. Or was he just signaling his wish for her to be gone?

She gripped her skirts with both hands, and decided that the very best thing to do would be to simply leave him, before she embarrassed herself further.

He turned, just as she made the decision to leave. She released the grip on her skirts, smoothing her fingers over the covered wire of her hoops. A bad habit, and one for which her aunt had often chastised her. *Davina, hoops are to give your skirts a pleasing aspect. But gripping the frame with your fingers only calls attention to a woman's underpinnings.*

Surely, however, Marshall knew she had underpinnings? She knew exactly what he looked like naked.

"My mother and father did not share a room," he said now. He spoke in a normal voice, and yet she could hear him quite well despite the distance between them. Was the sound amplified because of the stone courtyard?

"I believe they were happy with the arrangement."

"Did they like each other?" she asked.

For a moment she didn't think he was going to answer her.

"I do not believe so," he said finally.

"My parents adored each other," she said. "My mother

died when I was very young, but my father kept her miniature in his pocket until he, too, died. He only slept on the left side of the bed, as if her ghost would occupy the right side. And he never used the second pillow."

If she were saying the wrong thing, then she would simply have to say it. He would no doubt criticize her for it, or look down his handsome nose at her and make her wish she were a thousand miles and a thousand years away.

"We do not know each other," he said.

"We are not likely to, if we occupy different rooms."

"Did my solicitor not explain to you the terms of this marriage?"

Perhaps she really should leave now, before this conversation got any worse. Not that it could. How many women were so blatantly obvious and hungry for love and affection? How many women actually questioned why their husbands chose not to sleep with them? She'd never before been a bride, and she wasn't entirely certain how one should act. But she had a sinking feeling that it was not proper to confront a husband the way she was doing now.

It would not be the first time she'd ventured a strange comment or opinion. Her aunt was forever going on about how she should be more circumspect.

"I only met your solicitor once," she said. "He spoke mainly to my aunt. Are there special rules I need to know?"

"I will come to you when I feel it's right."

"When is that?" she asked. "When the moon is full? Or your mood dictates?" She looked around the courtyard. "Or would a long-dead Egyptian send you the information in some way?"

She thought she saw a smile on his face, but it was gone so quickly she wasn't entirely sure.

When he didn't answer her, she was tempted to stomp her foot on the stone beneath her shoes. Or perhaps indulge in a tantrum. How was a rejected bride supposed to act?

"Do you always say exactly what you think? Or what you're feeling at that particular moment?" he asked.

"When you address another person, do you always refrain from using her name? Or looking at her?"

He looked directly at her, his brown eyes unflinching, his gaze so intent that she almost glanced away. But she was no coward. If she had been, she would not be standing here now.

"I'm not afraid of you," she said. She could tell that her comment surprised him. But when he smiled, she was equally startled. How utterly handsome he was.

"Then you're either a very stupid young woman," he said amiably, "or a very brave one."

For a long moment she regarded him, uncertain of what to say or even to think. The strangest feeling overcame her, not unlike the sensation she had when reading one of her novels. It was as if his words had triggered some emotion deep inside her heart. Some yearning or some excitement for which she was unprepared.

"I could be either," she said, as affable as he. "My father used to say that I had no end to courage. But that courage, like chocolate, should be indulged in sparingly."

"He sounds like a wise man. Did you never heed his advice?"

"As often as I could. However, that was not always."

She hesitated a moment, and then spoke again. "There is only my aunt left to me, and your uncle to you." She pressed her hands flat against her skirts, conscious of her aunt's words. "We're orphans and nearly without relations. Wouldn't it be a wondrous thing if we could find family in each other?"

He turned away again, his gaze intent on the far horizon.

Evidently she'd overstepped her boundaries.

"Pardon me," she said, forcing a smile to her face. "It is all too evident that you don't feel the same. What, then, can I expect in the way of a marriage? Are there more rules?"

"Only the most important one."

"Yes. Well." She lifted her skirts, turned, and began to walk away.

Perhaps she should say something in parting, but she couldn't imagine that he'd be offended by the fact she'd left him so precipitously. In fact, she had the decided impression that he'd be more than happy to see her leave.

"We have managed to achieve a significant level of firsts with each other, my lady wife," he said, turning. "Be content with that."

She faced him. "Do you call me that because you can't remember my name? It's Davina. It's common enough. I could go by something else, if you choose. And what firsts would those be, Your Lordship?"

"I have bedded you, and you nearly fainted in my arms."

She really was annoyed at the flush traveling up her chest to her face. It was too warm and too prickly, like a rash instead of simple embarrassment.

The grip on her skirt was so tight that she was sure she was ruining the fabric. She forced her hands wide, and patted the warm material she'd wrinkled a moment earlier.

"Is that entirely proper? Bringing up what happened in our marriage bed, I mean." She tilted her head back and straightened her shoulders.

"This is not going to be a proper marriage."

She nodded as if she understood. In actuality, she didn't understand anything, especially how a man who'd been so charming the night before could be so cold and distant the next morning.

She took a deep breath and forced herself to smile. "Is it your intention to simply treat me as you would a stranger? Or someone whose name you can't remember? An Edinburgh acquaintance, perhaps, that you haven't seen for a while?"

When he didn't respond, she turned to leave him again. When he didn't call her back, when he made no comment at all, she glanced at him over her shoulder to find him looking at her. She wished he didn't have such striking brown eyes or that way of regarding something so intently. She wanted to ask what he was thinking. She wanted, even more so, even more foolishly, to ask him what he thought of her.

Before she could counsel herself that such an act

was foolish, if not downright idiotic, she turned and marched back to him, stopping only when she was directly in front of him. His smile had disappeared but that intent gaze remained. She knew why, now, his look was so troublesome. His eyes were brown, true, but the center of them was black and wide, deep and dark like a loch with overhanging trees, causing the water to appear mysterious, and not a little frightening.

"Were you displeased with me last night?"

Oh, what a foolish girl she was. What a simpleton. But she didn't pull back the question. Nor did she mitigate it with an explanation. She simply let it stand between them, floating in the air unanswered. And then she made it worse, by adding yet another statement. "I thought it wonderful."

His eyes changed, so imperceptibly that if she hadn't been studying him so intently, she'd never have seen it. A light flickered, like an underwater lantern below the surface of the lake.

"I wouldn't be displeased to do it again," she said. "That is, if you have any interest in doing so. I would like, very much, to do it again."

This time, before he could say anything or, worse, not say anything at all, she left him, walking briskly across the courtyard and feeling his stare on her back the whole time.

Chapter 8

Marshall was never completely free of demons, not even in the Egypt House, one of his favorite places at Ambrose. There were times when the voices swirled around the statues and hung low above the marble floor. Occasionally he thought he saw a creature with a cat's head trailing a scarf behind a pillar, or the very tip of Amenhotep's beard showing beside a doorway. When those moments came, he told himself they were the same visions and the same voices he always heard. These were not Egyptian ghosts or specters from thousands of years ago. These were simply manifestations of his madness. If he were in the middle of a fallow field, he would see something that did not belong there. No doubt the earth would speak to him, or the weeds rise up and twist themselves into some sort of creature.

This time, however, he kept seeing something—someone—that truly shouldn't be there, and this ghost wore scent. He was accustomed to auditory hallucinations, as well as visions, but he'd never before smelled attar of roses in the morning air at Ambrose. Dust, yes, and that strange almost cedar smell emanating from some of the mummies.

But then, he'd never been married before, either.

Sometimes all it took to appreciate one day from another was for something unusual to happen. A storm in the middle of a sunny afternoon, the unexpected appearance of an old friend, a few hours without pain—they were all ordinary events made slightly unusual, enough that they were marked and remembered.

For Marshall, that moment of appreciation had come at dawn, when he'd awakened feeling the simple and curious emptiness of the day. Nothing hurt, nothing felt wrong. Above all, there were no memories or fragments of dreams to haunt him. If he'd had hallucinations the night before, he couldn't recall them.

Not one bloody, tortured man had visited him.

There was no broken furniture. No blood to be found on the walls or the floor. There was no one standing inside the door, waiting for him to rouse so that he could be regaled with the horror of his behavior the previous night.

Had marriage unexpectedly brought him peace?

It would have been pleasant to sleep beside his bride, but Marshall couldn't take that chance. He might have awakened like a banshee, howling through the halls of Ambrose. Or worse—he might have seen her as an enemy, someone to destroy, a legacy of his imprisonment in China.

Thanks to his jailers in Peking, for seven months his life had been proscribed down to the minute. Sunrise to sunset, each moment was marked and measured against the day before.

He'd been so damn hopeful in the first weeks, believing each day that someone would come for them. The sound of booted feet through the brick corridors had inspired hope that he and his forty men would be rescued soon. After all, they were emissaries of the Crown, representatives of the greatest monarch the world had ever known. Even the Chinese emperor could not ignore Queen Victoria's might.

But it appeared as if the world had forgotten them, and the whole of China and the British Empire battled silently and in secrecy.

After three months, Marshall settled into a routine. He began to view anything different that happened with suspicion. Any sudden noise was cause for alarm. Any deviation in his ordered existence meant someone was going to die, or the Chinese had developed some new type of torture. Nothing new was ever good.

Somehow he'd carried that suspicion back to Ambrose, living in that fashion for the last year.

Davina was new. His marriage was new. So far, he wasn't entirely certain how he felt about either. He had a suspicion, however, that nothing in his well-ordered world was going to remain the same.

Davina McLaren Ross. Davina. He repeated her name several times in the silence of the room, and each time it sounded as if a bit of magic had rubbed off on him.

Davina.

Here was a woman who was not overawed either by

his consequence or by his past accomplishments. She hummed with intensity, her eyes sparkling, her cheeks pink with passion.

She'd actually raised her voice to him. *Were you displeased with me last night?* On the contrary, he'd been amazed. Enchanted.

How odd to be so fixated on one's wife. *Wife*, a word he tested several times, speaking it aloud in the silence of his office. She was nothing like he'd expected. But then his life was filled lately with unexpected events, not the least of which was his own madness.

He could still see her standing in the courtyard, a tension in her stance, a fiery sort of energy that was too much like fear. She'd determinedly forced her chin up and stared at him directly, very concisely telling him that she wanted him to be a husband in all ways.

He'd sent his solicitor for a kitten and the man had brought him back a tiger. His amusement was short-lived. Kitten or tiger, it mattered not. Davina McLaren Ross was an impediment to his life. She was going to be a distraction, he could tell. Hell, the night before had proven that only too well.

It was one thing to keep her distant with an air of indifference. What did he do about his own interest?

Of all the scenarios he could have envisioned about his marriage, Davina McLaren fit none of them. Their relationship was no more than that of two cordial strangers—or two strangers who'd been forced together. Yet the meeting earlier had proved to be uncomfortable, and unforgettable. The night before had proven even more difficult to forget.

Why the hell had he let her walk away?

Once he'd been facile in group situations, capable of speaking on a vast array of topics to myriad groups of people. He could converse in six languages, could swear in ten, and had been fluent in the easy quip, the impersonal banality.

For years he'd believed less in constancy than in variety. He couldn't even count the women he'd bedded, and if forced to pick each one of them out of a group, he couldn't swear he could do so.

Life had been an unending round of pleasures: the best food, the best wine, and the loveliest women. He'd been awarded success for simply being himself; charming, urbane, and filled to the brim with tact. He was handsome, titled, wealthy, well-educated, and had impeccable antecedents.

China, however, had put an end both to his social life and to his indiscriminate hedonism. Pride dictated that his nights be spent alone. Celibacy was easier than worrying whether the hallucinations would visit him and how quickly tales of his madness or his addiction to opium would spread.

Even in his marriage he had to be vigilant.

Still, he'd wanted to kiss her this morning, and thread his fingers through her hair, loosen her very proper plaits to see if she smiled at his daring. He wanted to kiss her throat to see if her pulse beat as strong as his.

Instead he'd sent her away. Prudent Marshall. Wise Marshall. Mad Marshall. He stared down at the desktop, seeing not the blotter, but her face.

I wouldn't be displeased to do it again.

Resolutely he pushed Davina from his mind and returned to his task. Several moments later Marshall stood, stretching. This office looked out on Aidan's Needle, so close that he could open the window, reach out, and touch the tip of the obelisk. He remembered the workmen warning that the obelisk was being erected too close to the Egypt House. If it ever fell, the structure might well be damaged. Marshall had given orders that work was to continue just as his father had wished, perhaps as a fitting memorial to the man. As apart as they had been in life, his parents had been close in death. His mother had died in May, and his father followed in June. Aidan had not lived to see his most prized acquisition set in its place of honor.

Marshall sat at the desk once more and pulled a sheaf of papers toward him.

In the last years of his life, his father had become almost maniacally acquisitive. Even after his death, so many shipments had arrived at Perth that Marshall had no choice but to simply warehouse the lot. Upon his return from China, he'd begun the transfer to Ambrose of his father's Egyptian treasures. Each week, another wagon or cart arrived from Edinburgh, and each week, Marshall was surprised by what his father had purchased or taken from Egypt.

As long as he could remember, Aidan Ross had been fascinated with Egypt and its culture. He'd studied Champollion's notes on the Rosetta Stone and conferred with scholars with a similar interest. More than once— and more than once in his mother's hearing—his father had expressed a desire to live his entire life in Egypt.

His mother had made no comment whatsoever. She'd simply raised her right eyebrow and fixed a look on his father that would have frozen a pharaoh.

Once Marshall had been as acquisitive as his father, but he'd been fascinated with Asia and the Far East. He no longer had a love for all things Oriental. He no longer wanted anything around to remind him of his travels to China or his ultimate imprisonment there.

I wouldn't be displeased to do it again.

He wasn't surprised to hear her voice in his mind. Her declaration had been surprising, perhaps even shocking, and certainly tempting. She wanted him to be a husband. Perhaps she'd deluded herself that there was something likable about him, something to admire about Marshall Ross, Earl of Lorne.

If so, he should go about the business of explaining that she was wrong. There was nothing in his nature or his character to recommend him as a spouse. She believed him to be someone he wasn't. All he could offer was his title and his wealth, both of which could be passed to an heir, or a daughter. For that reason alone she'd been brought to Ambrose. Perhaps last night he'd given her a child and there would be no further necessity for him to visit her.

My parents adored each other. What a fresh and unspoiled innocence. She wanted the same from their marriage. What would she say to the truth about him?

Perhaps she never needed to know.

She was beautiful, and he'd been lonely. The occasion of his marriage had given him an excuse to bed an attractive woman. He'd needed her, temporarily, and yet that momentary weakness made him feel strangely vulnerable now.

"We learn to accept what we know," he said aloud. Amenhotep smiled benignly at him from the corner.

Not too long ago, he'd seen Amenhotep walk, a hallucination that had shaken him badly. What had Davina said about courage? Courage wasn't like chocolate at all—it was the bitterest alum, a taste that curled the tongue and soured the stomach. Courage was the enemy of peace. Courage kept a man struggling to live when it was easier to simply give up and surrender.

I would like to do it again. Here she was, in his mind once more.

What answer could he give to that? *So would I, Davina. If I were sane. So would I, if I were not afraid that I'd see things move and see you grow into a two-headed Hydra and then laugh at me with bulging red lips dripping with blood.*

Well, marriage was certainly not what she'd expected. She'd been amazed, fascinated, delighted, astounded, thrilled, annoyed, and made miserable—all within the span of twenty-four hours. What would the next day bring?

Davina was almost afraid to discover.

She brushed away her tears as she walked briskly back to Ambrose. All of a sudden the house that had been so empty was swarming with servants. She saw two of them through the large windows.

Instead of returning to her room, a feat necessitating having to travel past a footman and up the stairs where a maid was industriously dusting, Davina simply sat on one of the slate benches in the courtyard and pretended an interest in the branches above her head.

"Your Ladyship," Nora said, "you shouldn't be sitting out here in the bright morning sun."

The young maid was suddenly a welcome companion and a reminder of home in a strange place. "The tree shelters me from the worst of the sun," she said. "But I won't remain here long. Do you know if my aunt has awakened yet, Nora?"

The girl hesitated. "I'm sorry, Your Ladyship. You didn't know? Mrs. Rowle left Ambrose over an hour ago."

Davina turned her head and looked at Nora. "No," she said, in violation of her aunt's dictate to not reveal anything to the servants. "I didn't know. Did she say nothing? Leave me a note?"

Nora suddenly looked at a loss, almost the way Davina felt. She reached out and patted the girl's hand in reprieve. "It's of no consequence, Nora."

Nora responded with a curtsy. Never before had she bowed so low or held the pose for quite so long. Was it due to Davina's new rank? Or simply because the young maid pitied her? Poor Davina McLaren, married one day. She felt alone on a tiny island in the middle of a suddenly dark and menacing ocean.

"I'll fetch your parasol, Your Ladyship."

"Never mind. I'll return to my room," she said, standing.

The servants had multiplied, dusting close to the windows, intent upon those tables that were already shiny and without a speck of dust. Were they that curious about her? Had they no other duties?

As they mounted the steps, Nora turned to her. "There's breakfast in the family dining room, Your Ladyship. I've been shown around this morning. I don't think I'll get you lost."

"Thank you, Nora," Davina said. "I find that I'm not hungry."

She turned her head and met several pairs of interested eyes. One woman in particular, attired in a dark blue, long-sleeved dress with a row of black buttons down the front, stared back at her for one long, unsmiling moment. Her blond hair was almost too brilliant and her lips looked too colorful to be natural. In her arms she held a ledger. Davina suspected her identity before Nora spoke.

"That's Mrs. Murray," Nora said. "The housekeeper. And a very strict one as well."

"If she finds me so interesting, she should at least introduce herself. In fact, she should have presented herself to me the moment I was married."

Nora glanced at her, but didn't say anything.

"Very well," Davina conceded. "Perhaps not that very moment. But certainly after enough time had passed."

"I don't mean to defend the woman, Your Ladyship, but you've been married less than a day."

Davina didn't respond to that criticism, well deserved though it might be.

"Go and fetch her, Nora," she said. "We shall end all this staring and speculation right this moment."

There was no need for Nora to leave her side. It seemed as if Mrs. Murray had the same idea. She was advancing across the immaculate wooden floor, her glance sweeping from side to side with the intensity of an inspector. If the maid in charge of cleaning this area of Ambrose had not been diligent in her duties, Davina didn't have a doubt that Mrs. Murray would upbraid her fiercely.

The woman stopped five feet away, wrapping her arms around the ledger as she executed a perfect curtsy.

"Your Ladyship," she said, "welcome to Ambrose."

The effrontery of that remark struck Davina immediately, as well as the irritation she promptly felt upon hearing it. Who was Mrs. Murray to welcome her to Ambrose?

But she was conscious of Nora's presence at her side as well as the voice of her aunt, forever counseling Davina on decorum. *Anger is an emotion, Davina, as powerful as fear. If you let someone know they've angered you, you've given them a powerful weapon.*

"Thank you, Mrs. Murray. I've been told that you are the housekeeper. How long have you been at Ambrose?"

"For a great many years, Your Ladyship," she said.

What a very agreeable voice she had. Did she practice it? It was on the upper range of female voices, however, and could easily turn into a screech. The smile was similar in quality, easy, perfect, and absolutely charming. She must have practiced it for hours.

"Have you?" Davina said. "How very interesting."

"I have found it to be so, Your Ladyship."

There were scores of questions she would have asked the housekeeper if the woman had been somewhat older and less attractive. Or if the sudden twinkle in Mrs. Murray's lovely blue eyes didn't irritate her immensely.

"I need a few maids to assist me," Davina said. "And a footman or two."

"We have a full complement of guests, Your Ladyship. Our staff is seeing to their needs."

Davina raised an eyebrow. "And you've no one to spare to see to mine, Mrs. Murray? Or to the earl?"

"Your guests are leaving this morning, Your Ladyship. If you will be patient for a few hours, the entire staff of Ambrose will be at your disposal."

"I do not require the entire staff," Davina said. "Merely a few maids and a footman or two."

"May I ask why, Your Ladyship?"

She wanted to be insufferably rude. She wanted to inform the woman that she'd the position neither to question nor to refuse what Davina wanted. Instead Davina forced a smile to her face.

"I need assistance removing the Chinese silk from the walls of my suite."

Mrs. Murray looked surprised. Her lovely smile faded, and the twinkle in her blue eyes flattened. "That wall covering was extraordinarily expensive, Your Ladyship."

"You do not approve, Mrs. Murray?"

"It is certainly not my place to approve or disapprove, Your Ladyship," the woman said, but the look on her face belied her words. She very much did not approve, and that suddenly pleased Davina immeasurably.

Had she always been so petty? So vindictive? So jealous? Or had marriage brought out the very worst in her?

The two women stared at each other for some time, long enough for Nora to evidently become uncomfortable. The young maid rested her weight first on one foot and then the other, as if she'd turn and run if given half the chance.

"The afternoon will be fine," Davina said, still smiling pleasantly. "I wouldn't want to inconvenience our guests."

Servants could punish their employers furtively and quite effectively. The sheets would suddenly become rough as if they'd had starch applied to them. Meals would be warm, instead of hot. Hot water would be tepid as well. Any confrontation would result in the servants looking innocent of guile and the misery being piled on. She wasn't going to give Mrs. Murray any excuse to foment rebellion at Ambrose.

"Thank you, Mrs. Murray."

The woman nodded, this time not even bothering with a curtsy. She turned and began to walk away, and Davina called her back.

"Perhaps we could go over the menus for this week sometime this afternoon?"

"I only discuss the meals with the earl, Your Ladyship," came the response. Nor did Mrs. Murray bother turning around as she spoke, but delivered her comments to the wainscoting.

Davina stared after her, realizing that war had just been declared.

Theresa Rowle stared down at the note in her hand. She'd taken nearly an hour to compose the silly thing. If she'd left it behind, Davina would have read it in puzzlement. There was little of the flighty woman in the words she'd written.

That woman truly didn't exist, but it was necessary to maintain the pose of a female who thought of nothing more serious than her latest dress or her current hairstyle.

More than once she would have liked to reveal to Davina who she truly was, but it wouldn't be safe to take anyone into her confidence, not even her niece.

A tear fell, and Theresa blotted it away with her fingertip so that it didn't stain the bodice of her dress.

Would Davina find happiness in her marriage? Only God knew the future, but Theresa had done what she could to protect her. The world was not a kind place at times, but that was knowledge she'd always wanted to spare Davina.

The silly girl had done something unforgivable, and the resultant scandal had almost ruined her. But by marrying her to the Earl of Lorne, Theresa had done what she could to protect her, and to alter the course of her destiny.

Dear God, she hoped her instincts had not proven wrong.

She leaned back against the cushions. The carriage belonged to the Earl of Lorne, and it was far advanced over her own vehicle. The springs prevented her from feeling the stones and unpaved sections of the road. The wheels felt padded, and the gentle swaying movement of the carriage was comforting rather than jarring on the body.

If she hadn't been annoyed at the fact that she'd been summoned back to London so precipitously, she might have enjoyed the journey to Waverly Station. But there were times when a person had to reach beyond himself, weren't there? When a person's selfish concerns were supplanted by other, greater needs? Marshall Ross understood that, and had demonstrated his patriotism.

Theresa's wishes and wants were not, after all, as important as the Empire's. In her letter, she'd tried to explain to Davina why she was deserting her, that it was important she return to London. But how did she speak of things like sacrifice and duty when she still wore the persona of a vain and selfish woman?

The Empire must stand. Right must triumph over personal matters. Justice must win. And she must never stop acting the part of fool, not until her task was done.

Out of sight of her maid, Theresa tore the notes into strips and the strips into pieces, and then placed the pieces in the bottom of the reticule.

Chapter 9

The maids arrived after lunch. In the meantime, Davina and Nora occupied themselves with unpacking Davina's trunks and arranging her possessions.

Her dresses, shoes, and accessories were placed in the commodious armoire, and her toiletries in the bathing chamber off the bedroom. The rest of the Countess of Lorne's suite, although similarly decorated in blinding red Chinese silk, was quite spacious, consisting of two additional rooms: a sitting room, and a room that looked to have no discernible purpose.

"What do you think it was used for?" Nora asked, coming to stand beside her in the doorway.

"I don't know," Davina answered, staring into the empty room. "There's no mark on the floor where a desk might have been. No shelves, no chairs."

"The previous countess used to grow plants," Nora said. "Do you think she used it for that?"

Davina glanced at her, surprised. "A conservatory?" Two long windows stretched from a foot above the floor to the ceiling. A narrow door between them led to a small sunny balcony, ideal for growing things. But the room itself? Although the Chinese silk gave the space the impression of being small and enclosed, in actuality the room was spacious.

"I'll make it my library," Davina said. "There must be some extra bookshelves at Ambrose. And if not, surely a carpenter is employed here."

"I'll see to it, Your Ladyship," Nora said, showing a great deal more initiative than she ever had in Edinburgh. Davina couldn't help but wonder if Nora had already made the acquaintance of the carpenter. Was he young and handsome?

Davina had a small desk moved from the sitting room and positioned between the windows. From here she could view the balcony and beyond to the sweeping vista of Ambrose, rolling hills, and, far off into the distance, Ben Hegan.

When the maids arrived, Davina occupied herself with directing their activities. Each girl took a section of the offending fabric from the wall, rolling it tightly as it came loose. Beneath it was batting that had been glued to the wall. That took a little more time to remove, and resulted in patches of plaster missing.

"Take the silk, if you wish, and use it in your own rooms," she told them, and more than one young girl looked enthused at the prospect.

She wanted nothing to do with the color red or anything Chinese that might remind her of her surrender to Marshall. She knew that a dozen years from now, the sight of Chinese silk would bring her wedding night to mind.

She could not believe that a man who'd seduced her so ably and made love to her with such gentleness the night before could treat her as a stranger the next morning.

"What are you going to put there, Your Ladyship?" Nora asked.

"Paint will do as well as anything," Davina said. "A very light shade of blue. Like a robin's egg, I think."

Nora looked a little doubtful, but didn't offer any suggestions. By dusk the walls were stripped and the rooms looked oddly naked. She dismissed the maids with their arms filled with rolls of Chinese silk.

"Tell the housekeeper that the silk is a gift," she told Nora. "I don't want her giving the maids any difficulties if they decide to decorate their own rooms."

Nora looked as if she would say something, but in the end only nodded.

Davina closed the door behind her maid, wondering if she should simply order a tray from the kitchen as they'd done for their noon meal. Eating alone in her room would certainly be easier than facing Marshall. But dining in solitary would also begin a precedent, and she would not spend the rest of her life hiding from her husband.

Even if he was content to absent himself from her.

Marshall had neither invited her to dinner nor come himself to question her dining arrangements. Perhaps he would have been happier if she'd left like the rest of their guests. According to one of the maids, there had been a stream of carriages leaving Ambrose all day.

Was she supposed to have entertained their guests?

Or had their guests been entertained well enough by the fact that neither she nor Marshall had made an appearance?

Determined, she refreshed herself with a sponge bath and dressed in a sedate peach gown, suitable for the occasion. Her hair was left as it had been all day, and other than donning a pair of earrings given to her by her aunt, she made no other alterations to her appearance.

She thanked Nora absently, her mind already on the confrontation to come, and left the room.

The dining room to which she was led by a tall, imposing footman was evidently set aside for small family gatherings. This room was not as magnificent as the receiving room or dining hall. Nor did it possess any Chinese furnishings.

The room was large and strangely shaped, not quite a square. The fourth wall was curved, and boasted a series of mounted stag heads. The floors were thick wooden slabs, pocked in places. Two stone walls were painted with a mural of a hunting scene, while the remaining wall was filled with mullioned windows now revealing the darkness outside Ambrose. Six carved chairs sat at the oversized wood table, each chair furnished with a crimson pillow tied to the seat and back.

Marshall was already seated at a table that could accommodate eight easily. At her entrance, he put down his napkin, pushed back the chair, and stood, all in one fluid movement.

"I'm sorry, am I late for dinner?" she asked.

"I was told you were ordering a tray in your room."

She smiled, her face feeling unnaturally stiff. "Mrs. Murray was wrong."

"It is of no great consequence, Davina. The kitchen can provide whatever you wish."

He moved to the end of the table and pulled out a chair. She ignored him and went to sit at his right side. There was already enough distance between them; she would not add to it by sitting at the end of the table.

By the time he reached her, she'd already sat, arranging her skirts around her. She was being rude, but she didn't suppose it mattered much, one way or another. Marshall had already dictated the tone of their marriage.

"I realize that you've run a bachelor household for some time," she said with equanimity. "But I am your wife. Would it not be natural for me to be present at meals?"

He raised one eyebrow but otherwise had no reaction to her question.

Within a matter of moments, a footman had placed a napkin and silverware in front of her. A moment later a second footman had provided two goblets, an array of plates, and a small covered basket filled with warm bread.

"Cook prepared quail," Marshall said. "I recommend it."

"I'll have whatever you're having," she said.

He smiled. "I haven't much of an appetite," he said. "I'm content enough with soup."

"Then the quail will serve nicely," she said.

All Marshall had to do was nod at one of the footmen, and the young man disappeared to relay her order.

"I understand that you've been busy," he said.

She glanced at him. "You do not object, surely?"

"You're the Countess of Lorne. You can do as you wish."

"I would not presume upon my title, one that I've owned for only a day. Ambrose is your home."

"And yours," he reminded her. "I have no objections."

"Do you store furniture? Things that are unused, or not in fashion? Is there an attic where I can look around?"

"You have my permission to do anything you would like to do, Davina, that would make you feel as if Ambrose is your home as well. Cost is not a factor, and there are numerous craftsmen employed at Ambrose who are at your beck and call."

"I have already discovered that," she said. "A young carpenter who will suit very well."

"You're an organized little soul, aren't you?" he said, glancing at her and then away.

"My father used to say the same thing," Davina said, "but he did so without derision in his voice."

"Was I derisive? Forgive me."

"I do like to arrange my life in organized little bundles—chores that need to be done immediately, tasks that should be seen to before the day has passed, and projects that are ongoing and take more than a day or so to complete. Each day should count for something. Each moment one is alive should be measured, explored, and lived to the fullest."

"Have you always been this way?"

She considered his question for a moment. "I don't

think so, no. I think my father's death brought home to me the fact that life was a fleeting thing, not at all certain. We think we're guaranteed tomorrow, but it may not come."

"Very admirable," he said, and there wasn't a hint of a smile on his face.

"I'm not an example for anyone to follow. I'm impatient, and there are often times when I forget to be thankful. Mostly I try to live my life."

"And expound that philosophy to anyone who will listen?" he asked.

"In all honesty, I've never spoken of how I feel to anyone else. Another first, Your Lordship."

Even if Marshall did not find this relationship disconcerting, she did. How was she expected to be intimate with a man at night when he was a stranger during the day? The same man who'd announced a rule for their marriage.

That little smile around his lips had the most annoying effect on her.

"I wish you well in your tasks," he said.

Could he be any more dispassionate? He might be addressing a chair. She'd heard the same types of comments in Edinburgh.

Fine afternoon, isn't it, Garner? Think it will rain?

The primroses are lovely, Miss Agatha. The colors are spectacular this year.

Have you seen the new pencil? Quite an invention with the eraser mounted at the end.

Dear heavens, she'd uttered the same kinds of statements herself at many a social gathering. She'd also been hideously bored at the time.

"Please," she said, gesturing toward his soup. "You mustn't wait for me. I'd feel much better about interrupting your dinner if you'd continue."

"I truly did not expect you."

She nodded, accepting that. All the same, she wondered what, exactly, Mrs. Murray had told him.

"I'm not someone with whom you have to converse endlessly. Silence is a blessed thing in a great many circumstances. I've been surrounded by chattering women all day. A little peace would be commendable."

A few moments of silence passed between them. Although she was extremely conscious of his presence, the moments were not uncomfortable.

"I find being married an unnatural situation," he said finally. "I'm not used to having a wife."

"Then pretend I'm a guest in your house," she suggested.

An intimate guest, one with whom you might share a bed.

Would it be possible for them to have such a relationship? Did such a thing like that happen? It must, given human nature and the fact that people find pleasure where they will.

"Most of the guests have left. My uncle invited them, and he was instrumental in banishing them. Only two remain, and they'll be gone by morning."

"Had you no friends you wished to attend your wedding?"

He put his spoon down and regarded her as if she were a troublesome puppy.

"Then perhaps I shouldn't be a guest," she said

before he could speak. "Unless, of course, you wish to banish me. Where shall I go? Back to Edinburgh?"

He didn't respond. Silence stretched between them, marked only by Davina's thanks to the footman when he brought her meal.

Marshall kept her company while she ate, but it was all too obvious, when he pushed his bowl an inch or two away with his thumb, that he had no interest in food.

"You truly have no appetite, then? Are you ailing?"

He began to laugh, such a strange reaction that she halted in the act of eating and stared at him.

When his burst of merriment was done, she commented, "Surely it was not that much of a jest."

"On the contrary, lady wife, it is more amusing than you know."

She placed the fork on the edge of her plate, blotted her lips with her napkin, and then deliberately took a sip of her wine before speaking again.

How odd that each gesture seemed slower than usual, as if her body were preparing her for what her mind was about to learn.

"Are you truly ill, Marshall?" she asked softly. "Is that the reason you wanted to marry me, someone you've never seen before?"

He smiled, that curious half smile she was beginning to know. This time, however, there was a touch of mockery to it.

"I didn't feel it necessary to meet you, Davina, because I knew all of the important things about you."

"From your solicitor? He doesn't know me well enough."

"I know you are of a certain age, that you are as described, a woman, healthy, and capable of bearing children."

"I don't know," she said, "whether I am insulted, confused, or sad."

"There is no reason to be insulted. On the contrary, most marriages are like ours." He glanced at her. "I forgot, except for your parents' idyllic union, of course. What a pity that you had to grow up thinking that love was something one found within a marriage."

"I've seen enough of society's marriages, Marshall," she said, pasting a smile to her face, "not to judge everything by my parents' example."

"As to confusion," he continued, "I don't know why you would feel any of that. I've made myself abundantly clear, I believe."

"And sadness?" she asked softly.

"That is your choice, Davina. I do not doubt that a great many women would commiserate with you, being married to the Devil of Ambrose."

He picked up his wineglass and studied her over the rim of it. "I do respect you, you know. For courage alone, I applaud you."

"For marrying you? In all honesty, I had little choice in the matter, as my aunt was fond of reminding me."

"I'm not commenting upon the occasion of our wedding, but on our wedding night." He placed the glass back down on the table.

When she didn't respond to that goad, he only smiled. "And perhaps to this morning when you were so determined that I continue my husbandly duties."

It was one thing to say something to him in the heat of emotion, quite another for him to tease her about it now. She looked down at her plate, not at all surprised that her appetite had departed also.

"Or tonight, when you entered the dining room to see me here."

If he wanted confrontation, she would give it to him. She would not be the little Edinburgh mouse recently transported to Ambrose.

Perhaps there were numerous reasons to be wary—the surly housekeeper, the strangeness of Ambrose, the feeling that there were secrets here that she couldn't begin to fathom, not the least of which was her husband.

But Davina had the feeling that if she began to be afraid, even rightfully, then she would never stop. She must cultivate an air of indifference, of apathy, of any other emotion rather than fear. Fear could eat away at her until there was nothing left but tears.

His right hand reached out and pulled the wineglass closer. A slow, deliberate movement that made her recall his fingers on her body. Was it possible that her new husband craved wine more than he did her?

"Was bedding me nothing more than a chore to you?" she asked.

There, she finally managed to jostle the smile from his face. That dratted perpetual half smile that indicated he thought her amusing, or charming, or precocious, like a small child or a cute puppy.

"Should I comment upon your ability to shock me, my lady wife?"

"That is all I have managed to do, Your Lordship," she said with a smile. "Perhaps that's how our marriage will be. You constantly disappointing me, while I annoy you."

"I never said you annoy me," he said calmly.

"But I should prepare myself to be continually disappointed?"

He smiled again and slowly pushed the wine-glass away with one finger. "I feel suitably chastised, Davina. Reminded of my duty as your husband, and as a man." One eyebrow arched upward as he looked at her.

She'd never seen a less cowed individual. Instead she was the one who felt reproached.

"You may do as you wish, Your Lordship," she said with as much of an air of indifference as she could muster. Truly, she didn't feel very indifferent around him. Instead he annoyed her, challenged her, made her feel emotions she'd never felt in a concentrated form and in a short time.

"I'll come to you tonight, Davina."

She didn't know what to say, but the necessity of speech was taken from her when he stood, threw his napkin down on the table, and strode from the room without a backward glance.

She stared at the meal on the plate in front of her. She couldn't quite decide what she was experiencing at this moment. Fear? No, not fear. Anticipation? That hardly seemed proper, did it?

Very well, she was doomed to perdition, then. Because that's exactly what she was feeling. Her fingers tingled, her breath was tight, her heart raced, and her mind recalled every moment of the night before.

Her aunt had always told her that a lady, a true lady, never had to worry about behavior. A lady was a lady down to the very center of her being. Decorum was second nature, politeness was always expected and delivered, but most of all a lady never stretched the boundaries of propriety. A true lady defined them.

That particular lecture had been given to her numerous times after *her abandon*—her aunt's way of referring to the scandal she'd caused. Davina hadn't volunteered that there were other occasions when she hadn't been the perfect lady, when she'd committed small, inconsequential acts of anarchy: leaving a party surreptitiously, claiming illness when she felt perfectly well, and hiring a public coach to travel through Edinburgh with only a maid for company. No, her most egregious, most inappropriate, and most offensive act had been to bed a man not her husband, and compound her shame by shedding her virginity with a great deal of enthusiasm.

She stood before the footman could assist her and left the room, retracing her steps back to her chamber. An hour later, she couldn't help but wonder, as she sat on the edge of her bed and watched as the second hand ticked slowly around the face of the mantel clock, whether her earlier, more youthful abandon had somehow altered her nature. Had she become incorrigible?

A proper lady would not be waiting impatiently for the arrival of her husband. A proper lady would no doubt be lying in bed beneath the covers, hands folded in a prayerful attitude, her supplication to the Almighty being that this chore be done and over with, quickly.

Very well, perhaps she wasn't proper after all, despite her aunt's attempt to mold her into a lady. The Queen demanded a certain type of behavior, and outwardly all society attempted to emulate her. But Davina couldn't help but wonder if the whole of society was truly as dutiful and proper as they appeared.

Had Victoria been?

How very odd to be sitting on the edge of her bed engaged in treasonous thoughts. But were they? Rumor had it that Victoria had been a devoted wife until her husband died a few years ago. Not merely devoted but besotted. Perhaps she had not been as proper in the confines of her bedroom. Perhaps she had been as fascinated with Albert as Davina was with Marshall.

Being a woman, surely, couldn't be any different from queen to countess.

She thought she heard a footstep and slid from the bed, gathering up the fabric of her peignoir, another frothy creation imported from France, so she could walk. At the time she'd picked out her trousseau, she'd done so grudgingly, and only because her aunt would have chosen for her if Davina hadn't indicated her selections. She'd not given any thought at all to how she might appear in all this fabric. At the moment, she was certain she looked like a small yellow cloud.

This garment, however, was not quite so modest, and there was no doubt whatsoever that she was naked beneath it.

Very well, she wasn't proper it all, because she had

no intention of lying in her bed until Marshall arrived. Let him see her nearly naked. And then let him turn around and walk out the door.

She wanted a kiss, and not just any kiss. She wanted his kiss. She wanted to feel the way his lips molded to hers, and the subtle sorcery he employed in opening her mouth with his. She wanted to feel his lips on her neck, throat, breasts, and his fingers all over her body. There was something so magical about his lovemaking, and she wanted to experience it again and again.

As if to demonstrate how wanton she truly was, she recalled the shape of him, his strong, muscular back that tapered down to narrow hips, and curved and perfectly rounded buttocks. His legs were long, and his feet dusted with black hair. He wasn't hirsute, this husband of hers, but there was no doubt that he was all male.

She wanted to surrender to him, to become sensation and feeling, simply a creature who existed for the sheer pleasure of being. When it was over, when night encompassed the world and there was nothing but the soft sounds of Ambrose settling around them, she wanted to lean into him and kiss him and thank him with a touch of her hand against his shoulder, or the stroke of her fingers along his naked back. The connection of that moment, tenuous and undemanding, meant that she wouldn't have to return to being a separate individual quite so soon.

Lovemaking was more than just bodies merging. The will itself slipped away as if it were no more than an unnecessary cloak. All that was left was the essence of the person, raw and exposed. In that perfect moment following pleasure, she'd felt closer to Marshall than to anyone in her life, experiencing a sense of connection that was the opposite of loneliness.

She looked around her. The chamber was a disaster, simply put. The shiny silk and batting had been stripped from the walls, but there were patches of plaster that still needed to be repaired before the room could be painted.

It was hardly a romantic bower.

Before she could talk herself out of it, she left the room, turned, and walked down the corridor to a set of double doors that quite obviously led to the earl's suite of rooms.

There were no footmen stationed at either side of the door or at the end of the hallway, ready to give aid to any of the family should they need assistance in the middle of the night. Was it Marshall's decision to have no servants in attendance? Perhaps he didn't like someone roaming the hallways at night. Or perhaps he simply guarded his privacy.

She knocked once on one of the two doors and waited only a moment before knocking again. When the door wasn't readily answered, she debated returning to her chamber. If she did, would he come to her?

Would she have to remain in her room and wait for him to call on her? Impatience was a character flaw and one she freely admitted to, along with a quick temper and an occasional tendency to be impulsive. And jealousy. She'd never before thought herself capable of jealousy, but that had been before meeting Mrs. Murray.

She stared at the door and then grabbed the handle, expecting some resistance. However, the door gave way easily, swinging inward and revealing a room that was even stranger than her bedchamber.

For a moment she could do nothing more than stand there, mouth agape. The earl's chamber was easily double the size of hers. If there was a sitting room, it was beyond this bedchamber. The bed was mounted on a dais, three steps up from the rest of the room. And in the middle, hanging from a plaster rosette, was a magnificent crystal chandelier, its prisms sparkling in the glow of the sconces on the walls.

What was difficult to comprehend was that all four walls of Marshall's chamber had been lined, not with Chinese silk or batting to hide any imperfections of the plaster beneath, but with mattresses. Laid two deep and lengthwise, they lined every wall, stretching well above her head.

Marshall's height.

She took a step backward, uncertain whether she should go or stay. When she heard his footsteps, she realized that the decision had been taken from her.

"I believe I've asked this question earlier," he said, appearing in the doorway. "Perhaps you didn't hear me, my lady wife. Were you not told that this was to be a certain type of marriage?"

In her filmy peignoir and nightgown, she felt even more naked than if she'd been stripped bare. By her actions, she felt exposed and revealed, every single one of her faults and frailties revealed. Above all, she

felt like a child who'd wandered into an area specifi-
cally off-limits and about which she'd been lectured
repeatedly.

She felt like a fool. Still, curiosity kept her rooted to
the spot. "Why?" She looked around the room and then
faced him again.

His eyes glittered, and his hands were clenched into
fists at his sides.

"Why, Marshall?"

"Get out."

The two words had the effect of thunder in the quiet
room.

Davina turned and left the room, startled when he
followed her, slamming the door hard behind him.
Before she could speak, before she could offer an explanation, he pinned her by the shoulders against the
wall. She flung out her arms, and he gripped one wrist,
his hand as firm as any manacle.

"Your husband is mad, lady wife," he said, breathing
the words next to her ear. "Did no one tell you?" His
cheek was abrasive against hers, his skin hot.

All she could do was shake her head within the confines of his embrace. Her blood suddenly felt as if it
were freezing, and her heart was beating so loud she
could barely hear.

Marshall pulled back, smiling. "Did no one tell you
I was a monster? A devil? And now you've entered hell,
my lady wife."

If she could have spoken, she would have apologized
for her intrusion. But this man did not want her words
of contrition. His brown eyes were chips of stone; his

smile had disappeared, and in its place was a face stiff with anger.

"Hell, madam wife, is where I scream to God in His heaven. God doesn't hear, but my demons do, all twenty-two of them. They visit me in hell, bloody and faceless, without hands and feet and sometimes carrying their heads. You want to know what you've found, lady wife? My hell. Welcome to hell."

"Marshall." That was all she was allowed to say before his mouth clamped down on hers. His lips were tender, the anger in his words and voice not transmitted to his kiss. She sagged against the wall, confused.

He freed her hand, and she placed it flat on his chest. A moment later he pulled back, and she was shocked to see the look in his eyes. There was such pain in his glance that she moved her hand to his face, her thumb brushing the corner of his mouth.

One single tear slid from her eye and tickled its way down her cheek. She'd not even known she was crying.

"Forgive me," she said, her voice broken and laced with tears. "I am so sorry."

"For what? For being married to a madman?"

"If you're mad, Marshall, the world should be filled with madmen."

He laughed, a short bark of a laugh completely without humor. "You have seen me at my best, Davina. Or if not at my best, then certainly adequate. You've not seen me screaming and throwing myself at the walls because they were bleeding. You've not witnessed my fits."

She resolutely refused to look away.

She didn't know him, true. And they had loved each other only once. But he'd been kind to her, and gentle, where another man might not have been.

"Marshall," she said softly.

He pulled back even further.

"I'm not afraid of you," she said. "Do you want me to be?"

"You would be safer to have some fear, my lady wife."

She opened her arms, and the look in his eyes softened. She took one step closer to him, and he didn't move, either toward her or away. One more step, and she was standing on tiptoe to wrap her arms around his neck.

In moments she was in her bed, in the ugly room that had magically ceased to be ugly. The man above her was not a monster at all, but a force of nature itself, a man with pain in his eyes and sorcery at his fingertips.

The yellow peignoir she'd wanted him to admire was gone in a movement she barely registered. From far away she noted the sound of fabric tearing, and then his hands were on her naked body. His dressing gown was flung to the floor, but she'd no time to marvel at the physique of this madman, a devil, her own personal demon.

He was beside her on the bed, pressing his palm against her forehead. He smoothed her hair back as he leaned over her. "Do you want this?" he asked, and it became a demand more than a question.

As she looked up into his eyes, she knew that he

wanted her surrender. Perhaps he needed her to capitulate, a payment for what she'd discovered, for invading his privacy.

"Yes," she whispered without a trace of fear. "Yes."

There was no more speech between them, no words, no protestations, no reassurance. She was trembling, but she wasn't afraid. When he touched her thigh, her legs spread wider. When his thumb brushed against a nipple, she pressed his hand beneath her breast as if offering herself up as a sacrifice for his ardent mouth.

For the next hour, he didn't speak, would not allow her to talk. He stroked her body, his lips following his fingers; his mouth learned her as intimately as his touch. When she sighed and closed her eyes at the feelings he evoked, he leaned over her and whispered against her closed lids until she opened them again.

"Come back to me, Davina."

She looked up at him to find him smiling down at her.

He was suddenly inside her, full and invading. Her hands went to his hips, her nails scraping against his skin. Relentlessly she pulled him to her, trapping him inside her by wrapping her feet around his calves.

He bent his head and kissed her, smiling against her lips, and she felt wild and abandoned. Pleasure swept through her body, pooled in secret places, made her fingers and toes tingle, harnessed her breath, and set her heart to beating furiously.

As she fell headlong into delight, Davina had the oddest thought—if Marshall were the devil, she'd gladly go to hell.

Chapter 10

When Davina awoke, Marshall was gone, vanished as ably as a dream. At first she didn't believe it, and stretched out her hand to the right, telling herself that Marshall had just moved a little farther away. But then she tested her theory by rolling over, keeping her eyes closed in wistfulness, and sliding her hand across the soft sheet.

She found only emptiness.

How foolish she was to want to cry. She'd spent hours in this man's arms, had felt incredible pleasure with him. Very well, Marshall had left her, but she told herself it was no doubt due to the press of business. Being an earl must carry with it several obligations of which she was ignorant. How silly to think that his decision to leave her truly had anything to do with her.

Yet it would have been nice to awaken with him beside her, to stretch out her hand and gently touch his face, to thread her fingers through his hair and feel the abrasiveness of his morning whiskers.

Davina sat up, knowing by the brightness of the light shining through the curtains that the day was well ad-

vanced. Normally, she woke an hour or so after dawn.
Morning suited her better than afternoons.

She dangled her feet over the side of the bed and
contemplated the room around her. Exploring Ambrose's library would have to wait.

She dressed, intent on finishing her chamber. The
carpenter arrived a little later to build the shelves
Davina had requested. For hours there was nothing
but the incessant sound of the carpenter and his helper
at work. The banging of the hammers became almost
commonplace, as routine as Nora slipping through the
adjoining door to see if Michael or his helper wished
a meal, a beverage, equipment or supplies, or anything
else that an increasingly solicitous maid might be able
to supply.

Michael was not averse to such attention. What man
would be? Nora was young and pretty, with blue eyes
and curly brown hair. She was shorter than Davina, and
more diminutive. But she had a smile that made anyone
witnessing it want to smile as well, and when she cast
it in Michael's direction, there was little doubt that
Ambrose's carpenter was a trout and Nora an expert
fisherman.

As for Marshall, Davina did not see her husband all
day. Nor was she about to send him a message. What
would it say? Are you well? Come to me? Forgive me?
Thank you?

She spent a few hours responding to well-wishers
and distant family, relatives whose existence she barely
remembered, but who evidently thought it opportune to
remind her of their ties now that she was a countess.

Stationery had been delivered from John Elder & Co. in Edinburgh with her new name. She'd not thought Marshall would have anticipated her wants or needs. Yet, in his way, Marshall was as solicitous of her as Nora was of Michael. Except that Nora was beside Michael whenever she could be, letting the man know—without a doubt—that she was fascinated with him. Marshall was a ghost.

Davina stared out the window, adrift in thoughts of her husband. Her memories of the night before were interrupted only by the entrance of plasterers into the sitting room. Her face felt flushed as she stood and crossed the room to her library.

"We're almost done here, Your Ladyship," Michael said, moving back from the wall. The shelves were lovely, built against one wall so snugly that they couldn't be moved. The cornice was still being carved, and when the whole of it was done, Michael was going to have his helper rub it down with oil that would bring out the grain of the wood.

"They look wonderful," she said, appreciating his workmanship.

"I had a bit of bother with that cupboard, but I finally worked it out. The third shelf's a bit deeper than the rest. I made it so for them big books, but it lets you in right enough."

She crossed the room to investigate, and found that Michael was indeed correct. There was a cupboard cut into the wall and framed with wood.

"It was underneath all that batting," Michael said.

"Did you open it?" Davina asked.

"Not my place, Your Ladyship."

She nodded, wishing he'd come to her earlier. Luckily, however, the space between the shelves was high enough that she could lean forward and pull at the edge of the cupboard. The door was wedged securely in place, and it took several moments until Davina could manage to get it free.

She opened the door tentatively, wondering if some vermin had found a nest in such a secluded burrow. Nothing greeted her but a pile of books. No, not books. Journals. Three shelves of journals. She extracted one and brushed its spine clean. The front page was delicately inscribed with a name she instantly recognized. Julianna Ross. She closed the journal again and held it close to her chest. Julianna Ross, Countess of Lorne. Marshall's mother. She replaced the book along with the others and slowly closed the cupboard. How very odd that it had been concealed. Why?

Why had she not simply destroyed the journals instead of hiding them? Or had she wanted to keep them for just such an occasion as this: their discovery by a descendant? Davina wasn't quite a descendant, but she might become the mother of one.

"What are they, Your Ladyship?" Nora asked.

For the first time since her marriage, her new title grated on her. Nora's habit of completing every sentence with "Your Ladyship" was growing tiresome as well. But she didn't berate her in front of the others. Nor did she have an answer to appease her curiosity. The journals suddenly felt private and personal. She didn't want to tell the other women, because they were certain to spread the news. Suddenly it felt as if the Countess of Lorne had reached out solely to her, and like it or not, Davina was the steward of a dead woman's words.

"There's plenty of time to determine what they are later," she said, closing the cupboard door firmly, and hoping no one would question her further.

Marshall closed the door, sealing himself in his study. He wouldn't go to Davina tonight. Even though he wanted to—dear God, he wanted to—he'd remain in his chamber.

She was too fascinating, too alluring. She made him forget, exactly, who he was. She made him forget the pain and the agony his life had become, and for that reason she was more dangerous than opium.

You must resist the pull of the drug, Your Lordship. It promises happiness but it only brings destruction. It is not your fault you have come to crave it, but what you do from this moment on is your choice, and your responsibility.

The pull of the drug? The Crown had provided the most skilled treatment for him, by the most intelligent and learned men, and they were all fools when they talked about opium.

He'd walked away from it, finally. He'd endured the cessation of the drug, the physical pain, the mental delirium. Yet even after his body was purged of the opium, his mind was poisoned by it. If he'd known what his life would have become, he would have begged his captors to kill him.

Now he was faced with another torment. A wife who promised him absolution when he was undeserving of it. A temptation who made him feel clean and safe and sane when he was with her.

He wanted to warn her that she should be sparse with her smiles. Each one made him want to place his palm over her lips, trembling in their curve, because he could not bear the tenderness of such an expression.

Her eyes were like the enchanted pools of a hidden forest, touched with magic. Yet those eyes had the power to reveal all her emotions from joy to sorrow.

Her face was all subtle curves and angles, a perfect nose, a chin with perhaps too much stubbornness about it, high cheekbones, and barely tamed brows. Her ears were shells of the most fascinating curve, as delicate and feminine as the nape of her neck exposed by her bent head.

Her teeth were white, and she flashed them often; even her most commonplace expressions ended in a half smile, as if she mocked herself. Her hair was thick and curly, a russet shade that curled around her shoulders to frame the symmetry of her face. Held tight in his fist, her glorious hair prompted him to think of silk and fire in one errant thought.

She'd a way of walking that made an onlooker think she was comfortable with the body Providence had given her. He'd been transfixed that first morning, watching as she walked toward the Egypt House.

He'd been besotted ever since.

For two nights he'd been fortunate, as if God Himself had taken pity on him for the travails of this past year and had blessed him with this temporary companionship. For two nights he'd lain with her, slipping not into sleep but a restful doze that mimicked peace.

The danger, however, was too great. He could fall asleep. Worse, his visions could visit him when he was with her. She was too vulnerable alone with him. Too fragile. Too sane.

He'd avoided society for a year—he could avoid Davina. He would visit her once a week, no more than that. Perhaps in a month or two she'd be with child. Or he would be dead, and she'd be a very wealthy widow.

Despite the fact that he'd spent the majority of his adult life in diplomatic service, ever since China he'd felt uncomfortable in social situations. The thrust and parry of saying nothing while appearing amenable strained his temper and bored him to tears.

He didn't care about the fate of governments or political figures. He doubted he could summon up one minute of compassion for any member of Parliament. Nor would they, if any of them knew the whole story, give him absolution for what he'd done. The less kind and perhaps more honest of his peers might attempt to put themselves mentally in his position and then congratulate themselves that they would never sink to his actions. But then a comfortable home outside London was not the same as a Peking prison cell.

A long time ago, Marshall had understood that he was not so much the Earl of Lorne as he was the property of the Crown. Now he was not even that, only an emissary who had failed, not poorly but magnificently, his mission to China an object lesson for all his successors.

In the last five years, he'd learned too much about human nature. He'd been surfeited by compliments from sycophants who'd cared little if he'd lived or died as long as he said a good word about them to the Queen. Five years had been ample time to teach him that greed was the most powerful motivator of the human species, that deceit was a common enough element in the people he met every day.

He'd learned, too, that there were a few people in the world capable of friendship and loyalty, but they were as rare and as priceless as black pearls.

Davina might be one of those people.

Yet he couldn't bear to see that look on her face. A look not of disappointment as much as regret—that she'd married him, that she shared his name, that she'd given him her body and the freedom of her responses.

Nor did he want to frighten her by letting her witness his ascent from the hell of his nightmares. Better she hate him than be terrified of him. Better she be confused and uncertain than aware of what he truly was.

He'd been powerless to prevent the deaths of twenty-two men. Men who'd put their trust and their lives in his hands.

Reason enough for nightmares.

He sat in his chair and reached for the decanter of wine, and wondered how long the night would be. Would his visions come at midnight? Or would they visit earlier, having been deprived of two nights of haunting? He sipped at his wine and prayed for sleep, for a moment of rest before he must battle his demons.

Davina ordered a tray in her room, fully expecting that Marshall would come to her later. She bathed and perfumed herself and then sat in the sitting room awaiting him. Another hour passed, and she realized that she looked too expectant, too anxious. Instead of performing a tableau that could easily be entitled "New Wife Awaiting Absent Bridegroom," she should go to bed.

By half past eleven, Davina knew that Marshall was not going to join her tonight. She sat up in bed, with the pillows propped behind her, and regarded the soft pink peignoir at the end of the bed. Should she don it and go in search of him? After yesterday, she was reluctant to enter his suite. What else would she learn about her husband?

She sat there for nearly half an hour, attuned to any sound around her. Her eyes became accustomed to the dark, enough to realize that a quarter moon was shining. There wasn't enough illumination to determine what shapes were in the darkness, but enough to mark the passage of the night.

Impatient with herself and her inability to sleep, she put her legs over the side of the bed and slid down from the tall mattress. She lit the lamp on her bedside table and then regarded the shadowed room. All her belongings had been put away. The walls had been repaired where the batting had pulled away some of the plaster. When she gave the order, painting would begin in earnest, and she'd have to find a place to sleep in the interim. She knew better than to assume she'd sleep beside her husband.

What task could she find to occupy herself in the middle of the night?

Needlework had always been a little difficult because it strained her eyes. She dabbled in watercolors occasionally, but needed sunlight for that, not the yellowish light from the gas lamps. She'd brought her personal library from Edinburgh, but none of the books looked inviting. She might explore Ambrose's library, if she knew where it was. Besides, there was every possibility that she could encounter Mrs. Murray on her rounds, and she really didn't relish that.

There were a few books she hadn't yet read—the journals of Julianna Ross. For a few moments, she engaged in a war of sorts with herself. Julianna's journals were not meant for anyone to see. She herself had kept a journal for some time, but had given it up. Her life was not substantially interesting to transcribe it to paper. Nor was she willing to divulge every single one of her thoughts for others to read.

Did she have the right, then, to read someone else's thoughts?

Perhaps if she simply read a few pages, Davina could better ascertain whether the journals were of a personal nature or more prosaic. Perhaps Julianna did nothing more than discuss menus or her garden.

Davina carried the lamp into the room she'd made her personal library. The odor of newly planed wood perfumed the air. Bending down, she pulled open the cupboard door. The arrangement of the journals wasn't difficult to determine. They began at the far left and continued to the right in chronological order.

She grabbed two of the books to the far left and returned to her bedchamber, retrieving her spectacles from her bedside table. Only then did she mount the steps and slide beneath the sheets again.

Gilt-etched leather made up the covers of the journals, reminding Davina of books her aunt had bought her from Florence. She opened the cover delicately so as to not damage the spine, now cracked with age.

On the frontispiece "Julianna Magreve Andrews" had been scratched out and "Julianna Ross" written above in a flowing and beautiful script.

Can love come so suddenly? Does it happen in the time that it takes to utter a sentence? Oh dear God, if it does, it has happened to me. I have fallen in love. I have fallen in love. Shall I say it again? I, Julianna Andrews Ross, have fallen in love. Such an emotion, love. Such a horrible and torturous thing to feel and yet marvelous and wonderful and entrancing all at the same time.

He came to sit at my side today when I was in the garden. I was sketching, and he sought me out. I pretended not to be aware of him at first. I wanted to be detached. But then I turned and he was looking at me.

Aidan. Such a wonderful name. It fits him, somehow. Aidan. It goes with his black hair and his smile. Such a lovely smile he has. Such a lovely manner about him.

Davina sat in the middle of the bed, drew her legs up, and balanced the book on her knees. She soon forgot her qualms about reading the dead woman's journal, being captivated by Julianna's story.

Marshall's mother was evidently in love with her husband, but it didn't seem as if the emotion was reciprocated. One entry in the second journal was telling:

He is going back to Egypt. Even though I am heavy with child, he is leaving. When I questioned him as to why now, he only looked away. Can he not bear to be with me? Am I so repulsive that he would much rather be in Egypt?

He will return, he said, in time for the birth. Yet he and I both know that isn't the truth. He will return when he feels the inclination to do so, and I will bear my child alone.

I would much rather hate Aidan now.

The next entry was commonplace, regarding a new spice Cook had used in what was evidently a delicious stew. A few entries later, Julianna recounted a plant cutting a neighbor had brought. Nowhere did she mention Marshall's birth, and he was mentioned only in passing toward the end of the journal.

I wanted to give Marshall a brother or sister. Perhaps it was for the best, given his difficult birth. What a joy he is to me. Why should I ever long for another child, with such a son?

Davina went back to the cupboard and retrieved a few more books, choosing a journal dated 1857, thirteen years earlier. Julianna had died in 1862. Did she know that she only had five years to live? Was there any inclination in her writings that she was conscious of the passing years?

The tone of Julianna's entries was generally happy, and only once did she seem less so.

Aidan is coming home. I received word via his factor today. The season in Egypt is finished, and his health has suffered for it. And so the Earl of Lorne has come home to be earl again.

Their marriage was not, evidently, a happy one, each living a separate life from the other. Davina skipped ahead several weeks to find an entry after the Earl of Lorne had returned.

Aidan lives for the dynasty of a forgotten age, in touch with his treasures as he has never been with human beings. I have seen him stroke the statue of a long-dead queen or gently touch a bandaged hand of one of his mummies with more tenderness than he has ever shown to another living soul. Does he not understand that those of us who draw breath also need attention?

Did Marshall emulate his father? Did he, too, want a marriage in which two separate lives never touched?

Davina picked up another journal, and then almost immediately wished she hadn't.

I have returned, just this afternoon, from the specialist in Edinburgh. He is quite an avuncular man, given to nodding often, which sets his large mustache to bobbing furiously on his face. I found myself concentrating on the ends of the mustache rather than the sound of his voice, which is rather high and whiny. I suppose a man cannot be blamed for the sound of his voice, but it seems to me that he would make an extra effort to counteract the appearance of femininity by adopting a more sober kind of dress. Unfortunately, my doctor chooses the rather appalling shade of plum for his waistcoats. But who am I to criticize the fashions of others? I am no portrait of elegance myself. I have no patience for it. Now, I have no time for it.

There, the very reason for my journey to Edinburgh. I cannot delay the words any longer, but in my foolishness, I think that if I do not write them down, they are less real. Instead my doctor's diagnosis will simply hang in the air, not fastening itself to me. How foolish I can be, sometimes. I cannot help but wonder if other people have such reluctance to face a terrible truth?

I feel as if my body is collapsing in on itself and will disappear until I am no more than an envelope. All they will find of me is a tiny, much-folded square of Julianna.

But I am delaying again, am I not? Silly woman. My reluctance to write the word will not prevent death from coming for me, eager and intrusive.

I had the oddest thought returning from Edinburgh today. Thank the dear Lord that Aidan is in Egypt. Otherwise I am sure that he would choose to use my body as one of his experiments and mummify me according to what he has discovered about his beloved country and its rather horrifying practices. I shall make it abundantly clear to Marshall that I am simply to rest in the family crypt, and nothing untoward is to be done with my remains.

There, I've said it again. My remains. Dear God, I am so frightened. I did not intend to die when I went to Edinburgh. I thought it womanly trouble. I am of that age, and gladly acknowledge it. I can no longer bear children, even though I have never lost the urge to practice for the act. Those days are long gone for me. They have been long gone for a time, unfortunately. When one's husband ignores one the only choice is take a lover or become a martyr. I do not have the tolerance for martyrdom, but I find adultery even more onerous.

I can't help but wonder occasionally if Aidan finds comfort in the arms of an Egyptian woman. I should like to kill him if he does.

In all actuality, he deserted me long before he started returning to Egypt with such regularity.

And I grew accustomed to his absences regardless of where his body resided.

I am dying, the doctor says. I have a cancer. In his very high, very squeaky voice, my physician informed me that he would do everything in his power to make the end as pleasing as possible, but that it would not be painless. I do not like pain.

There the journal ended.

Davina extinguished the lamp and lay alone in the darkness, her heart aching for a woman she'd never know.

Chapter 11

At dawn Davina awoke, certain that something was not quite right. What had awakened her? The journal she'd read just before falling into a troubled sleep? Or the fact that Marshall had never joined her last night?

She pulled the bellpull, but after five minutes Nora still hadn't arrived. Nor had a footman, inquiring after her needs.

She gave the bellpull another tug, but didn't wait until Nora joined her to dress. She dispensed with metal hoops, choosing a smaller set with tapes. A petticoat or two would be proper enough, and she laced herself very lightly in preparation for a good deal of physical work.

She chose a serviceable dress that was still too new for the task she'd given herself. Unfortunately, however, she'd not been allowed to bring any of her worn day dresses, her aunt deciding that she'd have no reason to ever need to wear a garment with a frayed hem or a threadbare collar.

You're going to be a countess, Davina. A countess does not go on foraging expeditions. If you go walking

*in Ambrose's woods, you will do so with a parasol and
a servant or two to beat the bushes out of your way.*

She had no intention of walking in the forests that
surrounded Ambrose, but she did want to explore the
attics. Instead of her more substantial shoes, she chose
casual slippers. She'd probably rue the choice, but the
leather shoes that laced up the side were uncomfortable
as well as heavy. By the end of the day her big toes hurt
and her heels pinched. She'd much prefer to walk around
in slippers even though it was like being barefoot.

Without Nora, the only way to fix her hair was to
plait it in one loose braid and secure it to the back of
her head. She did so, frowning at herself in the mirror.
After last night her eyes looked shadowed, the expression in them troubled. She'd not slept well.

Just when she'd dropped off to sleep she heard something that sounded oddly like an animal screaming in
pain. She'd been so distressed by the sound that it was
a very long time until she'd fallen asleep again.

She opened the door to her bedroom, wondering
where the maid's quarters were. Nora was always very
dependable, and if she'd not arrived, it was because
she was ill. Davina hoped it was only a minor ailment,
a complaint that could be rectified by a day spent in
bed.

Was there a physician living at Ambrose? A dozen
questions occurred to her, but each of them flew out of
her mind when she noticed the flurry of activity in the
direction of the earl's suite.

She flattened herself against the wall as a footman
ran past her, toward the room. The doors were open

and a parade of people were entering and leaving, some more hurriedly than others.

Davina pushed past the knot of people in the doorway. A footman jostled her, and she pushed him impatiently out of the way. He retaliated by pushing back and cursing at her. When he turned and glanced down at her, he flushed and bowed low.

"Begging your pardon, Your Ladyship," he said, finally moving out of her way.

Davina would have spoken to him but she suddenly saw Nora. The maid was leaning against one of the mattresses alongside the wall. One arm cradled a china bowl, its rim splashed with blood. A cloth, also bloodstained, was clutched in her hand. The color was stripped from the girl's face until it looked oddly gray.

Fear curled in the bottom of Davina's stomach. Her knees wobbled as she pushed herself through the crowd of people.

Something was horribly wrong.

She pushed her way closer to the bed. Marshall lay flat on his back, two men standing on either side of the mattress. One of the men was his uncle, but the second man was a stranger.

Marshall's right arm was bandaged. Blood dotted the sheets and trailed to a shattered window not far away.

"What happened?" she asked. At another time, she would have noted the absolute calm of her tone and congratulated herself on it. Now it was enough to push the words past the sudden constriction in her throat.

"You should not be here, Davina," Garrow Ross

said. He nodded to the footman who'd been so annoyed at her. "Thomas, see the countess to her room."

The footman stepped forward and would have bowed to her again had she not stopped him with an outstretched hand.

"I have no intention of leaving," she said. "Not until my question is answered. What happened?"

"There are some questions that should not be asked, lady wife," Marshall said. "You would not like the answers."

They exchanged a long look.

"Did you have one of your fits?" she asked, reaching out and touching his leg beneath the covers. A thoroughly shocking thing to do, especially in front of other people, but she needed to be reassured that he was all right. That simple touch was enough for the moment.

Garrow looked startled. "You know about his fits?"

She nodded. "What did you see?" she asked, ignoring Garrow and focusing her attention on Marshall.

"Is there a reason for such hysteria?"

Davina glanced behind her to find the housekeeper standing there, addressing a young maid who was blotting her eyes with her apron.

"Girl, get yourself to your room, and don't leave it until you can compose yourself. Your time will be taken from your half day off. Now go."

The young maid melted away, and it was then that Mrs. Murray looked in her direction. "The staff must remember their comportment at all times, Your Ladyship, even in difficult situations."

The words sounded uncannily like those she'd heard

all her life, but Davina didn't respond. Now was not the time to make a scene. Instead Davina turned and addressed the stranger.

"Who are you, sir?"

"He is a friend of mine," Garrow said in answer to her blunt question. "Who just happens to be a physician. A wedding guest of yours, who thankfully agreed to stay a week or so. Without him, I'd have been sorely pressed to treat Marshall."

"Which you have done," Marshall said. "And now all of you can leave. Jacobs, see the countess to her room."

Jacobs moved from the rear of the room and came to stand beside Davina. He exchanged a glance with Marshall and nodded before turning to Davina.

"Your Ladyship," he said, "if you please."

She glanced at Marshall but he didn't look in her direction.

"Marshall?"

"Go away, Davina," he said, without an inflection in his voice.

"It's for the best, Davina," Garrow said. He hesitated for a moment and then spoke again, in a low voice that couldn't be overheard. "I think that until he's well, you shouldn't be alone with him."

What utter rubbish.

She didn't make the comment to him, but remained silent instead. Sometimes older people, older men, often took silence for assent. They reasoned that a woman would not dare to disagree with them. Silence gave her the freedom to ignore their dictates and do what she chose.

"Marshall?"

He stared at the ceiling. "I want all of you out of my chamber. Now."

Once more Jacobs bowed to her, and this time she allowed him to escort her from the room.

But before she left, she stopped in front of Mrs. Murray. "There is nothing wrong with a little honest emotion, Mrs. Murray. Comportment has its place, but so does humanity. We cannot all be made of stone."

The two of them faced each other, neither speaking. Finally Davina simply walked away, Jacobs beside her, and Nora trailing behind.

She thanked Jacobs at the door and sent Nora back to her own chamber to change clothes and wash the blood from her hands.

Davina closed the door and leaned her forehead against it, wishing that she might begin the day again. She'd awake and Marshall would be beside her. They'd kiss, share a laugh, and plan their day. Except she couldn't go back and rearrange life to her liking, could she? If she could, she'd have her mother alive as well as her father. And her marriage? She'd still marry Marshall, and what kind of silly fool did that make her?

Garrow's friend peered into his face.

"Your Lordship, do you know who you are?"

"Of course I know who I am," Marshall said, feeling some degree of satisfaction when his identity came immediately to him. "Marshall Ross, Earl of Lorne. Is that sufficient enough for you? Or do you require additional proof?"

He noted the glance exchanged by his uncle and the other man. Was he being treated like a child? His right arm still hurt like blazes and his ribs felt as if they were bruised.

He didn't volunteer the fact that while he knew exactly who he was, Marshall wasn't entirely certain what had transpired in the last twelve hours. The last memory he had was of deciding not to visit Davina.

Davina. She'd looked at him as if she were frightened. What the hell did he do about that? Nothing— she was wise to be afraid of him.

He sat up, pushing away the physician's solicitous hands and ignoring his comments.

"Out of my room," he said, addressing the servants still milling about.

The footmen obeyed right away; a maid had to be propelled out the door by one of the young men. The housekeeper looked as if she'd like to remain in place. Only after they exchanged a long look did she nod and leave the room.

He turned to the physician. "Thank you for your assistance, sir, but as you can see, I no longer have need of you."

"I'm Polonius Marsh, Your Lordship," the man said, performing a sketchy bow. "I would like to leave you with a few instructions for the care of your arm."

"What about my arm?" He glanced down at the bandage.

"You have cut yourself, Your Lordship. On the glass from the window. A very nasty gash it is."

He craned his head to see the window in question,

wishing that he could remember. Sometimes it happened that way. Sometimes he had perfect recall, able to remember exactly which demons had appeared to him and in which guise. Other times his mind was wiped as clean as a blank slate.

He stood, feeling the room swim around him for a moment.

"You should rest, Your Lordship. You've lost a considerable amount of blood."

"I doubt I shall die of it."

"You'd be better to rest. Recuperate and let your blood multiply."

"I don't want to remain in this bed," Marshall said, realizing that he was fully clothed. Hadn't he undressed at all last night? Dear God, but the demons had come early.

"I can give you something for the discomfort, Your Lordship. Your arm is going to pain you."

Marshall almost smiled at that. "I won't take it," he said. "Better a little pain than to lose my senses."

"I assure you, sir, you would be better served by remaining prone for some time."

Marshall walked to the wardrobe, grateful to note that the room didn't swirl around him. "I'll be fine, Doctor. Thank you for your care of me."

"Marshall."

"Don't pontificate, Uncle," Marshall said, beginning to remove his shirt. He was used to the sight of his own blood—he'd seen enough in China. But he didn't have to inflict that sight on his servants.

He walked past his uncle, again thankful that his steps were steady and sure. Out of the corner of his eye he studied the window. The shards still remaining in the frame could have sliced his head off. Perhaps he should give some thought to installing bars on the inside of the windows.

If his privacy hadn't been so important to him, he would have installed a footman in his room as a body-guard. Or have Jacobs sleep in the next room. But he'd lived seven months in close contact with forty men, and he now prized his solitude.

He walked to the door and stood beside it. This time his uncle understood. Dr. Marsh was a bit slower to comprehend.

"Your Lordship, I do protest. You need to remain in bed."

"Thank you for your kindness, Dr. Marsh."

Implicit in his comment was a farewell. Garrow nodded, signifying his understanding. Dr. Marsh would be on his way home by afternoon, after an intent con-versation about the wisdom of keeping the events in this room confidential.

When the door closed behind them, Marshall braced his left arm against the door and swore softly. His right arm hurt abominably, and there was a thudding headache in the middle of his skull that threatened to burst from his forehead. But his physical symptoms didn't bother him as much as the sick feeling of regret he felt.

When would it end? One morning he wouldn't awake. Or he would awake in hell, a prisoner there forever.

"Lord Martinsdale, I must tell you that I don't feel comfortable doing what you're asking," Theresa said, staring at the man seated on the opposite side of an enormous mahogany desk.

She'd often thought that Lord Martinsdale summoned those who reported to him in this office in order to intimidate them. The chamber had no impression on her.

The portrait of the Queen was mounted on the wall behind him, slightly elevated to give the impression that Victoria was overseeing all that transpired. The bookcases along three walls were mahogany, the carved cornices matching the columns of the desk. Burgundy curtains were draped across the windows framing the door on the fourth wall.

It was, simply put, the office of a man of power, and one who didn't mind wielding it.

"Is it not a bit late to be using that particular word, Mrs. Rowle? There were numerous occasions when you were not comfortable. Besides, the situation is ideal for someone of your talents."

"Hardly ideal, Lord Martinsdale. The man is a relative by marriage."

He fixed a severe look on her, as if he could compel her to act by a glance.

"The man is a disgrace," he said. "That is the best I can say about him." He gestured toward the documents on his desk, documents he'd revealed to Theresa not five minutes earlier. "Surely you can see that for yourself. I would do anything, even trade upon your relationship with the man, to snare him."

"But you're not the one who is to snare him, Lord Martinsdale. You have left that task for me." She managed a smile by sheer will.

"I can think of no one better, Mrs. Rowle. In addition, I've been led to understand that he appreciates the company of intelligent, refined women." He bent slightly from the waist. "Not to mention beautiful."

Victoria's England was a strange place. Theresa would have shocked Martinsdale if she'd mentioned the word *bull* instead of the more acceptable term *male cow*, but Martinsdale saw nothing wrong with urging whoredom on her.

"You want me to encourage him to my bed. If that were not enough, you want me to spy on him?"

She knew her cheeks were flushed. She was of an age when heat raced through her body like a wildfire, indicating that nature was nearly done with her.

"Yes, Mrs. Rowle, I do. The Empire appreciates your patriotism."

Some years ago, she'd been widowed at the Battle of Balaklava. Ever since then she'd been struggling to find a purpose in life, one that would enable her to want to wake in the morning. She still missed James, and would until the day she died, but she'd found her purpose.

All in all, she didn't do much for the Crown. There were advantageous friendships she'd cultivated in London; she'd attended a number of important parties. When she heard something of interest, she reported back to Lord Martinsdale. Sometimes she suspected that the information was valuable. Rarely did she ever find out if she'd been of use.

Now, however, Martinsdale wanted her to pose as a seductress.

"I have long thought that we did not use you to your full advantage, Mrs. Rowle."

She stood, advanced on Lord Martinsdale's desk, placing one hand on either side of a rather ornate brass and crystal inkwell. The silly thing belonged in a lady's boudoir, not on the desk of such an important personage.

"I cannot do this, Your Lordship." She'd preached decorum to Davina from dawn until dusk. How was she supposed to transform herself into a fallen woman? Dear God, what if Davina found out?

He sat back in his chair and regarded her somberly.

"In all honesty," he admitted, "we didn't think about it until your niece married. A rather opportune marriage, that. I congratulate you on your cleverness."

She didn't know whether to leave the room that instant or stay in place, hoping that he would say something less idiotic and of more value. She opted for remaining.

He began fiddling with a few of the papers on his desk, stacking them and making a point of appearing incredibly distracted. But Theresa knew what kind of mind worked behind those bushy white eyebrows.

"It is an ideal situation, Mrs. Rowle. You are the ideal woman. If you do not act for your country, then for God's sake act for those hundreds of people the blighter has sold into slavery."

She abruptly sat down.

"Is there no other way?"

He smiled, and this time she was certain he wasn't going to answer. But he surprised her.

"We've detained his latest ship, but someone must have warned the captain. The hold was empty, and if there were poor souls on it once, they're at the bottom of the ocean now. But we cannot continue to engage in acts of piracy, Mrs. Rowle. We are the British Empire."

He looked so absurdly puffed up that she couldn't prevent her next words. "I do wish you'd been so forceful in regard to Garrow's nephew. The Earl of Lorne suffered a great deal for his patriotism. Does Her Majesty know the extent of what happened to him?"

For the first time since she'd entered the room, Lord Martinsdale looked uncomfortable.

"I do not believe so. Despite the fact that Her Majesty is a formidable figure—"

"Do not continue with that thought," Theresa said, holding up a hand. "Do not say that she is a female, and therefore must be protected. It is only men who are under the impression that women are protected from the world. We are not sheltered from any of life's inevitabilities, Lord Martinsdale." She fixed a look on him of such irritation that he glanced down at his desk rather than at her.

"It was an ill-suited remark, and one for which I humbly apologize."

In her decade-long relationship with the man who sat opposite her, she'd never heard him come close to an apology.

She nodded, absolving him with the gesture. "But the fact remains, the Queen does not know of Marshall's sacrifice," she said.

"She knows the whole of it, Mrs. Rowle, but not the details."

"The details?" She stared at Lord Martinsdale incredulously. "That's what you're calling torture?" The man didn't answer. "Why wasn't Garrow stopped when his nephew was taken? Did you simply ignore what he was doing at the time?"

He leaned back in his chair and studied her over the steeple of his fingers.

"We actually didn't know the extent of Ross's involvement in the coolie trade until the earl was taken. It was the Chinese who gave us the information. They believed sending the earl to them was a diplomatic slap in the face. Only after they were convinced we knew nothing about Garrow Ross's slave trade did they consider releasing the earl." He smiled. "It also didn't hurt that we burned their palace in Peking."

Theresa stood, grabbed her reticule, and frowned down at Lord Martinsdale.

"What kind of proof do you need?"

Martinsdale was quick to reply. "Get me anything that will indicate his contacts in Macao or his knowledge of what is being transported on his own ships and I will ensure that he pays for his activities."

She nodded. "How?"

Lord Martinsdale looked uncomfortable again. "We have an agreement to turn him over to the Chinese, Mrs. Rowle."

She thought about that admission for a moment. "Tell your superiors and tell the Queen if you must, that I will do my best."

Lord Martinsdale had the temerity to smile as she left the room.

Chapter 12

Nora was still shaking when she returned to Davina's room, although she'd changed both her dress and her apron. There was, thank heavens, no more blood on her.

"I was coming to wake you, Your Ladyship," Nora said, her voice sounding choked. "The physician grabbed me and said I was needed in the earl's room. I've never seen the like, all that blood and the earl acting like he didn't know what was happening."

"Well, it's over now, but our exploration of the attics can wait for another day. I want you to go back to your room, Nora."

"My room, Your Ladyship?"

"Take the day to rest," Davina said. When it looked as if Nora would fuss, she only held up her hand. "I shall not take it from your wages, Nora. Not when it's my suggestion. Go on now."

Nora looked as if she'd like to protest, but she finally only nodded, leaving the room and closing the door behind her silently.

Davina was grateful for the respite. With Nora gone,

she didn't have to pretend to be composed. She could weep to her heart's content, or simply stare out the window, worried and uncertain about what to do.

For nearly two hours that's exactly what she did.

He'd told her he was mad, and she'd refused to believe it. What did she do now? Believe him?

You are too stubborn, Davina. An echo of her father's voice as well as her aunt's.

She'd always been a little proud of her obstinacy, deeming it a character attribute. After all, stubbornness indicated a fixed set of ideals, a certain purpose, and control over one's thoughts. Had she been wrong all along? Was it truly a virtue or simply a flaw?

Had she seen only what she wanted to see and not the truth? Even so, she couldn't banish the thought that the man who'd touched her so tenderly could not be a raving lunatic the next moment. It didn't seem possible, even though she had the proof in front of her.

Was he a lover or a madman? Could he be both? He was her husband. He could not be mad.

Why was she cowering in her chamber like a silly schoolgirl? If she believed in him, then why was she allowing Garrow, the physician, and a score of servants to care for her husband when she was more than able to do so?

Davina bathed her face, smoothed the wrinkles from her dress, and inspected herself in the mirror before leaving her chamber and marching down the hall to the earl's suite.

She'd expected to encounter some sort of resistance but there was no one in the corridor, and when she opened the door to his room even Marshall was gone.

There was only one person in the room, and it was Michael, the carpenter, carefully removing the last of the glass from the window.

Even the bed linens had been changed, the counterpane perfectly smooth. There was not a sign of blood anywhere.

"Where is the earl?" she asked.

Michael turned and bobbed a half bow as he performed his task. "I don't know, Your Ladyship. He goes riding of a morning. You might send for the stable master."

She'd no intention of sending for anyone when she was more than capable of going in search of the man herself. She thanked Michael and made her way down the stairs, out the door, and to the road leading to the stables located some distance from Ambrose.

By the time she entered the wide double doors of the stable and sought out the stable master, she was past being worried and well into being annoyed.

"Have you seen the earl?" she asked.

At first the older man looked nonplussed, but he recovered quickly. "I don't know, my lady. I've not seen him today. Or yesterday, for that matter. Mr. Ross I put in a carriage not five minutes ago. Ready to see the back of this place, he said. Wouldn't be surprised if he stayed in Edinburgh for another year. We don't see much of him round about. Only when something special happens."

His grin lit up his face. "Begging your pardon, my lady. Like your wedding."

"You've no idea where my husband is?"

"No, my lady. Like I said, I haven't seen him."

She turned and was leaving the stable when he called her back.

"Have you gone to that place of his?"

She glanced over her shoulder at him. "What place?"

"Where he has those statues and odd things. Aidan's Needle. Where he holes himself up. They call it the Egypt House."

"The building beside the obelisk?" she asked.

"That's the one. You'd best try there, then. It's where he goes most days. Especially on a day like today with the storm and all."

Only then did she realize that it had begun to rain.

Heavy drops of rain splashed against the ground and marked the dirt with a slight depression as they hit. The Egypt House was on the other side of the hill. She'd no choice but to walk through the rain, and doing so did not add to her mood.

She'd been worried about him. She'd cried for him. She'd spent an hour, maybe two, in such confusion that she'd doubted herself, her emotions, and even her wits. In all this time, he'd been fine. Better than fine, if he was well enough to get out of bed and seek respite somewhere else.

She stopped in the middle of the lawn and stared up at the gray clouds, uncaring that her face was being washed by the rain. At this moment she wanted to shake her fist at the sky. Or perhaps at Marshall himself.

Aidan's Needle was nearly black, the rain sluicing off the obelisk.

Davina faced the Egypt House. Where in this sprawling structure was Marshall? Should she even try to find him? He'd made it all too clear that they were not to have any contact but the type that he initiated.

What was her life to be? Was she to spend her days attempting to find tasks to do, and her nights waiting vainly for her husband?

The door to the Egypt House remained closed, a barrier representing her marriage. She was not to go inside. She was to be patient and malleable, a dutiful wife with no curiosity and little courage.

She strode toward the door and turned the handle, surprised that it opened easily. No one greeted her. No one told her she wasn't welcome. Not one voice was raised in protest for her appearance. The silence was so acute that she would have been very surprised to find anyone in the building.

But the mystery of Marshall's whereabouts faded as she turned her head and viewed the whole of the building, her mind trying to make sense of what she was seeing.

The structure had been gutted. The second and third floors were gone, leaving a deep balcony on both floors overlooking the cavernous space, which had been given up to Egyptian relics. Huge stone statues, columns that stretched from the floor to the cupola ceiling, clay pots of every size and description, odd wooden figurines of men with the heads of jackals, and hundreds of statues of cats.

In the middle of the space were four large coffins.

She took a step away, clutching at her skirt, and made an effort to control her breathing.

A shaft of sunlight parted the clouds, speared into the Egypt House, bathing a section of mural. Four men in formal pose, their ebony bodies oiled, carried trays of amber and gold beads, dozens of ostrich eggs, and copper-colored amphorae to the gods. Caskets of myrrh, daggers sheathed in gold, deep purple grapes were brilliantly colored, as if the artist had done the work yesterday.

She might not have been in Scotland at all, but in Egypt. Or perhaps some odd combination of the two, a place carved out of this time yet steeped in antiquity.

She was sodden, her skirt dripping a path on the stone floor, marking her progress. The building was cool, and she was beginning to shiver. She wrapped her arms around her waist. She shouldn't have come without her shawl. She shouldn't have gone walking through the rain. She shouldn't have allowed annoyance to dictate her actions. Perhaps she shouldn't even be here now.

Was there anything she *should* do? Leave, perhaps. Go back to her room like an obedient and unwanted wife. Begin her own series of journals, just like Juli-anna's. A wiser woman would. A wiser woman would not have gone looking for her husband.

Oh bother. There had been more repercussions for her obedience than her wantonness. She'd been meek and mute, and all she'd gotten for her troubles was to find herself married. Married to a man who insisted upon placing her in a neat little compartment where she had no intention of remaining.

She might as well be shameful. When she'd shocked the matrons of Edinburgh, all that had happened was she'd been banished from society. All in all, she'd been content with her books, and with being saved from attending endless rounds of boring entertainments.

"Marshall?" She spoke barely above a whisper, but the sound echoed in the cavernous space. She spoke his name again, this time a little louder. The sound reverberated and then ended in a curious dead silence, as if swallowed in all the statuary and fragmented pieces of columns.

There was no answer, no sound at all but the scrape of her muddy slippers against the stone floor.

The rain had subsided to a drizzle, and she was oddly disappointed as she left the Egypt House. She was in the mood for rain, for heavy thunderstorms and pounding thunder. She wanted lightning and danger, and wanted to be out in it, challenging the elements. Maybe she'd stand on the highest hill and dare God to send her a thunderbolt. She felt reckless in a way that was unfamiliar.

Not the best mood to encounter Mrs. Murray.

Davina entered Ambrose, nodding her thanks when a maid helped her close the heavy door. Mrs. Murray was standing on the staircase, ostensibly inspecting the portraits on the wall for placement and dust. She glanced away when Davina looked in her direction.

"Mrs. Murray," she said, passing the woman on the stairs. She hesitated, wondering if ignoring the woman would be the best course of action. A problem ignored was never solved, however.

Mrs. Murray simply nodded, but that was the only acknowledgment she made of Davina's presence.

"I need to meet with you," Davina said. "About Ambrose."

Mrs. Murray didn't answer.

"Tomorrow morning?"

"If you have any problems, I'd be happy to assist you now, Your Ladyship. However, I have always discussed day-to-day matters with the earl."

"That was before he was married," Davina said. She was in the mood for a battle, and Mrs. Murray was proving to be the perfect combatant. "As the Countess of Lorne, I believe I should be consulted now," she said, but to her disappointment, Mrs. Murray only nodded and smiled.

In the next moment, the other woman descended the staircase, leaving Davina staring after her. For a moment she contemplated following the housekeeper and then decided against it. Instead she returned to her room to find Nora waiting for her.

"I couldn't stay in my room, Your Ladyship. Not if you needed me."

Had her aunt paired her with Nora because the maid possessed the same streak of stubbornness as Davina?

"I'm feeling a little under the weather," she said, hoping that Nora would take the hint and leave her.

"And it's no wonder," Nora said, grabbing a towel from the bathing chamber and beginning to scrub at Davina's wet hair. "You'll catch your death being soaked like that, Your Ladyship."

Within moments she was out of her clothes and wearing one of her sturdier wrappers. This one was not designed to attract her husband's attention, for which she was devoutly grateful. She couldn't bear another one of the Paris creations that made her look like a pastel cloud.

Nora bent to start a fire, and Davina didn't stop her. A roaring blaze would be a delight right now. Even if it was summer, she was chilled to the bone.

She sat back against the window seat and turned her head, watching the rivulets of rain travel across the glass. Without too much effort, she could transport herself through the window and into the ornamental gardens, past the well-manicured lawn. But she couldn't escape, however much she wished it.

He was here. Her husband. Her fascinating, enigmatic, utterly handsome, and charming husband.

"I think we need to send for your aunt, Your Ladyship," Nora said abruptly.

"Why is that?"

"I'm to keep you safe, and I don't think I can do that in this place."

Davina turned to look at the maid still kneeling in front of the fire. There was a look of such irritation on Nora's face that Davina knew it had nothing to do with the fact that the fire was catching slowly.

"Your diligence is commendable, Nora, but I don't need you to keep me safe. Nor do I need to send for my aunt. I'm a grown woman."

Nora stood and placed the matches on the mantel. "I think we should leave, Your Ladyship. I think we should go back home."

"This is home," Davina said. "Like it or not, Edinburgh is no longer home. Ambrose is."

Nora looked around her, the expression on her face leaving no doubt as to what she felt about her surroundings. When she spoke, however, it was to voice an opinion not of Ambrose but of its master. "They say he turns wild, and no one knows when."

"Does anyone know why?" Davina asked. She focused her attention outside. The rain had subsided, and what was left was a gray and cloudy day.

"What do you mean?" Nora asked.

Rather than discuss her husband with the maid, Davina only shook her head. "Never mind, it doesn't matter."

"You need to dress, Your Ladyship," Nora said.

"In a moment." The view from this window faced the rolling hills and woods that adjoined Ambrose's perfectly manicured lawns. In autumn, when the trees had lost their leaves, she'd be able to see the obelisk, and the very top of the roof of the Egypt House.

Nora, however, was not done with her revelations. "The earl doesn't like his servants about much. He's a great stickler for privacy. He speaks with each person he employs and makes it all too clear that they aren't to carry details of him anywhere, else there will be punishment."

Davina turned to look at her. "What sort of punishment?"

"I don't know, Your Ladyship. There haven't been many who've left Ambrose. The pay is better than in Edinburgh, plus His Lordship tucks away a bit of money for the future. It's a fair place to work, if you don't mind the strangeness of it."

That should be the motto for her marriage. *It's a good marriage, if you don't mind the strangeness of it.*

"It's a very mysterious place, is Ambrose."

"I find that men are very mysterious creatures, Nora. I don't understand them at all."

"Shall I send word to your aunt, Your Ladyship?"

"No, Nora," she said firmly, "you'll not send word. If you're unhappy here, I can arrange for you to be sent back to Edinburgh. I'd also be more than happy to give you a good recommendation. I'm sure you could find a position more suitable to your nature."

"I wouldn't want to leave you, Your Ladyship," Nora said, looking offended. "I won't be leaving Ambrose without you, miss," she said, and for once she didn't use the ubiquitous title. "I've been asked to care for you, and care for you I will."

"I don't need anyone to care for me, Nora," Davina said softly. "I'm perfectly able to care for myself. But I thank you just the same. You take your responsibility seriously, and that is something for which you should be commended."

But she wasn't a puppy in need of rescuing, or a poor, downtrodden woman of the street. She was a newly made countess, married to an earl of some renown, living in a magnificent home with dozens and dozens of servants to command. Anything she wanted would be given to her. Any task would be quickly and expertly performed.

Why, then, did she interpret Nora's look to be one of pity?

"Are you certain you don't wish to return to Edinburgh?" Davina asked.

Nora merely clamped her lips together mulishly and shook her head.

"Very well," Davina said.

This was the most intimate conversation the two women had ever had. Years of training on how to behave around servants came to her rescue then. She held her head up high and managed a small smile.

"Thank you, Nora. That will be all."

Nora nodded once, and then turned and left the room without a backward glance or another word spoken. Davina watched as she opened and then closed the door behind her. Where was she going now? To the kitchen, perhaps, to seek out a new friend, someone who would listen to her complaints about her mistress? Or to the servants' quarters?

How very odd to be jealous of Nora suddenly. She wanted to switch roles with the young girl whose future would probably always be serving someone else. Yet the girl never seemed to suffer from lack of friendship, and she almost always had a smile on her face. Life was amusing for Nora. And wasn't it a sad realization that she truly did envy the young girl?

Davina turned her attention back to the day. The edges of the clouds were ragged, as if they were pages torn from a book and placed against the sky. Laid one atop the other, they were each a different tone of gray.

The tops of the trees swayed in the wind, evidence of the storm's renewed fury. The ornamental hedges and carefully planted flowers in the English garden shivered in the gusts. The rain began as a soft shower, a delicate patter that lasted for a few moments before heavier raindrops brought the smell both of dust and of fresh air.

Suddenly the drumbeat of the rain drowned out every other sound. The rainspouts at the edge of the roof were flowing with water. The sky was dark gray, the clouds lowering.

This was no pretty English shower. This was a Scottish storm, teaching the unwary to be more mindful of the changing weather. Lightning suddenly darted from the sky to the tip of a tree, as if God had extended a finger to prove His might. The crash of thunder was accompanied by a high-pitched sound, as if the tree screamed as it was being torn in two.

Davina loved storms, and it seemed oddly fitting that this day was marked by such a display, as if nature—or God—understood how she felt and was replicating each one of her emotions in the rain and wind and thunder.

When she was a little girl, days like this were magical to her. The sky opened up and transformed into something powerful, threatening, and awe-inspiring. Somehow, however, she was never afraid of storms. She recalled sitting in the middle of her bed cross-legged as a child, her arms folded around her waist, her eyes closed tight, reveling in the sounds of the storm around their secure haven of a house. The rumbling thunder or the crash of lightning close by never scared her. She was more enthralled with the power of God than she was frightened of it.

Only later, when she realized that God wasn't, perhaps, as protective as her father had always said, that bad things happened even if she said her prayers, only then had she become afraid. Not of storms, but of other things beyond her control. When her father wouldn't wake, when her aunt didn't return from London when she was expected. When a marriage to a stranger loomed. All events over which she had absolutely no power.

She wanted to be angry instead of filled with sadness, but anger didn't make the sorrow go away. Besides, at whom did she get mad? Marshall, for being himself? Herself, for her foolishness in Edinburgh? Her aunt, for insisting upon this marriage?

Even if she chose to become mad at everyone and everything, it wouldn't ease this day. Or make her feel less unwanted.

Theresa stared at herself in the mirror, awaiting the inevitable summons. In a moment, the maid would come to announce that Garrow Ross had arrived.

She'd sent him a message, inviting him to dinner. After all, they'd already met at Davina's wedding. They'd even been seated together.

Tonight she'd flirt outrageously, and maybe giggle like a schoolgirl. Thank heavens the man believed himself excessively handsome and more than a little charming. She'd deduced that during the wedding dinner.

Her role would not be easy. It had been many years since she had lain with a man. How did a woman pretend pleasure? She wished there was a woman acquaintance she might consult. She almost smiled at that thought— she'd be even more of a scandal than Davina had been.

Just as she predicted, the maid knocked on the door.

"Show Mr. Ross into the sitting room and offer him some whiskey. I'll be down shortly."

She was ready. She looked rested, attractive, her eyes possibly revealing a bit too much reluctance, but that was to be expected.

For the Crown and the Empire. How very odd that the thought didn't reassure her in the least.

Chapter 13

Davina awoke the next morning filled with a sense of purpose.

She took great pride in learning, had often been intrigued by industry or a discovery about which she'd read. Therefore, she'd consider two avenues of investigation: Egypt and Marshall. If they overlay each other from time to time, then that was good. But she had absolutely no intention of remaining in her room, a dutiful bride. Nor had she any intention of being like Marshall's mother.

She picked up the latest journal, and the page fell open to where she'd finished reading last night.

Today was a good day. The pain was manageable, and if I concentrate upon other things, I might even come to believe that I carry a child. This growth has rounded my belly as when I was heavy with Marshall. What halcyon days those turned out to be, and I never knew it. At the time I was too concerned with whether my appearance, as large as I had become, would repulse Aidan. Then there were the usual concerns shared by every soon-to-be mother. What if I make a dreadful mistake? What if I accidentally harmed my child? Would I have a boy or a girl? If it was a boy, would that mean that Aidan would no longer find a reason to come home from Egypt? His duty done, his chore finished, he would be free to stay in his beloved land.

The answers came soon enough, and I was a good mother, I think. Marshall has grown to be a devoted son, a wondrous man. I am truly in awe of his accomplishments. Sometimes I have to remind myself that I gave birth to him, so filled with admiration for him am I.

I am not with child, however, as much as I would like to pretend, or send my thoughts back to those better days. But I need to tell my child the enormity of this secret. As my time grows closer, I cannot say I face it with any more equanimity. In fact, I might even confess to be more afraid today than I was two months ago upon learning of my diagnosis.

Adversity must come to us all. The kirk would have us all believe that it is our lot in life to suffer, the better that we should appreciate the approach of heaven. Heaven seems like such a faraway and unfriendly place now. I'd much rather remain at Ambrose.

As for Aidan, I have not summoned him. I am afraid that if I do so he will not come, and I could not bear knowing that, at the last, it was all pretense.

Davina put the journal away, tucking it into the drawer in the side table, and slid from the bed to stand at the window surveying Ambrose.

The air felt wet and heavy. On the horizon was a hint of a sunny day, but closer still the storm clouds hung low and nearly black.

Her mood was a little bit of both as well: sun and storm. The courtyard was dotted with puddles where the stones were concave or well-worn. The morning sun would make quick work of them if another storm didn't come.

The lawn between Ambrose and the Egypt House would be wet; she'd need her sturdy shoes. Her dress? Something new, of course, but comfortable.

She was going to find purpose for her new life.

Marshall saw her coming down the hill, oblivious to the storm clouds. If pushed to honesty, he would admit to looking for her, to anticipating her arrival. The woman who'd come to the Egypt House the day before would not be content to remain cloistered at Ambrose.

From the moment he'd seen her, he'd known she was different.

He stared down at the blotter, but instead he saw the determined face of his bride. Part of him welcomed her intrusion into his life, exalted in the fact that she was stubborn, opinionated, and quite evidently used to getting her way. Another part, a section of his mind given up to protecting the rest of Marshall Ross, wished he had never agreed to this farce of a marriage.

His arm, bandaged beneath his sleeve, still ached. There, a warning of what he could do if he let down his defenses.

Still, she offered a form of companionship, and he

was damnably lonely. His demons brought terror but never friendship.

He took the back stairs to the main floor and waited for her. When she entered, she didn't immediately call out for him. Instead she stood there a moment as if to get her bearings, her gaze drifting over some of the statuary and canopic jars.

Marshall didn't move, didn't want to startle her further. Her self-imposed restraint reminded him, oddly, of himself. When he was at his most rigid, he was attempting to control his emotions. He wondered if she was doing the same. Was it anger that kept her so silent and still? He suspected, suddenly, that it was fear instead, a thought that shamed him.

He took a few steps forward. The tension of her stance was greater than before. He wondered what prompted it, and felt as though he should know.

She turned her head and unerringly found him among the statues.

"Did you know that the Hundred Years War actually lasted one hundred sixteen years?"

"I must confess my ignorance," he said, coming to stand in front of her.

"One of Egypt's pharaohs was the longest reigning monarch in history. Did you know that? The second longest was France's Louis XIV, who ruled from 1643 to 1715. I think that's fascinating, don't you?"

"Do you never grow tired of knowing things?" Marshall asked.

She didn't look at him when she answered, concentrating instead on the statue in front of her.

"I've been asked that question all my life. And always in such a tone. As if knowledge is something that was only allotted to a person in measures. Is it so bad to want to know things?" She glanced over at him. "I know a great deal. Unfortunately, I have no use for some of my knowledge, other than to claim that I know it. The seven wonders of the ancient world, for example. Can you imagine a conversation where that would be needed?"

At his smile, she nodded. "You see?"

"What are they?"

She frowned at him. "Are you testing me? I do know them."

"Perhaps I would like to know them as well." His smile grew brighter.

"Very well." She began to recite them. "One, the Egyptian pyramids at Giza. Two, the Hanging Gardens of Babylon. Three, the statue of Zeus at Olympia; four, the Colossus of Rhodes." She glanced at him again. "A huge bronze statue near the harbor of Rhodes that honored the sun god Helios."

"I know what the Colossus of Rhodes is," he said, his smile firmly moored in place.

"Five," she continued, "the temple of Artemis at Ephesus. That one is the most difficult for me to remember for some reason. Six, the mausoleum at Halicarnassus, and seven—the lighthouse at Alexandria." She smiled in triumph.

He applauded her, and she curtsied to him, still smiling.

"If I allowed you to think, in any way," he said, "that I was denigrating your curiosity, I apologize. Such was not my intent. In fact, I can't but admire such a trait, since I, too, have been accused of it most of my life as well. However, in my case, I am supposed to be knowledgeable, being the Earl of Lorne."

"While I am simply Davina McLaren." She amended her name a second later with a smile. "Davina McLaren Ross."

"The Countess of Lorne," Marshall said.

"You say that as if the position conveys a great deal of power. Does it?"

His smile would have to suffice for an answer.

"If I asked you any question in the world, would you feel compelled to answer?"

"In the interest of scientific study?"

"Because I'm the Countess of Lorne."

He nodded. "Of course."

"Then why do you not come to my bed?"

She'd done it again. Flummoxed, he stared at her.

What in hell did he say to that?

"What are you doing here?" he asked, instead of answering her.

"I've come to learn everything I can about Egypt," she said, deciding to give him the truth. "I'm not allowed to be a wife, and I've found that decorating my suite has not taken any time at all. Mrs. Murray seems to resent my intrusion into her domain. Ergo, I have nothing to do but learn."

"Ambrose has a well-stocked library."

"Why should I learn from books when there is a museum at Ambrose? I will not be a bride confined to a tower, Marshall." There, her famed stubbornness, the obstinacy of which she'd once been so proud.

"This is not a fairy tale, Davina."

"Do you not think I realize that?" she asked, feeling an unexpected burst of amusement. "I'm not a princess, and, Marshall, you are not a prince."

She lowered her head and stared at a statue directly in front of her. Larger than life-size, the man seated on the throne looked as if he might well have given her the death penalty had he been alive. She felt like taking a hammer and breaking off one of his ancient toes.

Reaching forward, she picked up a shard of a pot from a table, marveling at the colors still visible on the terra-cotta, faded aquamarine once brilliant teal, and amber once orange.

"Were you here yesterday? When I came looking for you?"

Silenced stretched between them, but he finally answered.

"Yes."

She nodded, having expected his response.

The building was filled with beauty. One mask in particular captured her attention, lit as it was by an errant shaft of sunlight.

"Is it gold?" she asked, reaching out to touch the edge of the mask.

"Yes," he said, grabbing her hand and enfolding her fingers with his.

Of course. The mask was thousands of years old, and her touch, however gentle, might harm the object.

"It looks like a man with a ram's horns. That one,"

she said, gesturing to a tall ebony statue of a woman, "has the head of a cat."

"Bastet," he said.

To her right, a young man in an ornate headdress stood holding a crook across his body, almost as if he were defending himself. Beside him, another statue depicted a woman attired in a gold garment kneeling on one knee. Her hands were outstretched to reveal her blue and green wings tipped in red. On her head was a red orb supported by two golden horns.

"Isis," he said, correctly interpreting her confusion.

Everywhere she looked there was something fantastic, from the tables that looked formed of gold to the reed chairs painted in a design not unlike the mural. A sarcophagus shaped like a monkey rested next to one holding a mummified ibis. A golden urn, painted in vivid red and green stripes, stood next to a tall vase proudly displaying only a staff.

"It was once a peacock fan," Marshall said, fingering the wood.

"I've never seen the like, not even at the Grand Exhibition."

"A great many items you saw there were replicas," he said.

"And these aren't?" she asked, surprised.

He shook his head.

"They are my father's acquisitions. He loved Egypt."

She looked up, and then around the building, before fixing her gaze on him again. "It's a beautiful place, but there's nothing alive here."

When he didn't speak, she asked the question that had been niggling at her.

"How did you hurt your arm?"

"I don't remember," he said. "Take that truth and use it as you will."

"How do you bear that? Not knowing?" She studied him. His eyes were bloodshot; his face drawn. Whatever had happened to him the night before last had not been pleasant.

"Is that why you leave me? Is that why you've stayed away? Did you know that such a thing would happen?"

He didn't answer. When he did speak, it was to repeat a familiar refrain. "I told you this was not going to be a typical marriage. Now you know why."

"Because you're mad." She sighed and faced him. "I think something is wrong, and I don't know what it is. But I don't believe you're mad."

"Or the Devil of Ambrose?"

"Then we're a pair, are we not?" she asked, feeling absurdly lighthearted. "I am the Sinner of Edinburgh."

There, she'd managed to startle him. He looked as if he would say something and then changed his mind.

"If we're strangers," she said, "then rectify the situation. Teach me about yourself. I've always been an avid student."

"And the course is to be Marshall Ross? You would have me divulge all my secrets?"

"Why not? I would tell you."

She stopped, struck by a thought so odd that she could only stare at him.

"What is it, Davina?"

She shook her head, feeling foolish. "I haven't any." She paused. "I have no secrets at all. I never held anything back from my father or my aunt. I was always probably too vocal, too explanatory about myself. I never had a hiding place where I kept anything secret. I never had any close friends while growing up, someone with whom I could share a secret. The whole of Edinburgh knows about my shame, so I guess I have no secrets."

"Oh, but you do," he countered. "You know a great deal about the Earl of Lorne. Many people in Edinburgh would be more than happy to learn what you know."

"What do I know about you, Marshall? That you're a magnificent lover? I suspect more than a few women know that. What else do I know?"

He shook his head, but didn't comment further, and she wished he would say something else, something that would keep her there, anchored to the spot. As long as they talked, they established some kind of relationship. Friendship, even a budding one, was better than simply being lovers—lovers who knew nothing but the contours of each other's bodies.

It had already occurred to her, neophyte that she was, that pleasure with someone she knew was so much greater than with a stranger.

She closed the distance between them.

"Shall we see what I know about you?"

She allowed herself the freedom of his stillness, all ten fingers sensate. His brow was wide and deep; a curl of hair obscured her fingers, and she brushed it back into place, gently. His lashes were ridiculously long, his eyebrows thick; the planes of his cheeks carved hollows near his mouth. His nose was aquiline, but not too sharp; his chin definite, but not too pointed. It was to his mouth her fingers returned time and again, tracing the full borders of his bottom lip, the unsmiling contours of his upper, delicately exploring the seam of them, then darting away as if too brazen.

She didn't allow her exploration to cease then, although it might have been wiser and safer to do so, but ran her fingers over the column of his neck. His shoulders were broad, warm beneath the linen of his shirt. She pressed one hand against his chest, her palm absorbing his heat and the booming cadence of his heart. Her fingers trailed down his arms, measured the curve of elbow, the skin of his wrists, the broad hands that lay quiescent beneath her exploration.

Placing her hands on Marshall was as deeply moving as it would have been to explore the features of her first child, a loving expedition of tender and trembling fingers.

She wanted to feel all of him, trace the angle of his ribs; dart beneath his shirt and feel his flesh; palm the strength of his ankles, the ligature of his calves; cradle the heat of him, feel him hard against her palms.

She stepped back, her cheeks scarlet.

A need pooled between them, each for the other, and if he denied it she'd call him a liar.

"Perhaps I do know a great deal," she said. How odd that it was difficult to speak; her voice was mired in thickness.

A wiser woman would leave, but the last week had proven that she wasn't exceptionally wise when it came to Marshall Ross.

Chapter 14

He should banish her from this place, but instead he turned on his heel and made his way to the hidden stairs. He didn't turn to see if Davina followed. She had too much curiosity to remain behind.

Climbing the stairs, he made his way to the large room at the end of the building. Once his father's office had occupied only a corner of the second floor, but Marshall had enlarged it substantially. First to house the more valuable pieces of his father's collection, and secondly for his own comfort.

He entered, holding the door open for her, and then watched as her eyes scanned the room, widening as they took in all the treasures his father had accumulated. He felt the same upon entering the room after an absence of only a few days. Mounted on the walls were large frames holding necklaces and bracelets, and what looked to be a headpiece crafted of gold. On another wall was a shelf entirely devoted to funereal jars, and as she fingered one or two of them delicately, he felt as if he should warn her.

"Those were once used to hold the internal organs of those who were mummified," he said.

Her hand jerked back, and she looked at him, startled. She was not, however, horrified as he'd half expected.

"Canopic jars?" she asked.

He nodded. "You know a great deal more about Egypt than most people, Davina."

"My father had an interest in the subject," she said. "But then, he had an interest in most countries. He was a geographer."

"I met him once," Marshall said to her obvious surprise.

"You never said so. Nor did he ever mention you. I am sure I would have remembered it."

"It was a very long time ago. I had just returned from Egypt where I had been visiting my father. He and my father maintained a correspondence for some years, I believe."

"I didn't know that, either. But then my father was a great letter writer. When he died, my aunt and I could not bear to destroy his letters. We simply packed them away." She smiled. "It took a dozen trunks."

She looked around the room. "What is your greatest treasure?"

He didn't have to force himself to choose. Instead he reached into his lower left drawer and withdrew a small pitcher wrapped in gauze. Of turquoise glass, with a stylized lip and arched handle, it was painted with hieroglyphs expounding the "good god Menkheperre given life." The details were as rich today as when it had been made three thousand years ago, one of seven vessels used to hold sacred oils for a burial ceremony.

Davina came and stood beside the desk as he unwrapped it, and by the expression on her face, he could tell that she was as impressed as he'd been on the first day he'd found it.

"It was the most profound moment of my life," he admitted, "holding something that old, that fragile, that somehow had managed to survive all those years."

Carefully, he wrapped the pitcher in gauze and replaced it in his drawer.

She sat at the desk. "Tell me about the first time you went to Egypt," she said.

"I've only been once," he admitted. "My first impressions were jumbled. I'd not yet seen any part of the world, so even the journey to Egypt was confusing and strange to me."

"Why did you go?"

"I think my mother thought it would be a good idea if my father and I were left alone to get to know each other. He'd spent the majority of my childhood in Egypt, only returning home once a year or so."

She propped her head on her hand and regarded him steadily.

"As it was, her instincts were correct," he continued. "Up until that time I felt a vague dissatisfaction about my father. Once in Egypt I realized I didn't know him at all. He was, essentially, a stranger."

"Did you resent him for being gone so much?"

He smiled. "One of the great revelations of that trip to Egypt. I realized that while he'd spent the majority of my childhood being gone, I'd spent all that time being angry at him." Absently he rubbed his fingers across the wood of his writing case. "After that season, whenever I thought of him, I knew exactly what he was doing. While I missed his presence in my life from time to time, I understood."

"Was he distraught by your mother's death?"

He glanced at her, surprised at the question. "I think he was. Why do you ask? Because of your own parents? People are different, Davina."

She smiled. "I know. Forgive my intrusion, I was just curious."

A moment of silence passed. "Did he go back to Egypt?" she finally asked.

He shook his head. "He died barely a month after she did." He reached over and placed his hand on top of hers. "Why do you suddenly look so sad? It happened a long time ago, Davina."

As if determined to lighten the mood, she asked, "What did you do in that season in Egypt?"

"I sifted sand," he said. "I used a shovel to try to displace thousands of yards of sand. After a few weeks, I was allowed to visit some of his excavations. I actually performed some rubbings—the very same hieroglyphs that I'm now studying. It was days of tedium broken up by moments of profundity."

She didn't speak, waiting for him to continue.

"My father was a student of Belzoni," he said, as if expecting that she'd know the name.

He glanced at her and correctly interpreted her ignorance. "Belzoni led several excavations from 1815 to 1819. He opened one of the Great Pyramids at Giza, and was the first to enter the tomb of Seti I." He reached behind him to the bookcase and retrieved a large book.

"There are numerous illustrations," he said, "if you're truly interested."

The volume was filled with plates, each backed with cloth, and each magnificently colored.

"I don't understand you or your father," she said as she carefully turned each page. "How can you possibly leave a country like Scotland to find another home?"

"It wasn't to find another home," he answered. "A Scot will never belong to any country other than Scotland, even if he changes his locale. Scotland's in your blood. You can belong nowhere else."

She didn't look at him. "But if you weren't looking for a home," she asked, "what were you looking for?"

"I was too young to be looking for answers when I wasn't even certain of the questions. As for my father, I think he was in thrall to Egypt."

He stood and walked to the window, staring out at Aidan's Needle. "Once I climbed up the cliffs at dawn, and watched as the sun tinted the sand in yellow and orange. I remember being overwhelmed by the beauty of Egypt, by the sheer age of it, by the hint of mystery that permeated the entire country."

He glanced over at her. "Perhaps that's what my father felt every day." He returned to the desk. "At the end of that season, I came back to Scotland with an appreciation for my father's curiosity."

"But not for Egypt?"

He smiled. "I loved every moment of it, every dirty, grubbing, boring minute of it. I discovered that I was just like my father in that I had an affinity for the past, almost a soul-deep need to know, to discover. You might say that Egypt began my interest in the world itself."

"And excavating?"

"I learned that it's part science and part imagination. You have the sarcophagus of a king and you envision his queen, their children, and the life they lived in a palace just now coming to light. Or the tomb builders themselves; where did they live, how? Were they married or single, did they have wives or sweethearts, children? You hold a pot shard cradled in your hand." He looked down at his empty, cupped hand as if an imaginary clay piece rested there. "You think: Who used this last? Was it destroyed by the press of earth, or did someone throw it away in a fit of fury? Was it crushed by an animal, left on the fire too long? What was the last meal made in it?"

"And yet you became an expert about the Orient."

He smiled. "Hardly an expert. I was interested in the culture; my uncle had business interests there."

"Expert enough that the Crown sent you on numerous diplomatic missions."

"Perhaps diplomacy was a result of that summer as well. My father and I were strangers. I had to find a way to communicate with him. It was not diplomacy as much as desperation."

"Did you ever go back to Egypt?" she asked.

"No. There was never time."

"What happened to you in China?"

He turned his head slowly and regarded her, wondering how much of the truth she could endure. She was stronger than most women he knew, and at the same time, more innocent.

"What do you think of the world, Davina?"

The question surprised her, he could tell.

"You might as well ask me what I think of life, Marshall."

"Then what do you think of life?"

She frowned at him, but she answered him anyway. "It's not always fair. Or nice. Or kind. Is that what you want to hear?"

He shook his head. "You've never seen the ugliness of it," he said. "Or the horrors of it. Why should I be the one to expose you to the world, Davina?"

"Because it might be easier if you do," she said. "It might be kinder if I have someone's hand to hold. Or if I could turn to someone and have him embrace me after each revelation."

She stood and took a step toward him, and he didn't move away.

"What happened to you in China, Marshall?"

He pointedly ignored her, reaching for an object on the shelf beside him. The small statue of a bird had an inscription below it encircled in an elongated oval.

"Do you see this writing?"

"Demotic?"

Once again, she'd managed to surprise him.

"No," he said, "something a little different. Demotic writing was used in formal texts or treaties. These are hieroglyphs. More commonly used for the general populace to understand."

She frowned.

"If you know how to read it," he said, smiling. "I spend my time deciphering hieroglyphs."

He sat again, waiting until she joined him.

Ever since he was a child he'd had an affinity for languages, but this one wasn't spoken. Instead it was carved in relief on every single piece of statuary his father had sent from Egypt. Even the necklaces and bracelets he'd found had been embellished with symbols. The writing of the Egyptians, unlike most of the languages he'd learned in his lifetime, required that he study it in depth. However, his quest to understand gave him something to do each day, a reason to arise from his bed and leave his room, and seek out another world.

Being married to Davina also gave him the same feeling, a thought that he didn't choose to examine at the moment.

He opened his desk drawer and pulled out a scroll of papyrus he'd been translating. "Every language has conventions, and hieroglyphs are no different."

He unrolled the scroll with great care and spread it flat on the desk between them, turning it to the side so they could both read.

"English is always read from left to right, for example. In hieroglyphs, it's not as simple. People and animals always look toward the beginning of the text. See this bird?" He pointed out a stylized figure of what looked like a raven. "He's looking to the left. That's where you begin reading. Most often, however, you'll find that the figures look to the right, which means you begin from the right side and read to the left."

"What about these columns?" she asked, tracing the four columns of text.

"The Egyptians liked symmetry. Sometimes you'll see two columns opposite each other with the exact same text, only with the writing reversed."

Her eyes were intent on the document before her, her fingers delicately tracing the lettering that had probably been done nearly two thousand years ago. "This form of writing," he continued, "is almost always written from the top to bottom, so even if there are lines of texts, you'll read the top sign before the one on the bottom."

"But not always," she said, glancing at him.

His smile broadened. "No, not always. But let's keep that assumption for now."

He pointed out one sign. "Think of space, first. The amount of unused or wasted space was kept to a minimum. Sometimes you'll have symbols above and below a sign when it should be before or after it because of that very reason. Also, the order of a sign could be changed simply because of aesthetic reasons. Or even because of honor."

She didn't ask the question, but it was there in her eyes.

"The word *god* and the names of the gods and goddesses had to be written before all other signs. The same principle applies to the word for *king*."

"And you've learned all this in a year?"

He shook his head. "Other scholars have discovered these idiosyncrasies in hieroglyphs. I've just read about them. And used what they've learned, of course, to add to my knowledge."

She pointed to what looked like a reversed nine. "What is that?"

"That's a symbol representing the number one hundred. To write five hundred, you would simply draw it five times."

"What does this say?" she asked, selecting a line of symbols.

"'He rejoices because of thy utterance.'"

She glanced over at him.

"I think it's a love poem," he said, "but I haven't finished translating it yet."

He carefully rolled up the scroll. "It's not all that difficult," he said. "The signs are often simplified, but you can still detect that they're individual signs. A cursive form of hieroglyphs was used for some of the tombs of the kings, especially the Eighteenth Dynasty, but this is easy enough to read."

Her hand stretched out and touched the wax tablet, and he found himself studying her fingers.

How very odd that he'd never been fascinated by the sight of a woman's hands, but hers were extraordinarily lovely.

She used them well, in an infinitely charming ballet of purpose. Those hands had trailed along his skin in invitation, had brushed back his hair from his forehead. More than once, she'd pressed open palms against his skin, as if trying to find a way to breach the barriers that stood between them and become part of him.

He stood and returned the bird statue to its place. When he turned, she was there, standing just in front of him.

She placed one hand on his arm. When he flinched she jerked her hand back immediately.

"Does it hurt?" she asked. A prosaic question, a commonsense one. A question of wifely concern.

"Only a little."

"Do not forget to have the bandage changed often."

"My valet, Jacobs, is quite diligent in many tasks."

"See that he changes it every day," she instructed. "I would not have you getting ill from an infection."

He reached out and grabbed her hands and held them between both of his. "I thank you for your concern, Davina."

She looked down at the floor rather than at him. "It's nothing more than any wife would do," she said, her voice low.

"Not any wife. Not one who's been ignored. Or dictated to. Or given no hope that this marriage will ever be anything ordinary. Not any wife."

When he would have dropped his hand, she held firm, and finally looked directly into his eyes. "I've been told, on more than one occasion, that I am intensely stubborn. I've been likened to the most recalcitrant ox. I can only caution you, Marshall, that I've not given up on this marriage. I believe, unlike you, that we could suit."

She traced her fingers up his uninjured arm, and he reached down and captured her hand with his own, brought it to his mouth and slowly kissed each finger. The center of her palm was a target for a kiss, her wrist a spot where he held his lips immobile, measuring her pulse.

"Thank you for your company," he said, stepping back.

She looked as if she'd like to say something, but didn't. Instead she turned and walked toward the door.

At the threshold, she turned. The tenderness of her smile was something that he'd implant in his memory.

"Will you come to me tonight, Marshall?"

He shook his head. The demons were too close, the episode yesterday too raw to trust himself.

She nodded, just once, as if she'd expected his answer.

And then she was gone, and he had only his regret for company.

Chapter 15

Davina returned to the Egypt House the next day, only to find herself alone. Marshall had simply disappeared, not to be seen anywhere at Ambrose.

That night, when she took dinner in the family dining room, she expected him to appear. By the end of her meal, even the stony-faced footmen were beginning to look at her with pity in their eyes. Or perhaps she simply imagined it, just as she imagined that Marshall might join her.

The Devil of Ambrose. Dear God, what if it were true? What if his delusions were only growing stronger, and he was genuinely afraid that he might hurt her?

Nonsense.

The man who'd touched her with gentleness, who'd laughed at her comments, who'd smiled so tenderly at her could not be a monster.

After dinner, she dressed in a silk peignoir he'd not seen, this one a pale green the shade of a newly unfurled leaf.

If he would not come to her, then she'd go to him.

The double doors of the earl's suite faced her at the

end of the corridor like a broad and daunting wall. She would not allow herself to think of the other times she'd made this same journey and the disastrous results. But her legs were trembling, and she could barely take a deep breath.

She was halfway down the hall when the doors opened. Her heart leaped, but then a second later she realized it wasn't Marshall coming to her, but Mrs. Murray.

The woman turned and glanced at her, the look held for too long to be respectful. Her lips quirked in a strange, almost triumphant smile, and then she made a show of adjusting her bodice. As if she'd been manhandled, as if someone had placed his hands on her breasts. Or as if she'd recently dressed in a hurry.

She bobbed a shallow curtsy, and then turned and walked down the other corridor so that the two women were not forced to pass each other.

Davina placed her hand on the silk wallpaper, feeling the texture abrade her fingertips. The temperature in the corridor dropped; the silence in the great house was otherworldly.

She carefully turned and walked back to her own suite, opening the door with measured care, closing it just as slowly and silently. The click of the lock was absurdly loud. So, too, the sound of her slippers on the wooden floor.

Davina removed the peignoir and laid it on the end of the bed, arranging the folds very carefully so that it wouldn't be wrinkled by morning. She mounted the steps and slid beneath the sheets, propping the pillows behind her back.

The Egyptians used stones for pillows. She, at least, had feathers.

What would an Egyptian woman do under such circumstances? She hadn't any idea. Would she weep? Or curse her husband? Or send an assassin to kill the servant?

How strange to realize that she was possessed of a bloodthirsty nature. She'd been annoyed before, and even irritated—at herself, her aunt, her acquaintances, life, and certainly at Marshall. Yet she'd never quite been as angry as she was right at the moment. Her fists clenched against the sheets. Her blood felt as if it colored every inch of her skin a bright Chinese red. She could feel the furious beating of her heart, so loud that her chest felt as if it vibrated. Her breath was shallow, as if her stays were too tight. But since she was wearing none, it wasn't fashion causing her rage, but her husband.

She sat against the pillows for at least a quarter hour, glaring at the door. At the end of that time, her anger had subsided somewhat, but another emotion was taking precedence—pity. Not for Marshall, and not for that hussy Mrs. Murray, but for herself.

To distract herself, she leaned across the bed and opened the drawer of the bedside table, and extracted Julianna's journal. She hadn't progressed very far since learning of the countess's disease. Right at this moment, Davina wanted to feel something other than rage or jealousy or self-pity.

She put the book down on her lap and stared at the door. Jealousy. She'd never been jealous before, but then she'd never had a reason to be jealous. She'd never before felt . . . what? Love?

She'd never before understood love, and had never before considered that one day she might feel the emotion. She'd simply thought that people were exaggerating, perhaps for literary license. Or perhaps there were certain beings who possessed the capacity of extreme empathy or who'd lived through their emotions more than their thoughts.

She could remember holding a book of poetry in her hands and wondering at the sacrifice of lovers, at the anguish they experienced. She remembered thinking that such an emotion must be indeed rare, or perhaps even a little dangerous.

If this was love, then love made her miserable, vulnerable, and heartsick. Love was not what she'd thought it might be. In fact, if anyone had told her that she'd feel this way, she would have walled herself away from other people, determined never to feel it.

She'd foolishly thought that love and physical pleasure were the same, and she was beginning to believe that the latter was much easier to obtain than the former. Alisdair had certainly proven that to be correct, but then she hadn't felt all that much physical pleasure with him.

Was her life to be forever like that, then? Living in blissful ignorance until a sudden revelation demonstrated how utterly stupid she'd been for the preceding months? Then she'd bask in her newfound wisdom, only to learn how stupid she'd been about something else? Life was, no doubt, going to be a series of shocks.

But not, surely, as unpleasant as this.

She could not be in love with her husband. History was repeating itself, was it not? But instead of disappearing to Egypt, her earl was simply disappearing.

Deliberately, she pushed all thoughts of Marshall from her mind. Instead she opened the book and focused on Julianna.

Garrow came to Ambrose today. I have not seen him much in the past few months, but I must confess that I was glad to see him today. He is such a fashionable man. My physician could take lessons from him in how to be more sober and less flamboyant in his dress.

Up until today our meetings have always been cordial, but there has been a degree of distance between us. Upon seeing me, however, he crossed the room and pulled both my hands into his. I was seated by the window on a chaise and clutched the coverlet lest he whisk me upward into a fervent brother-in-law's embrace, revealing that I was still attired in my bedclothes. Dressing seems such a chore lately, and such an unnecessary bother.

I moved my legs aside so that he could sit, and when he did so, he asked me what was wrong. I looked fully into his face, meeting his direct gaze with no thoughts of subterfuge. I am dying, I told him, and to my astonishment he only nodded, as if my fate was evident from the sight of my pale face and pinched features.

A spasm struck me then, inopportune as such things are, the pain traveling from the core of my belly and outward as if a hand reached inside me and gripped each of my organs in turn. I laid my head back against the chaise and prayed that it would pass. Such pains are commonplace lately.

Perhaps it is time to send for Marshall in London. If I do, it will be a sign of acceptance, my acknowledgment that these are my last days. Foolish as I am, however, I have not yet sent for my son. Evidently, hope still lingers in my mind.

Garrow told me that he would fetch me something for pain, and I wanted to ask him if he meant some of his Chinese herbs, but I didn't speak. At that moment, I was afraid my voice would sound feeble and old. Perhaps nature itself felt robbed of my old age and pinned dotage on me in addition to a cancer.

Garrow must have noted my feebleness as well, because he halted and looked down at me, and there was pity on his face.

He promised that what he would bring me would ease my pain, and coward that I was, I did not demur. I do not like the pain. It has not become a friend.

He returned to the room in a matter of moments, calling for the maid and a glass of wine. Despite my protests that wine did nothing for my pain, only gives me a raging headache, he mixed *several powders in the glass and handed it to me. Wine aids in digestion, he told me, and also masks the taste of the herbs. It will work quickly, he assured me, and I took the glass from him, drank it, and found that it was only a matter of moments before I felt some relief.*

There was one effect from the herbs he mentioned, but only after I had downed the glass, my stomach protesting at the sourness of the wine. I may have bad dreams, but that can be controlled by the amount of my medication. I didn't tell him that my dreams were troubling now. A lifetime of regret does not make for easy sleep.

The pain was gone in a matter of moments. The blessed man was right. From that moment on, I have been kept quite comfortable.

Even so, I have sent for Marshall.

Davina put the journal aside and slipped from the bed, walking to the balcony outside her bedchamber.

The air was warm, pressing on her skin. The moon hung like a pearl disk in the sky, faintly illuminating a landscape littered with differing shapes of black and emerald green. The courtyard was transformed into a light gray rectangle, and far away the obelisk became an accusing finger.

She missed her father. She missed her aunt. She missed life as she'd known it, regular and familiar and kind.

She felt off-center, out of place. She needed someone to embrace her, or she needed to be around familiar surroundings. She wanted to see the chamber that had always been hers, or walk into her father's study and smell the scent of his pipe still lingering in the air.

There was no one at Ambrose that she knew, except Nora, and she didn't know the girl well. There was nothing around her that was familiar or easy. Even her position as bride-turned-wife felt unknown and strange.

She felt adrift.

And in love.

Dear God, should it truly hurt this much?

"Is there nothing I can do for you, Your Lordship?"

Marshall glanced at his valet. "Nothing, Jacobs. Go ahead and retire for the night."

"If you're certain, Your Lordship."

Marshall didn't bother to answer. Every night it was the same, with Jacobs solicitous to the point of being intrusive.

"If you'd like, Your Lordship, I could remain with you. Perhaps the dreams wouldn't be so bad."

"I don't need a chaperone, Jacobs."

"No, Your Lordship." Jacobs puttered around, rearranging Marshall's shoes, pulling out the top drawer to inspect it.

"What is it, Jacobs?" he asked when the man made no move to leave.

"Does Daniel ever visit you?"

Marshall turned his head and stared at the statue of Seti I perched on one of the bookcases in his study. On countless nights before this one, Seti had actually spoken to him. Tonight, however, the long-dead pharaoh was silent.

"Daniel?" He shook his head. Jacobs's grandson had been his boyhood friend, and had enthusiastically been part of the last expedition to China.

"Get to bed, Jacobs. We'll talk of ghosts another time."

Mrs. Murray had dutifully replenished his wine, and he took a sip of it as Jacobs left the room.

He glanced over his shoulder and the moon was there, framed in the window, a sentinel to his night.

Lawrence walked out of the wall and saluted him with two smiles, the one that stretched across his mouth, and the one that slit his throat from ear to ear. With a jaunty wave of his hand, he traveled across the room and disappeared into the far wall. Lawrence had been his second-in-command, and one of the first to be killed by the Chinese.

At least he'd died humanely, or as humanely as possible. His death was quick, which was more than Marshall could say for the other men in his command. He fully expected to see every one of them tonight, just as he did every night when the visions came.

Could a man get tired of madness? One day, perhaps, he would. One day the prospect of being himself, of being the man he'd once been, would be so far away that he couldn't reach it, like a distant shore seen only on a clear day. He was floating in an ocean, and one day he would simply get tired of swimming. He'd let himself sink into the water and drown in insanity.

Peter appeared next. Peter was, without a doubt,

one of the ugliest men Marshall had ever met, and the marks on his face from his torture had not made him prettier. If anything, the welts and burns called into relief Peter's crooked nose and the angular nature of his features.

Peter was always an affable ghost, hardly ever condemning Marshall for his survival. The rest were not quite so generous. They reminded him, by their appearance, by their jeering smiles, how much guilt he bore for their deaths. If he was fortunate on this night, their wounds would not seep blood, leaving a trail across the floor. Their heads would remain intact, and attached to their necks.

If he were not so fortunate, they would begin to speak, gibberish at first. Then he'd be able to make out one word and then two, and then whole sentences of condemnation.

He raised his glass, downing the rest of his wine. He should change to whiskey, perhaps. The wine might not work and sleep would not come at all tonight.

Peter spoke to him, but Marshall only closed his eyes. He knew there was no one really there. If he did feel something brushing against his cheek, that, too, was only part of the hallucinations.

He heard sounds that should not be here in the close confines of his study. A waterfall, a rushing river, or was that the sound of his own heartbeat and the blood coursing through his body?

Dear God, but he wanted escape from this, and yet he knew deliverance wouldn't come. Not tonight, if at all.

"Your Lordship," came the voice.

Marshall smiled, knowing that the sound was only in his mind.

"They're coming for us."

He leaned his head back against the chair and closed his eyes.

"They'll be here in a minute, sir. What do we do?"

They would come, in his memory or his mind. Two men at first, and then two more. Sometimes they'd kill one of the English sailors in front of him. Sometimes they'd take him away, to a room down the hall, close enough that Marshall and the other men could hear him scream for days or for however long the poor man lasted.

"Don't show your fear, men," he said now. He took another sip of wine, knowing that his advice was idiotic, misplaced, and ineffective. What did they have left other than their courage and their pride?

"Don't show your fear," he whispered, and toasted the dead men who'd depended on him, whom he'd failed, and whose lifeless bodies visited him every night.

Chapter 16

The grass was a deep emerald green; the sky was a brilliant blue. The birds were chatty this morning, the sound of their chirps and squawks accompaniments to Davina's journey to the Egypt House.

The ornamental hedges had been sculpted into a twisting maze that both delighted and astounded her. The trees of Ambrose's forest were old, their trunks scarred and massive. New leaves clung to their branches, providing a large and expansive canopy.

There was something about the day that reminded Davina of her childhood, carefree days of walking hand-in-hand through the streets of Edinburgh with her father as he explained the history evident on each corner. Sometimes the child she'd been had wanted to be one of those faraway people, come to Edinburgh to visit the court. She'd wanted to be an exciting person instead of simply reading about intrigue.

A few bees passed her, and Davina wondered if she was about to be strung. But two darted in front of her and then simply went on their way, off to visit a few of the flowers.

The gardens were glorious. The engorged leaves and fragile, starlike white flowers of the crassula lived in perfect harmony with bright yellow primroses and clusters of dark purple bluebells drooping low on their curved stems. Wood sorrel, their petals open to the sun, proudly revealed their lilac striations. Next to them was the queen of the garden, the pink and white blooming phlox, planted in a magnificent border.

The Countess of Lorne had often written of her garden, and it was evident that she'd spent many hours in contemplation of what she would leave as a legacy.

The countess served as a lesson of sorts. Davina had no intention of living the kind of life Julianna Ross had lived. There was something so tragic about her unrequited love for her own husband, a love that Aidan never noticed.

What about her own marriage? There was nothing successful about her own union; witness the smirk she'd received from Mrs. Murray the night before outside Marshall's room.

She wasn't going to accept that kind of behavior from Marshall.

The warm breeze brushed against her cheek. Winter was her favorite season, and it was probably because ever since she was a child she'd been fascinated by the legend of the Calleach Bhuer, the hag who symbolized winter and was capable of changing from flesh to stone.

Spring was always more favorably portrayed as a young girl with flowers in her hair and Winter as a hag with unbecoming features and pale, white skin.

Winter, despite her appearance, might have been the more charming of the two.

In winter the world appeared dead, but it wasn't, only waiting. There were signs of life for the person who was careful to look: the grasses turning green beneath the melting snow, the first brave flowers pushing up through the ice. In the winter, dawn was always so much more spectacular, as if nature knew the dullness of the landscape needed brightening with color and drama. Blues, vermilions, greens—all the colors and shades of the rainbow merged together and splashed across the sky. The sunsets lingered, saying a protracted farewell before fading away into night.

But it was summer now, and on this morning, she was not as intent on the dawn as she was the Egypt House in the distance.

She needed to ask Marshall a question, just one question that might possibly decree the future. Not simply his, but also hers.

Davina hesitated at the edge of the courtyard, wondering if Marshall could see her from his office. Aidan's Needle pointed the way, the obelisk repeatedly drawing her gaze. Was he there? Or was he choosing to hide himself from her?

She entered the Egypt House, unsurprised that the door was unlocked. Who would dare broach the Devil of Ambrose's sanctuary? None but his wife.

For a moment she simply stood there, surrounded by all the magnificent relics of the past. Without too much difficulty, she could picture herself back in ancient Egypt. What would life have been like for her there?

Would she have married a man of substance? Or would she have been content to be a handmaiden? Would she have been frowned upon by Egyptian society for being invariably curious? Or would she have even considered society worthy of a second thought? Would she have caused a scandal in Egypt, too?

She rested her hand on the stone leg of a pharaoh and smiled at her bravery. No doubt in ancient Egypt such an act might be reason enough to be killed. A gesture of defiance, of bravado, for all that it had been committed against a statue.

"Marshall?" His name echoed around the large space, but he didn't appear. Perhaps he was simply waiting for her to leave. Well, he was in for a very long wait.

She wended her way through the array of Egyptian antiquities, stopping to admire a series of masks in a glass case. One, the head of Anubis, was crafted out of hammered silver. Another was made of plaster, the colors showing even after all the passing centuries.

At the bottom of the staircase, she hesitated, calling Marshall's name again. When he didn't respond, she mounted the steps, and entered his office. Everything was as it had been yesterday, except for the addition of a small ceramic coffin in the corner of the room. The size was no larger than a small child. The remnants of a reed mat clung to the top of it, but Davina stepped carefully around it, having absolutely no desire to peer inside. What would she do if she found the wrapped body of a child?

The same thing, probably, that she did when encoun-

tering another one of Aidan Ross's prized possessions—
the open sarcophagus proudly displaying its mummy:
She carefully avoided looking in that direction and pretended it wasn't real. She was not so frightened by such
trophies as she was repulsed by them.

It was one thing for Aidan to bring home furniture and statues and artifacts, but shouldn't the citi-
zens of Egypt be allowed to rest in peace in their own
country?

She arranged herself at Marshall's desk. From the
pocket of her dress, she withdrew her spectacles, balanced them on her nose, and retrieved the papyrus from
his desk drawer.

Opening Marshall's writing case, she picked up the
stylus and began laboriously copying the symbols from
the papyrus to the wax tablet, discovering that it was an
excellent way to learn the hieroglyphs.

She was so intent on her chore that she didn't hear
Marshall enter the room.

"Did you know that your eyelashes are so long that
they brush against the lenses of your spectacles?"

She placed the stylus on the desk and looked up at
him.

"You say that as if they are somehow deficient," she
said.

He didn't answer, merely leaned forward and kissed
her on the nose. She blinked rapidly at him, and then
concentrated on the papyrus in front of her.

"Did you notice how perfectly these lotus flowers
are formed? Each petal is just like the next. There
is such majesty and yet delicacy with each one.

They are alike, yet each is separate and somehow unique."

He came to the side of the desk and sat in the chair there. She should have, perhaps, given up his chair to him, but she wasn't feeling excessively charitable right now. Or excessively polite.

There was the matter of Mrs. Murray.

"Did you know that Egyptians prevented unwanted children with the application of crocodile dung?"

He looked startled. "No," he said. "I didn't."

"Did you know that the Roman emperor Caligula stole armor from Alexander the Great's tomb?"

"No."

Was that only word he was going to utter?

"He had a bridge of boats built across the Bay of Naples and he rode back and forth across it on a horse. He wore the armor, and no doubt thought himself greater than Alexander."

"Do you know that you use knowledge like a shield? When you're distressed, you start repeating the most fascinating facts. I really must get a look at that library of your father's."

"There's nothing left," she said, carefully taking off her spectacles and folding them. "Oh, the books are still there, but the room isn't. The house isn't, I mean. It was sold not long after he died. There wasn't any need, you see, for me to keep it. I wish I had, now. There should always be a place you could call home, some-place where memories are stored."

She looked around the room. "Not like this. Not filled with other people's memories. But instead, memories of your own. Something to remind you of your mother's smile, your first achievement, something that made you happy or proud."

"Do you always wax so philosophical?"

"I suspect you do as well," she said, looking at him. "However, you're loath to share your thoughts. Or you disappear for long stretches at a time, so that the opportunity never arises for you to share them."

He didn't say anything in response, but he sat back in the chair and regarded her silently.

For the first time she noticed that he looked tired. His eyes were reddened, and there were lines on his face that hadn't been there a few days ago.

"Whatever did you do last night?" she asked. "Besides avoid me?"

Again, he didn't answer.

"You're always so dour, Marshall, but more so today. Your expression makes me think that your thoughts are not exceptionally pleasant."

"Then I shall have to guard my expression."

"I wouldn't bother if I were you. Just continue to disappear. You're very good at disappearing. And staying away."

She smiled at him, but she knew her expression had an edge to it.

"Perhaps I should think of you as a challenge. Perhaps I should ask myself: How shall I charm Marshall today? How could I make him smile?"

"The effort is appreciated, but not necessary."

"Oh, I have learned that, Marshall." She smiled again. "I confess that I think a great deal about you," she said. Should she be telling him this? Perhaps not. But he was her husband.

"I can think of a great many subjects that would be better for you to concentrate on rather than me, Davina."

She brushed her hand in the air as if wiping his words away.

"Nonsense," she said blithely. "I'm a bride. And brides are allowed to think only of their husbands. At least for a short amount of time. No doubt I shall become more involved in decorating Ambrose in the coming weeks. Or perhaps I shall become an expert on the daily menu. Or, like your mother, I'll become proficient at gardens."

He looked bemused by her announcement.

"Or perhaps I shall never find anything more fascinating than you to study." She propped her chin on her hand and regarded him.

"I can show you the necklace of a Twenty-second Dynasty queen," he said, his smile as insincere as hers.

How very polite they were, and how very irritated at each other. At least she was irritated at him. Perhaps he saw her behavior as normal and usual.

"Anything but fixate upon you?" she asked, her smile disappearing.

He stood and walked to the other side of the room, opening a case she'd not noticed earlier.

When he returned, his hands were overflowing with gold links, chains embedded with stones.

He dropped them on the desk in front of her as if they were an offering, and perhaps they were.

"I'm very impressed with Ambrose," she said, staring at the necklaces. "And your father's collection. You're quite wealthy, and famous as well."

With one finger she rearranged one of the necklaces so that the links were lying straight. The jewel at the center was a beetle of some sort, only this insect was crafted of gold.

She glanced over at him, again seated in the chair beside the desk. "But I would trade it all for a marriage like my parents shared."

Had she stripped the words from his mouth with her candor? Had she horrified him?

She picked up the necklace.

"I had thought to give the entire collection to you. Not all of the antiquities," he said, at her quick look. "But the queen's jewelry. It seemed fitting."

"How can you own something that is thousands of years old? It shouldn't belong to anyone any more than the earth and the sky."

He didn't comment, merely straightened out the jewelry on the surface of the desk with one finger.

She suddenly grabbed his hand, and when he would have pulled away, she held on to it firmly. They both knew he was stronger, but he allowed her to hold his hand, to carefully bend back his fingers.

In the center of his hand was a deep, incised scar, round in shape, with an irregular border, as if he'd been wounded not once but many times. Radiating outward from the circle were other, smaller scars similar in size but not as deep. She turned his hand over, but the scars didn't carry through to the other side.

Gently she pressed two fingers against his palm.

"Tell me about this," she said softly, surprised. How odd that she'd never noticed the scar until now. He had, however, a curious habit of keeping his hands clenched. Except of course when they'd loved, and she hadn't been concerned with his hands at the time. "Did it happen in China?"

"Yes."

"How?" she asked.

"It's not important," he said.

"Does it hurt?"

"Rarely now," he said, gently withdrawing his hand from her scrutiny "It's bearable."

"A great many things are bearable to you, Marshall, that would not be so to another individual. Have you always been so stoic?"

His smile surprised her. "I'd hardly consider myself stoic, Davina. I don't make light of my injuries, but at the same time, I realize they're the price I paid for my survival."

He refused to be thought of as a hero, and judged his own actions in the harshest of ways. Such modesty should be a character asset, but Marshall took it to extremes, refusing to believe that there was anything notable or honorable about his behavior in China. Because he'd been captured, he could extract from the expedition nothing good or decent.

"Are you always that salt and pepper about everything?"

He looked at her quizzically. "Salt and pepper?"

"It's an expression my father used to use. Not everything is black or white. He used to say that life is mostly salt and pepper mixed together, an unsurprising shade of gray. The best times have a little sadness mixed in, and the worst times have a little joy."

"Your father was never in China."

"Have you never wished to continue traveling? Never wished that you were still in service to the Queen? Still a diplomat?"

He stared down at his hands before curling them into fists. "I'm hardly an example of successful diplomacy."

"Salt and pepper," she reminded him.

He nodded, but that was his only response.

There was a look in his eyes that she couldn't fathom. A look of caution? For the first time, she had an inkling that his past might be something he would never discuss fully. The pain might be too deep, the agony of his experiences too great to ever share.

"Did you fornicate with her?"

He looked confused. "Who?"

She frowned at him. "Mrs. Murray. Last night, did you fornicate with her?"

"Fornicate?"

"Fornicate. Copulate. What do I call it, Marshall? There weren't any books in my father's library that addressed the act."

"Thank God for that," he said.

She stood.

"Is that the reason she was in your room last night?"

There was that damnable smile again.

"I did not fornicate with Mrs. Murray last night. If

she was in my room it was either to deliver something or pick something up, not because I was beset with lust for her."

"But you did," she said, the suspicion so strong that she began walking toward the door. "You did once, didn't you?"

He looked away, but just when she thought she wouldn't get an answer, he nodded. "It was a very long time ago, Davina. I was not yet earl, and she was not yet the housekeeper."

She clenched the material of her skirt tightly, and then forced her fingers to relax.

"We both needed solace at the time. It doesn't matter now. You're my wife."

She nodded. "A very strange wife," she said. "You push me away with one hand, and pull me close with the other. Is that one of the rules of this marriage?"

He didn't answer.

"Am I not to feel anything for you, Marshall? Nothing at all?"

"It would be easier if you didn't."

"For whom? You? Or me?"

"You knew from the first, Davina, that this would be no ordinary marriage. If you weren't told before our marriage, I made a point of telling you afterward."

"Yes, you did."

Her own foolishness had made her think there might be something more between them.

"I broke the rules, though, Marshall," she said.

Without a further word of explanation, she simply turned and walked away.

* * *

For a week Davina remained in her room. Her meals were brought to her on a tray from the kitchen. Her occupations were reading and sleeping.

She'd never been so thoroughly bored. Or heartsick.

Not once had Marshall sent word inquiring as to her health. Not once had he knocked on her door. Not once had he sent her a note.

She might as well have been a guest he'd forgotten was in residence.

After three days, she'd exhausted her supply of books brought from home. At night she descended to Ambrose's massive library to take a few books. She did not encounter Marshall. Nor was the ever-present Mrs. Murray in sight. She returned to her room with an armful of volumes, some of which involved Egypt.

At the end of the week, she retrieved the last volume of Julianna's journal. For days she'd thought about not reading it at all, especially the last entry. There was something so sad about knowing Julianna's story from the ending first.

As she opened the last volume, she realized that the pages were written in a different handwriting. Still she kept reading, compelled to by the very nature of Julianna's story.

I have been sitting by the window all day, watching the workers erect Aidan's obelisk. He has returned, shocked, I think, to find his wife resembling one of his ancient mummies. I think, per-

haps, the mummy is more substantial. I'm afraid I look like a skeleton.

The delightful young girl I hired from Edinburgh had to be convinced to write the previous paragraph. Leanne comes highly recommended by one of my acquaintances, and has agreed to assist me in those tasks I can no longer perform for myself. I doubt that she knew, when she came to Ambrose, that she would also be required to act as my confessor.

Leanne is a beautiful girl, with long blond hair and a sunny disposition. She blushes quite prettily also, as I will no doubt see often enough if I put all my sentiments into words.

I used to count the months and weeks and then finally the days left to me. I am now counting the hours, I'm afraid. There will no doubt come a time when I begin to count the minutes as well, hearing each click of the mantel clock as a drum roll, an announcement to the angels that I am shortly to be among them.

I do not seem to care any longer if heaven or hell is my final destination. I simply want to be gone. It is time. Julianna Ross's role in life is done and played out.

If I regret anything, it is that I was not closer to people, that they didn't know how I felt about them. But most of the people I loved in my life are gone now, and perhaps I will have an opportunity to communicate with them once more.

I shall miss Marshall with all my heart. My

son has been very solicitous, and possesses more skill at hiding what he feels than his father. There was no look of horror on Marshall's face when he first saw me a few weeks ago. There is no revulsion now, only love and compassion. For that I adore him all the more.

Garrow has been a constant visitor, and we have grown close over the months. He provides me with his magic Chinese herbs and powders, and I no longer question the efficacy of them. I have managed to survive this long relatively pain-free. I have eventful dreams in which I visit with my parents and my childhood friends, but I do not mind those. For his assiduous attention and compassion, I shall always be grateful to Garrow.

We tend to remember people by the way they died, and not by how they lived. I hope that people will see my gardens and marvel at their beauty. I hope they will not question whether or not I was courageous at the end. I hope that when the time comes, I am sleeping, and death is simply part of a dream.

There were no further entries.

Chapter 17

Mist clung to the ground and to the trunks of the old trees. From the courtyard, Davina could see only the beginning of the maze; the rest of the hedges disappeared into the white gloom. There was not a squirrel or bird to be seen, as if nature was holding a convocation somewhere and they'd all disappeared to gather together. Even the trees seemed to be only partially there, the tendrils of the fog curling around the lower branches and obscuring them from sight.

Why did it feel as if the landscape was waiting, as if Ambrose itself had paused? An immense quiet settled over the great estate. Davina could hear nothing—no maids, no noises from the stables, no gardeners, no footmen, nothing but a cushiony silence all around her. As if time itself had stopped.

Time—a commodity that had evidently fascinated the Earls of Lorne as well. If not, both father and son wouldn't have been so intent upon Egypt's history.

She began to walk, brushing her hand along her skirts as if to dislodge the most tenacious remnants of mist. According to a footman stationed at the door to the family dining room, His Lordship had gone riding this morning.

A girlfriend's mother had been badly injured in a carriage accident on a day such as this. Ever since then, Davina was mindful of how unpredictable horses could be in this kind of weather. One might be startled by the wisps of fog, or not see a rabbit hole until it was too late.

How like Marshall to take chances.

She walked as far as the obelisk and stood next to it, surveying the fog-ridden countryside. Today the obelisk looked even more foreign than usual, shrouded as it was at the base with thick Scottish fog. She put her hand flat against the stone, her thumb tracing a portion of the hieroglyphs inscribed there.

A few moments later, she heard the hoofbeats of a horse echoing in the fog, and Marshall was suddenly there, leaning forward on his black horse and taking the incline down into the glen as if he were being pursued by demons.

He was dressed as he often was, in a white shirt, black trousers, and boots. He was coatless and hatless, a brigand upon a magnificent ebony horse.

Finally he slowed the horse to a walk, dismounted, and stood beside the animal, leaning his forearms against the saddle. Long moments later, he turned and faced her.

"Exhausting myself doesn't keep me from wanting you," he said as a greeting.

Warmth shot through her.

"Should I apologize?"

"I doubt it would do any good," he said, eyeing her as if she were a stranger.

She wished she'd taken more care with her appearance instead of simply grabbing the first dress her hand reached in the armoire. She'd not roused Nora to help her, intent upon this very confrontation.

Days had passed, and her anger had grown. Anger at being in love unwisely. Anger at being in love with a man who was insisting upon being a mystery. Anger at him for being so alone and refusing to share his life with her.

"You're young and innocent and untried, unseasoned in the ways of the world. Ignorant."

She almost took a step back at the unexpected attack, but she held her ground, folded her arms in front of her, and regarded him impassively. It was with some difficulty that she schooled her features to reveal nothing of the sudden hurt and shock she felt. How could he give her the most delightful of compliments in one moment and excoriate her in the next?

"You look terrible," she said. "Have you slept at all in the past week?"

"Little enough," he answered. "And you? Where the hell have you been for a week? Nora tells me that you've been eating, but that you haven't spoken very much."

"Perhaps I should consider myself blessed that you consulted Nora, and not Mrs. Murray."

"Are you still angry? It happened years ago, Davina, almost beyond my memory."

At that, she stared at him incredulously. "Is that

what you will say to your next wife? Poor Davina, I barely remember her. She was a mousy little thing. You know she wore spectacles. And she was forever given to quoting odd facts, always out of context."

"Not quite out of context," he countered, "but always amusing. And I doubt I would ever marry again after this experience. Are you dying? Is that why you've hidden yourself away?"

"You're forever going on about harming me, Marshall. Perhaps you'll kill me."

He took a step toward her, and it was only too obvious that he was controlling his temper with some difficulty. Why should he bother now?

"You say you do not wish to cause me injury, Marshall, but you have caused me more injury in the last week than anyone has in my entire life." She hated the fact that her voice quavered, but she faced him steadily.

He looked stunned by her admission.

"Is that why you've sought me out?" he asked, carefully stepping back from her. "To tell me how much I've harmed you?"

"No," she said. "I finally believe you. You truly do not wish a marriage. You do not want a friendship, and you certainly do not crave a companion. Fornication, however, is necessary between us to provide you with an heir. It's for this reason that I'm here."

"It's called fucking, Davina. If you refer to it at all, call it what it is. Fucking. A good, old-fashioned, Anglo-Saxon word."

She turned and began walking toward the Egypt

House, unbuttoning the row of buttons down the bodice of her dress.

"Then shall we begin?" she called over her shoulder. "It's nearly noon. And after a good, old-fashioned, Anglo-Saxon fucking, I'll no doubt be hungry."

Marshall stared after her, realizing that he'd never been rendered speechless by a woman. He'd challenged the might of the Emperor of China, had met with Her Majesty, Queen Victoria, and had been attaché at Paris, Lisbon, and Stuttgart. He'd been on Gladstone's staff. Never before had he been absolutely flummoxed, and not by any woman, but by his wife.

For a week she'd disappeared, retreating into her suite of rooms as if she were avoiding him. Nor could he blame her. He'd spent the last week certain that she was regretting their marriage. Certain, too, that she'd emerge from her room and demand to return to Edinburgh.

For that, also, he couldn't blame her.

Instead she'd become a termagant with flashing eyes.

He followed her into the Egypt House.

"Shall we do it here?" she said, looking for a bare spot on the floor. "Or in your office?"

Marshall grabbed her hand and pulled her with him, striding up the staircase that led to his office. Once there, he tapped on a door set into the wall so perfectly that it was nearly invisible. He opened it, revealing a small bedroom lit by the weak light from one narrow window. The door closed behind them slowly, almost as if giving her an opportunity to escape.

"What is this place?" she asked, looking around her.

The room was spartan, the furnishings only a narrow bed and one ladder-back chair.

He smiled. "A secret refuge. A place my father used when he didn't choose to go back to Ambrose."

"How absolutely clever. And so opportune. This way, we can fuck in the daylight and you can retreat to your chamber at night."

She smiled sweetly, but he wasn't fooled. She was blazingly angry.

"Why did you stay away for a week?" he asked.

"I simply did what you asked," she said. "I was avoiding the madman I married."

"And now?"

"Procreation," she said patiently, as if he were a half-wit. "I cannot do it on my own."

He leaned against the door frame and folded his arms.

"We should get it out of the way before gloaming, of course. Since you need to disappear at nightfall. I'm beginning to think that the moon must do something very strange to you."

"I've already told you why I leave you."

"Because you're a madman?"

"Yes, damn it."

"Then why don't you act the lunatic with me?" she asked calmly.

He frowned at her.

"If you're truly a madman, why aren't you one all the time? Why not at breakfast? Why not now? Is it only at midnight? Or at dawn?"

He didn't have an answer. Nor did he feel comfortable admitting that he'd never considered such a thing before this moment.

"You've evidently given my condition some thought."

"I've had a week to think of nothing else," she said airily. "Are you certain you don't drink some tonic?"

He smiled faintly. "Something to render me a different creature?"

"Well, perhaps you should at least entertain the thought."

"The only tonic I imbibe is wine."

"Then you shouldn't," she said firmly.

At his silence she sighed. "It's all right, Marshall. I've learned that I can deal quite well without you. I've grown quite accustomed to sleeping most of the day. And when that does not suit, I read. I've read a great deal in the last week, Marshall. I may trouble you to send to the jeweler's for another pair of spectacles. I do believe that there might come a time when I wear the very glass from mine."

"Should I succumb to base honesty? I've missed you, Davina. Even my footmen have commented to me about your absence, and Jacobs has mentioned your indisposition more than once."

She lowered her head and stared fixedly at his shirt.

"I should not be fascinated with you," he said.

She nodded. "In other words, I should be more experienced to have garnered your attention," she said. "A woman of the world, perhaps. Not a mousy woman of Edinburgh. Someone with blond hair, perhaps?"

"Mousy? Are you daft? I know, for a fact, that there are dozens of mirrors at Ambrose." He looked around the bedroom. "There's one there," he said, pointing to the far wall. "Look in the damn thing. You'll see what I see. You're a beautiful woman, Davina. But I'd never thought you to be so needful of reminding."

She frowned at him. "And you claim to be a diplomat? Every woman needs to be reminded, Marshall."

He took a step back, and was hit in the chest with a dozen hairpins. She unfastened the last of her buttons too forcefully, and then threw the button at him.

"I was wrong," she said ridding herself of her chemise with surprising speed. "I'm hungrier than I thought I was. I didn't eat breakfast this morning. So, if you don't mind, if we could do this quickly, I'd be very much obliged."

She put her hands on her naked hips and surveyed him, obviously irritated.

"Is there anything I need to do? I would think that seeing a naked woman would be quite enough. But if it isn't, please just advise me. After all, I'm not a woman of the world. However, I am a very good student. I can learn what I do not know. Once I make a mistake, I try not to repeat it. Therefore, we can suit very well if you'll just tell me at what part of the act you consider me deficient."

She bent and pulled off her stockings. Where had her shoes gone? Her hair was tumbling over her shoulders, and he didn't think that he had ever seen such a delightful sight as Davina, naked, sitting on the edge of the bed, one leg drawn up immodestly.

She noticed where he was looking and smiled back at him, an impish little smile that didn't quite match the anger in her eyes.

"Should I cower beneath the sheets, Marshall? Should I pretend to tremble? Do you only like fearful women?"

Her voice was meant to be cutting, he was sure. The fact that she could not mask the small smile that tilted her lips somewhat softened her mood and her message.

He leaned against the wall, wondering just how far she'd go in this little demonstration.

Just for the sake of comfort, he toed off his boots, but more than that, he was not prepared to go.

She moved the pillows behind her and then sat up against the headboard, one leg angled in a slightly more modest pose than before. But he could still see her breasts, quite large breasts for a woman her size. They weren't being modest at all. Instead, her nipples were pointing at him impudently.

"I'm getting hungrier," she said. "Would you like me to lie down flat on the bed and spread my legs? Would that make it faster?"

The temperature was rather warm in there, so he unbuttoned the top two buttons of his shirt. His pants were getting a little snug as well but he had no intention of removing them.

She slid down on the bed and contemplated the ceiling. "I wonder what the kitchen staff will bring me for lunch? I've asked them to serve me here. Do you mind?" She raised her head and looked at him. "I wouldn't want the soup to grow cold."

She smiled brightly at him, propped up on one elbow, and surveyed him intently. "You don't look mad. You're frowning quite fiercely, true, but is that how a madman is supposed to look?"

"What game are you playing, Davina?"

She looked absurdly innocent for a naked woman sprawled on his bed. His bed.

He'd barely slept during the last week and was incredibly tired. Why shouldn't he sleep for an hour or two?

The next two buttons were easily unfastened, and the shirt was suddenly gone. The damn pants were next.

She tapped her bottom lip with a forefinger. "Does a madman foam at the mouth like a mad dog?"

He wasn't entirely certain he was sane right at the moment, but he wasn't thinking of harming her. Perhaps he should warn her, nonetheless.

"I'm going to join you on the bed, Davina, and no doubt shock our staff if they are foolish enough to deliver your lunch."

"Oh?" She raised one eyebrow and smiled. "The act of a madman, Marshall?"

"Will you stop saying that?"

"Why?" she asked. "You use the term often enough. Too often, I think."

"Shall we consider a moratorium, then? No mention of madness or insanity for an hour or so?"

"Because you want to fuck?"

"Let's have a moratorium on that word as well," he said, removing the last of his clothes and bounding onto the bed.

The mattress sagged with his weight, rolling her toward him.

He reached for his wife, climbed on top of her, and lowered himself until his body was barely touching hers.

"Didn't anyone ever tell you not to taunt the Devil?"

Her smile was luminous. "Oh, bother, Marshall, you're not a devil. How could you be?"

"You're impossible," he said, but his voice sounded too kind.

She only smiled.

"Doesn't your arm pain you?" she asked. His bandage was smaller today, but it was still evident.

"Does it seem to?" he asked, smiling.

"Did the doctor leave you something for the pain?"

"I wouldn't take it," he said shortly.

"That sounds a little stubborn, foolishly so."

His lips brushed against hers in the lightest of touches as his hands ran from the rounding of her shoulders to the violin curve of her back, a delectable and seductive undulation of femininity. She cupped the back of his head with one hand, her palm curving along the line of his skull.

Her hair was really quite glorious, with its chestnut thickness revealing streaks of red and gold. Her form was perfect, her breasts full, and her legs long and shapely. But beyond her feminine endowments, she had the smile of a Madonna and the delicate complexion of a Scottish lass.

She wiggled underneath him; there was no other

word for it. So much for restraint. His fingers felt her, warm, wet, and welcoming. He slid a thumb through her folds and she trembled, widening her legs slightly.

An invitation he couldn't refuse.

He slipped inside her and stilled, his arms braced on either side of her, his breath halted in the act of possession. Or was it submission? Her feet wrapped around his calves, her hands pressed against his chest, his shoulders, and then crept around to link at the back of his neck.

She crooned his name softly, a siren song almost impossible to ignore, but he didn't move, trapped on the precipice of sensations so exquisite that he closed his eyes to savor the feeling.

"Are you absolutely certain there was nothing in your father's library about fornication?"

"I'm certain of it. I'd have learned more about it if there had been," she said.

"Good God," he said, opening his eyes. "I wouldn't have survived it."

He wanted her to be part of this enchantment, more heady and debilitating than any dream or imagination, and more important than his past.

She was lax in his arms, pliant to his demands, a woman not given to either laxity or pliancy. This, too, was a gift, and he recognized it even if she did not.

He kissed her, softly at first, and then more deeply. But he didn't allow himself to move.

Making love to Davina was like being in a giant tunnel of fire. He was unharmed, but not untouched, by the searing heat. Each moan she made drew the flames closer, each touch of her hands on his skin made them arc higher.

He drew back, looked into her face, taut with the strain of wanting, needing, and being artfully denied.

He bent forward and kissed her on the forehead, framed her face with his hands, brushed her hair out of the way with fingers that trembled slightly.

She might take herself away from him, or the madness might return. Either situation would draw him back to his memories, and it was for that reason that he stretched out the moment. He wanted to remember everything about her, from the slight hitch at the end of her indrawn breath, to the impatient drum of her fingertips and nails on his back.

He wanted to be able to recall the speed of her heart, measured by the press of his lips against the pulse at her neck. He wanted to be able to remember how it felt to be deep inside her, to fill the whole of her with the heat and the hardness of his cock.

She trembled, the sensation so faint that it was almost like an entreaty. Submission and power. But who was the submissive, and who the powerful in this joining?

He rose up on his knees and pulled her up until she was sitting astride him, her legs on either side, her breasts pressed against his chest. There was a look in her eyes of such confusion and desire that he threaded his fingers through her hair and jerked her head down for a kiss.

There was nothing polite about this mating. He bit at her lips and smiled when she did the same a second later. Her breath was coming in gasps now, a match to his. The two of them pulled at each other, hands clenched almost into claws, fingernails gently abrading skin, palms rubbing against heated flesh.

He pushed her up and then brought her down again, over and over, relentless. She murmured his name, and he swallowed the sound of it with his mouth on hers.

When she found her pleasure, it was with head tossed back and eyes staring mindlessly at the ceiling. Her hands had lost their grip on his shoulders, her entire body was trembling, her inner walls clutching his cock with so much force that the sensation propelled him over the edge.

Through it all, she softly called his name and marked herself in his mind forever.

Later, he would wonder how his body had been able to survive it. He was surprised to find himself intact. He wouldn't have been shocked to gather up his arms from one place, his feet from another. He was damn surprised his manhood was still firmly affixed to his lower body.

The woman who'd caused such an explosion of feeling lay compliant beneath him, a small smile wreathing her full, swollen lips.

Davina. He said her name in the silence of his mind, and the sound of it was almost like a love poem.

Davina was still, her soft breathing regular and rhythmic.

He rolled over and studied her. Her mouth was turned up in a half smile. Her cheeks were flushed and her hair tousled. He'd thought her beautiful from the moment he saw her, and each day only brought him greater proof of that fact. Smiling, frowning, sad, in every emotion or circumstance, she'd the grace and the body of a Botticelli angel.

She stirred, and her smile slipped as she made a sound—a protest against moving?

This woman had the capacity to make him see into himself. She challenged, with her brashness and her candor, all the façades he hid behind. Although she knew little of his past, and nothing—blessedly—of his present, she'd unerringly peered behind the curtain he held up for everyone to see.

He had the feeling that she'd discover everything that was to be discovered about him, every secret, every horror, every difficulty that he wished to keep hidden. Perhaps she'd understand it all, and offer up a series of excuses for his behavior. Perhaps nothing would shock or disgust her, and she would forgive him anything.

Davina had declared that he was not insane, and the world must simply accept that. His entire journey to madness would be accompanied by her devout and determined support.

At the same time, he didn't doubt that Davina would flatten his consequence just as adeptly. If the world bowed to him, all souls kneeling in a vast spread of human submission, he suspected one lone figure would remain standing. She'd grant him a look of such disdain that he'd know who it was from the toss of her head alone.

Davina. She should bear another name, perhaps, something more exotic. Rose? Adelphia. Glorianna.

He smiled at himself, envisioning her reaction to his thoughts.

He rolled over on his back and put his forearm over his forehead.

Why did he never have hallucinations around Davina?

"Are you going to leave me now?" she asked.

He glanced over to find her smiling at him.

"It isn't dark yet."

She smiled. "No, it isn't. She stretched her arms over her head, clasping her hands together. "I was wondering how one greeted a husband after an afternoon of loving."

"What did you decide?"

"With a hello, of course," she said, smiling. "As simple as that."

Chapter 18

J oy was an ephemeral emotion, racing through her
body like the faintest of breezes, dancing across her
spine, piercing the core of her with the most incredible
sweetness. She could not stop smiling.

Weak gray sunlight bathed the room, reminding her
that it was still daytime.

Was it entirely proper to be getting warm from a
smile? Or was it his look that heated her?

She stretched out her hand and he grabbed it, thread-
ing their fingers together as if they were children playing a secret game. She would have liked to have been
a child with him, but she was six years his junior. Such
an age difference would have meant that he wouldn't
have played with her at all, but would have thought
himself vastly superior and too old for childish games.
But at this moment, they could be playmates of another
sort, indulging in simply being human and adults and
grateful for it.

She suddenly wanted to give him something, make
a present of something valuable and uniquely her own,
a gift of honesty.

"I never thought that loving could be fun." She pressed her fingers against his smiling lips. "No, don't laugh. I mean it. It's supposed to be earthshaking and awe-inspiring and special, but I never realized you could feel joy as well."

"Joy?"

She nodded.

He closed his eyes and at the same time reached out and pulled her to him. "You unman me, Davina. Just when I am prepared for what you might say, you say something like that."

She pulled back. "Should I not have?"

He didn't answer her, merely pulled her close again. He was naked as was she, and they fit together with such perfection it had to be God-made.

"Tell me about the man in Edinburgh," he said.

She pulled back and looked at him.

He stretched out his hand, his fingers trailing over her hand. "I regret that you were shamed, Davina. Or hurt. Cruelty and falsehoods, isn't that what you said?"

She looked away, and then resolutely turned back to him. "It isn't what you think, Marshall." She took a deep breath. "If anyone was to blame for bringing scandal down on my head, it was I."

He seemed fascinated with the actions of his fingers as he traced a line across the back of her hand to her thumb. The silence brought with it a sense of resignation, a feeling that the time had come to finally admit the whole of it.

"I was curious," she said, determined to be honest. He deserved the truth. Or perhaps she gave herself the truth, voicing it aloud for the first time. "I wanted to know what all the books were about, all the poems, all the sonnets."

"Books that weren't in your father's library?"

She smiled. "There were enough to give me a good idea of what was to come. Or what I expected. It wasn't a complete surprise." She smiled. "It wasn't what I've experienced with you, of course. I never realized there was a level of skill involved."

His laughter startled her. A smile curved her lips in response. Should this be such an easy task? Surely she should be feeling more guilt. His amusement rewarded her for her courage, her imprudence. For the first time since that entire episode, she didn't wish the world away, or herself banished to a place where there were no people, no witnesses to her stupidity. "I was a foolish girl, intent on satisfying my curiosity. I allowed myself to be lured into a bedroom. Or perhaps I was the one who did the luring."

"In my experience," he said, "it's often a case of mutual attraction."

She shook her head. "He was a very handsome man," she admitted. "Titled, and quite pleasant, actually."

"And so, the inevitable ensued."

She nodded. "And so, the inevitable ensued," she agreed.

"Afterward?"

"We were discovered, of course," she said, surprised that her voice sounded so matter-of-fact. In actuality, it had been a hideously embarrassing moment, the maid having hastily summoned her employer, Davina's hostess for the garden party. At least a dozen people had clustered around the open door, witness to Davina's dishabille. Her greatest shame had not been at that moment, but later, when her father had been told of the incident. Her father's sigh and the shuttered look in his eyes had been as painful as an arrow to her chest.

"Then he vanished?" Marshall said now.

"No," she said, looking down at his hand on hers. "He was very chivalrous. He would have had us married by special license, I think, if he'd had his way. I was the one who refused."

His fingers stilled and then began tracing up one finger and down another.

"Are you not curious as to why?" she asked.

He glanced at her, a small smile on his lips. "Of course I am. But I have learned if I have patience, you'll eventually tell me what I need—or want—to know."

She frowned at him, but it made no impression on his smile.

"My father died," she said softly. "It was a horrid time, of course. I was almost relieved to discover a reason to refuse." She glanced at him. "In all honesty, I found him to be a stultifying boor," she said. "His charm was annoying after a few hours. He quoted poetry and then claimed it his own creation."

"Ah, not an original thinker, then."

"I doubt he thought at all," she said.

"So, you couldn't see yourself married to a man such as that, despite your foray into decadence."

"It wasn't all that decadent, if you must know. It was a disappointment, all in all. I expected to hear angels sing."

"And they didn't?" he asked, his smile growing broader.

She only shook her head.

The moment slowed, his touch on her hand becoming slower and more delicate. When had her hand become so sensitive?

She waited for the question, and when it came, she continued to smile, anticipating his response to her answer.

"Have you ever heard the angels sing with me?" he asked, concentrating on his fingertip tracing around the cuticle of one nail.

She wanted to show him what he'd taught her, that passion was a heady drink and there was intense delight in being sotted. That was the height of decadence, not the furtive coupling of a rake and a virgin desperate for education.

"I've heard the angels sing, Marshall," she said softly. "But what I enjoy the most are the Devil's whispers."

He raised his head, his gaze intent and direct.

"I should be furious with you," he said, the calm tenor of his voice rendering his words even more disturbing. "You should have saved yourself for me. You should never have known the touch of another man."

"And you, Marshall? Can I surmise by that remark that you came to my bed a virgin?" Her smile had slipped, and her gaze was as direct as his.

He ignored the question. Instead he linked his fingers with hers and pulled her forward. "I should be furious," he continued. "But if you had not been daring and improvident, reckless and feckless, you wouldn't have been persuaded to marry me. If you were not ruined, why would you?"

"Not persuaded," she said, their hands still linked. "Not persuaded," she repeated. "Threatened, shamed, perhaps. But never anything so subtle as persuasion."

She kissed his chest softly, then turned her cheek and rested it against the place she'd just kissed. Her hands explored him, hip and waist and chest, until he grabbed each wrist with his hands and held them still.

"You will only begin something if you continue that."

"Would that be such a terrible thing?" she asked. She rose on one elbow. "Don't people expect us to be a little selfish now? After all, we are newly married. We are not going on a wedding journey, but remaining here. Can we not concentrate each on the other?"

"Did you want to go on a wedding journey?" He looked startled, as if the thought had never occurred to him.

"I would have liked to have seen Egypt," she said. "But I would trade that for remaining in your bed."

Again she had the impression that she'd startled him. Good.

"Davina," he began.

She smiled again, wondering if he was going to chastise her for her candor. Instead he pushed her over on her back and loomed over her.

"I like the way you're formed," she said, pressing both hands against his chest.

"I'd no choice in the matter."

"Still, I like the way God formed you. You're all muscle where I am not. And much hairier," she added.

"I would hope so," he said. "Hirsute females are not the norm, I believe."

She cocked her head to one side and regarded him seriously. "Do you know a great many females?"

"That is not a question I have any intention of answering," he said with a smile. "Especially when I am lying naked next to my wife."

"Well, I for one think it is a shame that women do not have more experience, especially if they are to be wed."

He rolled over and placed his arms behind his head. "How would you change it? By having women be as experienced as men?"

"Who are these women who help you become so experienced? Do they simply disappear once they've educated a man? Women are supposed to be virtuous and men are allowed to be rakes. But if men are to be rakes, they must have partners, mustn't they? Who else but virtuous women?"

He raised up on one elbow and looked at her. "You've given this a great deal of thought, haven't you?"

"Not an excessive amount," she said. "But it does strike me as particularly unfair."

"Perhaps a woman must remain virtuous because there are consequences to her behavior. The legitimacy of an heir, for example."

"There are consequences to a man, as well," Davina countered. "The pox."

His startled laughter made her smile.

"And what you know about the pox, Davina McLaren Ross?"

"I read a great deal," she said primly.

He only shook his head, but there was a smile on his face, one that looked young and carefree.

"Tell me what you were like as a child," she said suddenly.

"I was a good son, my mother used to say," he said. "Although I must confess that I had imaginary playmates. Perhaps that was the Almighty's way of reconciling me to these damn visions."

"Or perhaps one has nothing to do with the other. I know what it was like to have imaginary friends. I did for a time, before books replaced my playmates. I think children who are alone often make allowances as such, don't you?"

He smiled. "I was the earl, the heir, and as such, I was supposed to be everything my father and mother wished for me to be. Without, I might add, being trained for it. My father was in Egypt most of the time and my grandfather died when I was eight."

"And so you taught yourself how to be an earl. I for one think you've done a wonderful job of it."

"Oh, but you're supposed to. You're my wife, and as such, you must be loyal. But there were times when I didn't deserve your loyalty at all."

"Because of China?"

"No," he said, surprising her. "Because of my misspent youth. I did not hesitate to act in ways that did little credit to my name."

She raised her eyebrows and regarded him.

"Did you seduce the maids?"

"Should I answer that question? The last time I was honest about my past you disappeared for a week."

She rolled her eyes. "Did you seduce the maids?" she asked. "Please, do not include Mrs. Murray in that answer."

"Only if they wished to be seduced," he answered. His smile had disappeared, and in its place was an almost saturnine look.

His face was gloriously handsome, and there was something about the whole of him, arresting and compelling, that made her wonder just how much those maids would have protested the seduction.

But his life had changed since his youth. His reputation was one of a man who'd devoted his life to service to the Crown. His list of accomplishments would have been impressive for an older man. Still, she didn't doubt that if he crooked his finger and summoned a woman to his side, the female would go with few reservations. Even Mrs. Murray.

"Tell me about your mother," she said.

She'd evidently surprised him. "What about my mother?"

"I'm torn between telling you the truth," she said, "and bargaining with you. We'll trade secrets, you and I. You'll tell me of China. And I'll tell you what I know about your mother."

He shook his head again, and this time the gesture annoyed her.

"Tell me about her."

"I don't know what you want me to say. She died a few years ago."

"I know of her death," Davina said. "Tell me about her life. I know she designed gardens. What else did she do?"

"She was the steward of Ambrose all those years my father spent in Egypt. The place probably would have crumbled to dust without her. My earliest memories are of her ordering the repairs to the curtain wall."

For a moment Davina remained silent, remembering the journal entries of a lonely woman, one who had spent the majority of her life longing for a man who wasn't there.

"Did she know about your father's fascination with Egypt when she married him?"

"What you're really asking is if she knew that my father was going to desert her for Egypt all those years?"

"Perhaps I am," Davina admitted.

"Evidently her parents were friends with my grandparents. While it wasn't a love match, they were acquainted with each other."

More than we were, but those words were left unspoken.

"But that still doesn't answer the question, unless he was fascinated with Egypt all his life."

"I think the fascination began when he was a young man," Marshall admitted. "He'd visited the country on his grand tour."

"How very sad for her."

He didn't respond.

"At least," she said, attempting to explain her comment, "if she'd had an opportunity to visit Egypt, perhaps she would have been as enthralled. They could have shared his interest."

"Do you do that often? Rewrite history? Does it matter what might have happened?"

"Perhaps your mother wouldn't have been so sad," she said, trying to take his questions seriously and not rhetorically as he'd probably meant. "If she could have understood exactly what he was feeling, or known why he devoted so much of his life to another country and another culture."

"How do you know she was sad?" he asked.

"I think that knowledge is worth a trade. What happened in China?"

His face changed. Just as quickly as that, his smile slipped, and there was an expression in his eyes that she'd never before seen, one that warned her that the topic would not be a good one to pursue.

"How do you manage to look startled and angry at the same time?" she asked.

"Why do you insist on knowing?"

"You can be a very formidable man when you wish to be, did you know that?"

"To anyone but you," he said. "You have no shyness whatsoever when it comes to addressing me on a variety of matters, my lady wife."

"Should I be shy, Your Lordship?"

Abruptly he sat up and swung his legs over the bed. She turned and stretched out her hand toward him, but Marshall was already putting on his trousers, and then his shirt.

Only once did he glance back at her, and when he did, his face was shuttered. "I do not discuss China with anyone, Davina, not even you."

When she didn't comment, he looked over at her again.

"Do you want to know why I'll never take anything for pain, Davina? I was fed opium in my food day and night in China. Days passed when all I did was sit in a corner nearly unconscious, certainly unaware. Then my jailers would amuse themselves by taking it away from me for weeks at a time. My body was on fire, and my mind was useless. I would have done anything for the opium. I would have killed my own mother."

Silenced stretched between them.

"Is that why you think you're going mad?"

He didn't look at her, intent on his task of fastening his shoes. "It's been too long. I've been free of the opium for nearly a year. I shouldn't be experiencing the delirium or the hallucinations."

"And you fault yourself, Marshall? Is that entirely logical?"

He gave her another look.

"Should you not simply be grateful that you survived and came home?" she asked.

"You're determined to see me as some type of hero, aren't you?"

She thought about his question for a moment. "I don't think so. I think you're fallible like any human being. I think you take a certain type of pride in being mysterious, in being reclusive. I think it suits your purposes very well to be thought of as the Devil of Ambrose. I don't think you like the company of people very much, but that's not part of your nature. I think it's because you've disappointed yourself. You've not lived up to your own standards. And the standards we set for ourselves are sometimes much higher than the standards anyone else would set for us."

"You're too young to be so philosophical."

"I'm not at all philosophical," she said. "I'm just interested in you. You're my husband, after all. I want to know why you've chosen to barricade yourself at Ambrose. At this moment, I've come closer to learning the truth that I ever have before."

He stood, looking down at her. "You don't understand, Davina. You do not know what I'm capable of," he said. "What I've done. You only see what you want to see, and while it might be a virtue to be so naïve in some situations, it can be dangerous here and now."

She sat up. "Are you warning me, Marshall, that you could do harm to me? If so, I don't believe it. I think you would harm yourself first, rather than hurt another human being."

"Tell that to the men who died under my command. Tell that to their ghosts, who haunt me regularly. Tell that to their wives and mothers."

She clenched her hands together and arranged her features to reflect only a calm acceptance of his words. Inside, however, she wanted to weep at the look on his face. He wouldn't accept her comfort at this moment, and so she didn't offer it.

"I don't believe you were responsible," she said.

"Davina, you've ignored the truth of what I've said. Are you that much a romantic? There's nothing good or decent or pure about what I've told you. It's ugly and frightening."

She nodded. "I'm not afraid of you, Marshall. If

it would make you feel better, I'll try to summon up some fear. I'll counsel myself that you're despicable, the Devil of Ambrose. I'll even write myself little notes to remind me."

"Stop smiling at me, and I might believe you," he said, shaking his head. "And don't think I haven't noticed that every time I call you lady wife, you refer to me as Your Lordship. You're not at all subtle."

He held out his hand to her.

She took it and stood naked in front of him. "If I cannot make a point in one way, Marshall, I have to make it in another."

"I did call you obstinate, did I not?"

She ignored the comment with a smile.

"May I stay with you, today?"

"Do you think to be my talisman, Davina? As long as you're here, I'll not see visions? I'll not hear any other voice but yours?"

"When you're with me, Marshall," she calmly pointed out, "you do none of those things." She shook her head as if to emphasize the point. "All you are is a tender lover, a most considerate man. The perfect husband. When you're with me."

"Then you don't know the true Marshall Ross."

She waved her hand in the air as if his comment was foolishness. "Let me stay with you. I'll show you what I've learned of hieroglyphs and you can teach me more."

"I'm tired of Egypt," he said abruptly. "Let's do something Scottish."

She tilted her head and looked at him, and then smiled.

"Scottish?"

He pulled her to him, the sensation of his clothing against her nakedness oddly arousing.

She linked her arms around his neck and pushed her body against his.

"I'll play any game you want, Marshall," she said with a smile.

Chapter 19

"**D**avina, you have to concentrate on the ball," Marshall said. "When you swing, keep your eyes on the ball."

She swung the golf club and barely tapped the ball.

Turning, she fixed Marshall with an annoyed look.

Because of the rain, Marshall had constructed a makeshift golf course in the middle of the Great Hall, insisting that Davina learn the finer points of the game. Now he sat behind her, judging her form.

"You're pulling back on the downswing."

"I'm hitting it," she said, turning and placing both hands on the hilt of the club. "That's better than I was doing."

"I'm surprised you've never played before, Davina. It's a Scottish tradition."

"I know," she interrupted. "The first rules of the game were written in 1744. I know *that*, but that doesn't mean I know how to play. The lamentable truth is that I don't think I'm very good at it, Marshall." She turned and frowned down at the ball, focused on it, and then swung with all her might. The ball soared into the air, hit one of the beams, and fell with a thud on one of the overstuffed chairs. "There! I made it to the fourth hole."

"I'm still winning," he said, not at all modestly.

A knock on the door interrupted her response.

When Marshall called out, Jacobs opened the door and stood in the threshold, staring at both of them.

"Sir," he said, his round face bearing a worried expression. "I have been recruited to speak with you."

"By whom, Jacobs?"

"The majordomo, Your Lordship, and three of the maids."

"Not the housekeeper?" Davina asked.

"No one wished to bother her, Your Ladyship," Jacobs said, sending a bow in her direction.

"Is everyone afraid of that woman?" Davina asked. For a moment she thought Jacobs was going to answer in the affirmative, but then he stopped himself, giving her only a little smile instead.

"I have been tasked, Your Lordship, with the obligation of attempting to protect Ambrose's miscellany, all of an historical nature."

"Miscellany?" Marshall asked.

"Your Lordship, shall I move some of the vases? Or cover the more valuable windows?"

Jacobs looked northward to a particularly beautiful example of stained glass art. "A bit of batting, sir? The window is three hundred years old."

"We are being chastised, Davina," Marshall said, turning to her.

"Put in our place," she said, lowering the golf club.

"What about the chandelier, Jacobs?" Davina asked. "I do believe Marshall nearly decimated that." A few crystals on the bottom tier looked sadly shattered.

"Would you like to give me some advice, Jacobs?" Davina asked. "I'm not entirely sure that Marshall is playing fair."

Jacobs looked horrified. "Thank you, Your Ladyship, no. I don't play golf."

"Good man, Jacobs," Marshall said.

Jacobs backed out of the room, his orders to the maids to fetch some batting clearly audible.

Davina and Marshall smiled at each other.

"Tell me what a birdie is again," Davina said. "And eagle and albatross."

"I don't think you need to worry about any of those," he said with a smile. "They all refer to excellent scores."

She sent him another irritated look.

"I could practice, you know. Then I'm certain I could beat you."

"Are you ready?" Marshall asked, smiling. "It's my turn."

"It's not very gentlemanly to look so enthusiastic about trouncing me."

"I'm excessively competitive," he admitted, his smile still evident.

"In fact, I think I should practice," she said. "I would very much like to beat you."

"It is not going to happen today," he said, and laughed when she hit him on the shoulder with her open hand.

She flounced to a chair and sat hard. "Go on, swing."

He propped the club against a small table, came to her side, and offered her a hand. When he pulled her up, he smiled at her. "You've been a very good student. For that you should be rewarded. I'll do whatever you want for an hour."

"Just an hour? I demand an afternoon. Better yet," she said, regarding him, "I crave one whole night. For one whole night you'll sleep at my side."

"Davina."

His embrace was loose, arms draped around her waist. He bent down until his nose brushed hers.

"Has anyone ever told you how intractable you are?"

She smiled at him. "Incessantly. Constantly. Forever."

"It's not yet night."

"No," she agreed. "It's a very, very rainy day and the thunder sounds as if it might go on for hours."

"What shall we do with the time we have?" he asked before kissing the curve of her ear. "We could adjourn to a quieter, more private place and discuss what we could possibly find to occupy us."

"Oh, but it's my choice," she teased.

"And what would you have me do?"

"Kiss me everywhere," she said somberly, not a hint of smile on her face. "Pretend I'm a hieroglyph," she added. "Learn my curves and symbols. What each means."

He glanced around, no doubt to ensure no one was

in the room other than the two of them and then he cupped her breast outside her dress. "This curve? What do you think is the greater meaning there?"

"Sustenance? Fertility?"

He surprised her by pulling her closer and wrapping his arms around her. He made no further movements, simply surrounded her with his body, as if she were a precious artifact that needed to be protected.

"What are you doing?" she asked, her voice barely above a whisper.

"Holding you," he said in the same soft tone.

He pressed his hands flat against the small of her back. His fingers splayed, reaching out on either side of her waist.

"Do not lace yourself so tightly," he said. "You've no need of it."

She smiled. "Would you have me be a wanton, Marshall?"

"With me, yes."

Her hands reached up and gripped his arms as her cheek rested against his chest.

The silence in the Great Hall was encompassing; the moment was oddly beautiful. She wanted to thank him for his care of her, but how did such a thought ever get verbalized?

Would he understand?

She wanted to tell him everything that he didn't know about her, those details about her life he didn't already know. Yet Marshall divulged information about himself with excruciating reserve. As if she'd judge him, or feel horror over what he'd done.

How could she feel anything but love for this man?

"Stay the night with me," she whispered against his throat. "Please, Marshall."

"Davina."

"You'll not hurt me. I know it. Believe me as I believe in you."

He didn't respond, didn't answer her, only held her within the circle of his arms. In that moment, she felt the faint stirrings of hope.

Marshall accompanied her to her chamber, opened the door, and entered the room, closing the door behind him. Facing her, he began to remove his clothing.

"Should I be shocked?" she asked.

"Should you be? You've seen me naked before."

"This is what I get for being brazen this morning?"

"Punishment by lovemaking? It's an idea. Would it work?"

"Very possibly," she said calmly. "I quite like bedding you." The very word was titillating.

"Shall I undress? Or would you prefer to disrobe me?"

"On the contrary," he said, his fingers halting in the act of undoing the buttons on his shirt. "I would much rather see you perform the honors."

"I have ugly feet," she said. "I've often despaired of them. I can never find shoes that fit me well enough, so consequently they are very large and ungainly. Plus I have very small and pudgy toes."

"I'm not interested in your feet."

She wished she could have begun this chore with a

great deal more equanimity, but Davina knew she was blushing. Warmth trickled down her skin to encompass the whole of her chest and shoulders. How odd that her fingertips felt cold.

Marshall crossed the room to sit in the overstuffed chair beside the window, still watching her.

He sat there fully dressed; his only concession to disrobing was his open shirt.

"Aren't you going to undress?" she asked.

"Impatient?"

She'd already dispensed with her hoops, her laces, and was in the process of gathering up her chemise. She hesitated when the garment reached her knees and stared at him. "I'm beginning to think that you deliberately goad me with words, only to see what I'll say in response."

"If that's the case," he said, smiling, "then you've not disappointed me."

She pulled off the remainder of her clothing and stood before him naked.

"I've never thought of myself as avant-garde, or an iconoclast. I might have caused a scandal, but it wasn't intentional. Nor was I all that brazen in my thoughts or actions as a girl. How odd that I've changed in the last two weeks. Just when a girl should be on the verge of becoming matronly and proper, I've become shocking."

"Hardly shocking to the world, Davina. Unless, of course, you intend to discuss what happens within this room. I myself would prefer that you not do so."

"Why ever not? The rumors that would accompany

your name would be very favorable indeed."

How very strange to see his cheeks deepen in color. Not a blush exactly, but enough color to give her the impression that she'd discomfited him.

How had she lived without him?

Dear heavens, what if she'd agreed to marry anyone else? Dear God, what if she'd married Alisdair? She would never have felt for Alisdair what she did for Marshall. She'd never have experienced this heady sensation of freedom that each day brought.

"You would let me do anything I wished, wouldn't you, Marshall?" she asked.

He looked surprised by the question, but answered just the same. "In what context?"

"If I came to you and told you that it was very important to me that we have swans and a lake, would you allow it?"

His eyes crinkled with amusement. "This is your home, Davina. If swans are important to you, then how could I refuse?"

"And dresses? May I fetch some of the modistes from France to Ambrose?"

"Are you planning on beggaring us, Davina? I warn you that it would be quite an undertaking."

"Or trunks of books?"

"Do we need new shelves in the library?" he asked, a half smile back in place.

How silly to feel tears peppering her eyes.

She went to him and knelt beside the chair, taking his hands in hers. "It is a good thing I married you," she said. "Otherwise you would have been too generous and giving." She smiled teasingly. "As it is, I'm excessively frugal by nature."

"No swans or modistes?"

"Except for books and shoes, I'm excessively frugal," she admitted.

He leaned forward, removing one hand from her grip, and tilting her head up to meet his gaze. "Then we shall have to enlarge Ambrose's library and find you another armoire or two for your new shoes."

He kissed her then, a light, friendly kiss that hinted at more.

She stood, and he did as well, removing his shirt and beginning on his trousers. A few more garments and he was gloriously naked. Gloriously. Naked.

What an absolutely beautiful instrument. Was that what it was called? It looked like a spear jutting out from his body, the shaft taut and firm, the end almost pointed.

"You have your own obelisk," she said, and smiled when his laughter echoed throughout the room.

She wanted to touch him, to stroke her hands the length of him. She wanted very much to study that absolutely fascinating appendage.

Marshall was looking at her, and that made her skin feel strange and tight and her blood heat. In fact, he was looking at her with the same hunger with which she no doubt looked at him. Is this what God had done, created in each gender such curiosity about the other that making love was a natural completion?

"Is it the same size with every man?"

She still had not moved, and neither had he. No more

than a few feet separated them, but it felt as wide as Scotland.

"Or is it in proportion to a man's body? Like an arm or leg?"

With one hand he lifted himself, as if in offering. "So you're satisfied, are you?"

"Should I truly answer that? Wouldn't it make you even more insufferable than winning at golf?"

"I promise not to become insufferable."

"Then of course you know I'm satisfied," she said. "But you haven't answered my question."

"I haven't the slightest idea how I rank among men," he said. "Perhaps I'm a little larger than most. Or simply average."

"Does it always stay that way? How on earth does it fit in your pants?"

He was smiling broadly now, but it wasn't the kind of smile that had an edge of ridicule to it. She had pleased him, she could tell.

Two of his fingers slid up the shaft, and she wanted to replace his hand with hers.

"It doesn't always stay this way," he said. "Seeing you naked has an effect on it."

She shook her head as if to negate what he was saying. "It was that way before I was naked."

"Talking about it with you has that effect as well."

"Can you find pleasure simply with words?"

She lifted her gaze to find that he was looking at her intently. "Words don't affect me as much as images. Remembering you, remembering entering you, now that affects me."

"The first few times were different," she said, taking a few steps closer to him. "Not like now."

"That's because you were innocent."

"I wasn't, actually."

"You were, more than you know. Or if you do not choose to recognize yourself as an innocent, then perhaps another word would suffice. Unaccustomed."

"Unaccustomed?" she said.

"To me."

He reached out and pulled her closer with one hand. His hands were on her shoulders, and his eyes were on her breasts, but she ignored what he was doing in favor of placing her hands on that beautiful instrument, hot to her touch. It quivered as if it recognized that she was there, nearly bobbing up and down in eagerness.

She felt breathless and yet utterly calm.

"Lovers must become accustomed to each other," he said softly.

When he turned and began to walk toward the bed, she followed, reluctantly surrendering her grip on him. She climbed up to the mattress and reached for him again, and he didn't demur when she gripped him between her palms and held him tight, fascinated at the length and strength of his erection.

She was seated at the end of the bed, naked and almost unconscious of the fact until his fingers slid across her breast in a gentle touch, so light and delicate it might have been a feather.

He knelt on the bed in front of her. She rose up on her knees and placed one hand behind his neck, extending her fingers upward into his soft black hair.

Gently, she pulled his head down for a kiss. He acquiesced but kept the kiss light when she wanted to deepen it. She pulled back to find him smiling at her, a teasing glint in his eye.

He pulled her up until she was pressed against his chest. Her fingers curled around his cock, and he made a sound deep in his throat. But he didn't pull her hands away.

They were so close that a whisper could not come between them. But he didn't kiss her again, choosing instead to tuck her head into that spot between neck and shoulder. His right hand traveled up from the small of her back and then down the line of her spine, repeating the movement until she began to anticipate the stroking of his hand against her skin.

His fingers splayed against her shoulder and then down her arm, his palm cupping her elbow before trailing down her forearm and wrist to the back of her hand.

His knuckles brushed against her nipple, and it hardened instantly.

"Marshall," she said, breathing his name against his throat. She was weak, filled with sensations. His hands were everywhere, smoothing, sliding, touching, and measuring. She felt as if he were learning her, that he would soon know each curve and joint, each separate crevice and mound, each muscle and bone.

Slowly, with great deliberation, he laid her down on the bed. In perfect silence, he entered her, their gazes locked.

This moment was silent and perfect and beautiful, like a baptism or a wedding.

Her hands held on to his shoulders, and then trailed to his back. When he bent his head to kiss her, Davina finally closed her eyes. Her last glimpse of Marshall was smiling, the look in his eyes one that made her want to weep. As he brought her pleasure, he also gifted her with love.

Even though most of his wealth had come to him courtesy of the ocean and clipper ships, Garrow Ross didn't particularly like anything nautical, including the stench wafting from the sea. So he settled for sitting in his office above the large warehouse he owned in Perth with the windows tightly closed and the shutters blocking out the tall masts of the ships docked not far away.

The accountancy report he read made for boring reading for anyone but him. His wealth—growing by the day—was represented by a substantial column of figures. All in all, it had been a prosperous month and looked to be an even more prosperous year.

The goods located in his warehouse were plentiful, most of them imported from the Orient, India, or the Continent. But the bulk of his wealth was not derived from goods that were purchased by the average buyer.

He was no longer the poor relation of the Ross family, looked upon a little askance because he was in trade. A fortune could purchase a great deal of respect.

He signed his approval of his accountants' records and then put the sheaf of papers to the left of his desk. His secretary would pick it up in a matter of moments. On the right of his desk was a leather folder, another missive from one of his captains.

In his pocket was a present for Theresa, a string of perfectly matched pink pearls. Theresa would be suitably grateful, he knew. She liked presents, and he'd seen that acquisitive glint in her eye.

Now all he had to do was ensure she never knew exactly how he made his money.

He smiled. It shouldn't be all that difficult. Theresa was a toothsome female, but she also tended to be vacuous. Unlike her niece, Theresa had no curiosity, no interests other than her wardrobe and her newest hairstyle.

Davina was an annoying chit. Well, let her play at being Marshall's bride. Such devotion might actually keep Marshall sane for a while. Then again, Marshall might lose his mind completely one night and snap the little bride's neck. That was all too possible.

Chapter 20

Moonlight spilled into Davina's bedroom, casting the chamber in a strange blue hue. It wasn't the moonlight that woke Marshall, however, but hunger.

His appetite had been affected ever since his imprisonment. The last year he'd been slow to put back the weight he'd lost in prison, a fact that Jacobs had mentioned on more than one occasion. There were also too many nights when wine dulled the edge of his hunger.

Tonight, however, he was ravenous. He could have eaten a side of beef if it had magically been produced in the middle of Davina's bedroom.

They'd slept for hours, curled into each other. He hadn't slept for so long in months. Hours of dark, sotted sleep devoid of dreams.

She was restless, preparatory for waking, and a part of him wanted her to awake, wanted her to know he'd not abandoned her after they'd made love. He studied her as she slept, wondering what it was about this woman that enticed him so much, made him want to smile at the same time he wished to kiss her.

He had not, despite the invitations, taken a mistress on his return from China. It was not truly him they wanted, it was the earl those women lusted for, the steward of Ambrose, the diplomat. His position, his person, his very identity was a commodity, and that he reluctantly accepted, but he wouldn't tolerate pretense in his bed. Therefore, he'd remained a celibate man until his marriage. Abstinence had been more tolerable than expedience.

Yet it wasn't simply pleasure he felt when looking at her. She was loyal, and witty, and possessed of her own courage. But admiration wasn't the complete answer, either. Some other emotion, something more important and less suitable to examination, made him want to protect her, shelter her, and keep her safe from anything and anyone who might harm her—even himself.

He pressed a soft kiss on her bared shoulder and then covered it with the sheet before leaving the bed. After donning his trousers, he glanced at the clock on the mantel, surprised that it was nearly midnight.

"Where are you going?"

He turned to find that she'd rolled over and was regarding him sleepily. She raised up on her elbow and smiled at him. Her hair cascaded over her shoulders, and she impatiently pushed it back.

"You look like some sort of enchanting mystical creature in the moonlight," he said.

"Is that a compliment to take my mind from the fact that you're leaving me again?"

"Only temporarily," he said. "I'm hungry. Are you?"

She shook her head. "You'll come back?"

"I'll come back," he said. "You're my talisman, remember?"

"Don't forget," she said, and curled up on his side of the bed, her hands gripping the pillow he'd used.

He left the room smiling.

As a boy, he'd haunted the kitchens, having an affinity for Cook's biscuits. Tonight he easily retraced the steps of two decades ago. On the lower floor the walls needed cleaning, and there wasn't substantial enough lighting in this area. He made a mental note to address both of these issues as well as new furnishings.

His grandfather had always been fond of telling him that inherited wealth traditionally lasted only three generations, but that the Ross family had been the exception to that rule. The old man had added a caution: "It doesn't matter what your title is, son," he'd once said. "If you're devoid of income, a fancy title is like peacock feathers on a chicken. Pretty, but useless."

Like his father, Marshall had an affinity for making money, even when he hadn't been paying any attention to his investments. His grandfather would be happy to know that Marshall hadn't stripped the family coffers. All the family ships had made a fortune in the spice trade and in importing cotton from the southern United States.

Cook had baked yesterday, and there was an assortment of loaves and rolls. Marshall put a few into an empty basket he found at the end of a shelf.

He carried a wheel of cheese to the large oak table in the middle of the kitchen and sliced off a portion. From the shelves on the right side of the sink he grabbed a plate and a mug. The plate he put down on the table, and the mug he carried into the larder. There, resting on the floor was a large keg that he suspected held ale. When he tapped into it, his suspicion proved to be correct.

He took a sip and smiled in remembrance. As a boy home from school, he'd slipped down here to meet his boyhood friend Daniel. Together they'd ended up being inebriated on more than one occasion. The ale might taste refreshing, but it had been brewed at Ambrose, and had a more powerful kick than some types of whisky.

Daniel had accompanied him to China, and had died there. Marshall had brought the news back to Jacobs himself. As the boy's grandfather, Jacob had been against the adventure, but he'd received the news of Daniel's death with great stoicism.

They rarely discussed Daniel after that day. But Marshall lifted his mug to Daniel's memory now.

"Here's to the old days, Danny."

Marshall heard a noise, a slight scrape of sound, and whirled. Was Daniel's ghost responding in kind? But there was nothing there. Nothing real, at least. He heard the sound again, coming like a faint knock.

Was it happening again? Had darkness brought about his lack of connection with the real world? Was he descending into madness again? If so, he was grateful that Davina was nowhere near. She was safe in her chamber.

He took a few steps out of the larder and stared through the window. He wouldn't have been surprised to see his visions hovering there in the darkness, floating some feet above the rain-dampened ground. His visions were not susceptible to the rules and boundaries of nature. They existed within his mind, and were therefore capable of anything.

"Richard?" There was no response.

He called out a few more names, but none of them materialized.

The sound came again, delicate, almost muted. Suddenly a hand pressed against the glass, fingers splayed. He steadied himself, waiting, but the fingers didn't come through the glass and the figure didn't seep through the solid wall. Just that hand pressed against the glass.

Perhaps this visitor was more mortal than hallucination.

He took his knife with him and reached the kitchen door, pulling it open. He stood on the stoop and stared at the visitor, wondering if it truly was a hallucination, or if nature and fate had conspired to bring him his past in the flesh.

Davina walked down the grand stairs and through a series of hallways that led to the East Wing. The Pharaoh Wing, she'd heard one of the young maids call it because of the statue at the end of the corridor. Evidently Aidan could not bear to be parted from this particular rendition of Seti and had him carted to Ambrose proper.

She'd been to the kitchens only once, and that had been with Nora leading the way. As the Countess of Lorne, she needed to inspect all areas of Ambrose, despite the fact that Mrs. Murray ruled the estate with her dictates and ever-present ledger. There was no waste at Ambrose, nothing unaccounted for, little food left over for the poor, and the great house ran with surprising dexterity and economy.

Davina was pleased by that revelation for two reasons—it meant she had no need to seek out Mrs. Murray in an attempt to educate her on frugality. In addition, the housekeeper would be occupied in her efforts to keep Ambrose running as smoothly as it had been. She wouldn't have time to concern herself with Marshall.

The sound of voices alerted her to the fact that Marshall wasn't alone. That explained why an hour had passed and he hadn't returned to her room.

She turned the corner and entered the kitchen to find Marshall sitting at one end of the table piled high with food. Seated beside him was a younger man.

As she approached them, the stranger turned to her, and she was startled by the brilliant blue of his eyes. However beautiful their shade, they could not deflect from his shocking condition. He was too pale, and almost gaunt. His face was narrow and all angles, his brow prominent, his jawline sharp. There was not one ounce of spare flesh anywhere on his face.

She'd never before seen anyone who so closely resembled a skeleton.

He was dressed as a sailor, one evidently parted from the service, since he wore no hat and his uniform had seen better—and cleaner—days. The dark blue jacket hung from his shoulders, and revealed almost fragile-looking wrists.

Marshall stared at her for a minute, as if deciding

whether to introduce the stranger to her. Finally he nodded, a gesture that demonstrated his reluctance more than any words.

"Jim, I'd like you to meet my wife, the Countess of Lorne. Davina, I'd like you to meet Jim."

There was no other information forthcoming. Nor did Jim appear surprised at the paucity of that introduction.

"Welcome to Ambrose," Davina said. She added a smile to her welcome.

Her aunt would have been proud of her composure.

"Thank you, Your Ladyship."

Now what was she supposed to say?

"You'll stay with us for a while, certainly?" There, a little more politeness. "I will send one of the maids to ready a room for you."

Jim didn't say a word, but his face was suddenly suffused with color. Her heart went out to the young man. It was not his fault, after all, that Marshall was being rude.

"I don't want to be any trouble, Your Ladyship. I just came to see the earl. I don't need to stay."

"Unless you have someplace that you must be, Jim," she said kindly, "is there a reason why you cannot remain with us for a little while?"

She did not miss the look that Jim sent Marshall. Nor was she oblivious to Marshall's small smile. A gesture of welcome, evidently, from the grin that joined the flush on the young man's face.

"Thank you, Your Ladyship. I would like to stay, very much. I'm a little tired. It was a very long walk from Edinburgh."

"You walked?" she asked, shocked. "And how long did that take you?"

"Days," he admitted. "I'm not used to walking, but I've not been out of the navy long."

"What Jim is not telling you," Marshall said, "is that he was very ill for a very long time. You'll stay, then?" he asked.

"I will, sir. Thank you," the young man said, looking as if he might cry.

Marshall stood and left the room, only to return a moment later. "I've sent the scullery maid for Mrs. Murray," he said.

Davina sat at the table, poured another cup of ale for Jim, and busied herself slicing cheese that probably no one would eat. At least she was doing something, occupying herself with activity rather than looking at Marshall or their guest.

The moments passed silently, in a tense silence broken only by commonplace sounds. She didn't ask any questions. Nor was Marshall generous with answers.

When Mrs. Murray appeared in the doorway, Davina was almost happy to see her.

The other woman was beautiful as usual, her hands folded neatly in front of her. The ever proper Mrs. Murray, even at this hour of the night. She was attired in a dark blue wrapper with white piping on the color and cuffs. Her hair was braided and wrapped in a coronet at the top of her head.

Davina had disliked her from the very moment she looked up to find the woman staring at her. Now, knowing what she did about the woman and Marshall, her jealousy was understandable. Although the woman excelled at her position, Davina would just as soon she left for Edinburgh.

The two of them looked at each other, and for a brief instant of time, there wasn't any pretense in either of them. Perhaps it was the lateness of the hour, or the strangeness of the circumstances, but Davina could almost feel Mrs. Murray's antipathy.

Marshall outlined what was needed, and Mrs. Murray nodded. "I'll have a room prepared immediately, Your Lordship."

"Thank you, sir," Jim said. "Not just for your hospitality. But for everything."

Marshall only nodded, but didn't explain Jim's comment.

"You were in China, weren't you?" Davina asked the young man.

Three sets of eyes turned to her.

Davina clasped her hands together and refused to look away from Jim. He stared down at the table and then at Marshall and finally at her.

"Aye, Your Ladyship. I was in China."

"Jim was one of your men," she said to Marshall.

He didn't answer. Neither did he look away.

If Mrs. Murray hadn't been standing there, looking too interested for a good servant, Davina would have continued her questions. Instead she forced a smile to her lips, bid them good night, and slipped from the room.

But she was determined to speak to Jim at her earliest opportunity.

Chapter 21

Marshall didn't return to Davina's room but to his own. She would be awake and want answers, and there were some things that he couldn't discuss now. Perhaps he couldn't ever divulge them.

Jim. He'd never expected to see the young man again, and especially not in that condition. He'd been close to starving. Marshall had deduced what Jim had not said—separation from the navy, while something he'd desperately wanted, had not been easy.

He probably hadn't been able to find work. Or perhaps Jim had been unable to work because of his experiences in prison.

China dug its tentacles into a man's soul and never let loose.

Instead of heading for his bed, Marshall went to his study, unsurprised to find that the lamp was lit, the decanter of wine refilled—all was in readiness for his comfort, thanks to the efforts of Mrs. Murray.

He sat and poured himself some wine, knowing that sleep might not come at all tonight. Seeing Jim had brought back memories he'd managed to tamp down in Davina's presence.

She couldn't be his talisman all the time. No one could wipe out the sounds and sights his mind furnished only too easily now.

He'd been taken prisoner hours after arriving in China. The Treaty of Tientsin had not been signed by the Chinese, and it was an embarrassment to the Empire. Queen Victoria had sent him to China for the purpose of acquiring the emperor's signature. The Chinese, however, were still angry about the importation of opium into their country, and not willing to sign a document that would legalize the trade of the drug. To show his displeasure, the emperor had ordered Marshall and his men, all forty of them, imprisoned at once.

Davina had once asked him if he missed being a diplomat. The truth was remarkably simple and remarkably sad. He could no longer, in good conscience, represent the British Empire. If the Queen had not known of opium's effect on the Chinese people, then she'd been a fool. If she'd known and willingly blinded herself to it, then she'd been worse than criminal.

No longer would he do the bidding of a corrupt government. Nor would he sell his soul for anyone ever again. But because he had, once, because he'd shamed himself and his name, he was doomed to nights like this.

Dawn was hours away, as was sleep.

He felt nauseous and his ears were ringing. Not now. He couldn't bear the visions tonight. The past had rushed in and captured him unawares. He would be defenseless against the men he'd given up to their deaths.

He left the study, intent on the Egypt House. As he passed Davina's suite he hesitated for a moment, tempted almost beyond his strength to remain with her. Finally he continued past the door. He started to sway at the top of the landing but he caught himself, holding on to the banister with a clenched hand.

As he descended the staircase, Marshall caught sight of himself in the mirror on the opposite wall. The man in the reflection looked out of focus, his eyes crazed. Behind him he could see the beginnings of a cloud. A shape, forming in the wall.

Peter, coming to bedevil him again? Or Matthew, perhaps, with his enduring patience?

Let the specters look for him tonight. Let them wander through the halls of Ambrose, unseen and searching. He wasn't going to make it easy for them.

The Egypt House was dark, eerily lit by the moon. A perfect night for a haunting. He was surprised his father's spirit hadn't begun to walk. Aidan would be the perfect ghost, buried in the family crypt in an Egyptian sarcophagus.

Marshall lit the gas lamps at the base of the stairs. At the top, he swayed again in the act of lighting more lamps. He would not sit in the dark tonight and see blood as a black pool. Let them bring him gore in all its vibrant color. Let them seek him out and deliver hell to him in grand measure tonight.

He sat at the desk, his nausea returning in force.

Davina's perfume wafted up to him, a reminder that

he could have been next to her in her bed. He would have held her while his world swirled around him, hoping that she'd be enough to keep these night terrors at bay.

She wasn't, and to test her in such a way was dangerous.

He heard the loud, bright tones of the Chinese zither, the guzheng, and the guqin, accompanied by the flute. Smells came to him, not exotic perfumes or rice dishes but the distracting scent of roses. Davina.

She'd never appeared in a vision before, but perhaps it was only a matter of time.

"Marshall?"

He looked up to find her standing there.

"If I'd known that you were given to wandering around so much at night I would have donned my heavy shoes," she said, glancing down at her feet. "As it is, I've only my slippers, and they've been ruined by the dew."

Was she a ghost? The air around her wavered. But his visions had never spoken of such things as feet before, and it gave him hope that she might be real.

"My apologies," he said. "Send for a dozen from Edinburgh."

"The slippers don't matter," she said, coming into the room. "My husband does."

She came and sat on the chair beside the desk, and placed her hand on top of his. Her skin felt warm, as warm as her expression. She was real, then. Either that or his visions had become so advanced that he could no longer tell what was true and what was fantasy.

Wasn't that the definition of insanity?

"Your husband craves a bit of solitude."

She didn't comment to that, and he was grateful for her silence. The air shimmered, and Paul appeared just over her left shoulder, his disembodied head looking just as it had when the Chinese presented it to Marshall at his noon meal.

"What is it, Marshall?"

He shook his head and then changed his mind about that particular gesture when his nausea was abruptly made worse and his dizziness increased.

"Go away, Davina."

"What did I do?" she asked.

"Nothing. Just leave me alone."

She stood, but didn't move away from the desk. He wished to God she'd leave before anything else happened.

Blood pooled on the carpet at the doorway, and then spread on the carpet like long fingers, reaching out for him.

"What are you seeing?"

He closed his eyes. Coming here was not a good idea. He had no locks on the doors and there was no bellpull to summon a footman to take her away.

She took a step closer, and he was powerless to prevent her approach.

"Tell me why, Marshall. Tell me why I must stay away from you. Are you afraid you might run me through with one of your sabers? Or are you afraid that the craving for opium might be so much that you would harm me?"

"I could kill you," he said, and closed his eyes at the look on her face.

How many days had she been married? Barely a month. Not even that. In that time, she'd felt passion, despair, anger, jealousy, and hope. She'd laughed and wept, empathized and agonized. She'd doubted herself and him. She'd mourned for a woman she never knew, and examined her character with great intensity.

Yet, in that time, she'd also fallen in love. Not mildly or sweetly or even easily, but roughly, and raggedly, and with reluctance. Once loved, however, Marshall Ross could not be unloved.

He stood, wavered, and caught himself with his hands on the edge of the desk. He looked at her, and then swiftly to the left. She followed his line of sight but couldn't see anything in the corner other than another stone pediment, no doubt the base of a missing statue.

She turned back, to find that his features had taken on a stern cast, his lips thinned, his eyes narrowing. If she were a recalcitrant servant, or a tradesman who'd provided an inferior product, she might have been frightened at that moment. But she was the Countess of Lorne, Davina McLaren Ross, and the title alone gave her some bravado.

She stiffened her back and faced him. "What do you see, Marshall?"

He shook his head. "Davina, I think it best if you leave."

She folded her arms and stood where she was. She

had absolutely no intention of leaving the room. He would have to bodily carry her from here. His head turned suddenly, and he stared at something on the far wall and then on the floor.

"What is it, Marshall?"

He sat again, placed his elbows on the desk blotter, and covered his eyes with his fists. "Please go, Davina. Please leave me."

"You're seeing things, aren't you?" she asked. "Tell me what you're seeing, Marshall, please."

He laughed, and it was a sound curiously lacking in amusement. Instead it held a hint of desperation, so much so that for a moment she contemplated doing what he asked and leaving him. But she could no more desert him at this moment than she could someone in pain. Because it was evident, from the look on his face, from his every gesture, that Marshall was in agony.

She came around the side of the desk and knelt on the dusty floor. Placing her hand on the arm of his chair, she let her fingers brush against his sleeve at the wrist.

"Please, Marshall," she said softly. "Let me help you. Let me do something to help."

"Take the last two years from my memory," he said slowly. "Give me wisdom and guidance so that I was not such a naïve fool. Take my memory of China from me. If you cannot do that, Davina, leave me."

"I can't leave you, Marshall."

He looked toward the other end of the room. Whatever he'd expected to see was still there. His eyes widened ever so slightly, and she could tell that he forced himself to look away.

"You don't see anything, do you?"

"No," she said gently. "There is no one here but you and me."

"My mind knows that you might be correct," he said. "My mind always knows that. My eyes, however, tell a different story."

"Then you must simply command your eyes to ignore what they see."

He turned his head and smiled at her. "As easy as that, is it? My monsters aren't horrifying at all?"

"They probably are," she said. "I'm sure I should be terrified. But wouldn't it be easier to face them with someone else at your side?"

"No," he said tiredly. "Your being here will only put you in jeopardy, and lengthen their visit. They want me to themselves, you see."

"Why?"

"Do you never grow tired of your own curiosity? Does it never wear you down? Is there never a day when you awake and you say to yourself, Today I will simply accept all that I see? I will not question the entirety of the world today?"

"No," she said softly. "There isn't. Especially not about you. Especially when you're in pain and there's something I can do to help."

"There is nothing you can do, except leave."

"Because you're the Earl of Lorne? Because you must face everything alone? Has there never been a time when you've reached out to other people? I'm your wife. Doesn't that mean that I should stand with you?"

"What is it about you that makes you hammer at something relentlessly?" he asked.

"Obstinacy? The courage of being right?"

"You mustn't be this loyal, Davina. I don't deserve it. I'm responsible for the deaths of twenty-two men under my command."

"Did you shoot them?" she asked.

He looked startled at the question.

"Did you run them through with a sword? Or poison them? Or injure them with your mind? With a glance? With a wish? Are you that powerful, that you can kill with simply a thought?"

She smiled as she ran her hand up his sleeve.

"You did not kill them."

His glance flickered over her. "But I did." At her silence, he continued. "I did kill them. It was a choice between my life and theirs, and I chose them to die. So don't tell me how virtuous I was and how noble. Don't say that I think I'm somehow special among men. I know exactly what I've done and how."

"I don't believe you."

"Believe it. I chose them by name. I was given the choice to die or choose one of my men, and I did so. Peter was the first one I chose. He was tortured. It took him two days to die. You want to know about obstinacy? Peter was too damn stubborn to die."

She stood, looking down at him. He stared straight ahead as if addressing one of his specters.

"Matthew was the next. I chose him because he was an irritating son of a bitch. He needled me constantly. He didn't scream as much as Peter."

He glanced at her, his smile almost tender.

"Now you know what happened in China. Are you satisfied? Are you happy? Is your curiosity assuaged?"

She had no words for him, nothing that could travel past the constriction in her throat. Nor did he seem to expect anything from her, and that fact alone forced her to speak.

"I'm going back to Edinburgh. It's evident you find the addition of a wife to be rather restricting. I would not like to keep you from your dour moods or your self-flagellation, Marshall. No doubt, with me gone, you can be about the business of filling your universe with guilt."

She folded her arms and stared at him. "You certainly have the right to forbid me to leave, Marshall. And you can certainly forbid the stable master from arranging for a carriage. And should I take a horse instead, I'm sure you could report me to the magistrate for stealing. No doubt should I indicate that I had the desire to walk to Edinburgh, as Jim accomplished, you will imprison me in my room."

"You know I would do none of those things, Davina."

"No? You've given me to believe that you are the most horrible person alive, a monstrous character. Why wouldn't you do any of those things? Surely the man who killed twenty-two of his own men would not hesitate to punish a recalcitrant wife."

"Damn it, Davina."

She tilted her head a little to the side and regarded him steadily. "Isn't it odd, but I just realized that my name goes quite well with a curse word. *Damn it, Davina*. It certainly sounds complementary, one word to the other, so to speak. I think I shall have to get used to hearing a great deal of it, at least if I am to live my life the way you want me to do it."

"What way is that?"

"Accepting everything you say, of course. Believing that you're a hideous monster, that you're mad. I cannot cower in the corner like some poor little damsel, waiting to be rescued. I'm not afraid of dragons, Marshall."

He looked at her. "Why do I have the feeling that you're not afraid of anything?"

"Then you'd be wrong," she said firmly. "I am very much afraid of a great many things. I don't particularly like the darkness, although I dare myself to be out in it. I hate to be sick. I loathe it. When I get a headache I'm cross because I have a headache, not because it hurts. But I never was truly afraid of things until I came here. Before I became a wife."

"And have I made you afraid?"

"Not of you, Marshall. Nor what troubles you. I'm afraid that I'm willing to give you my heart and my soul, and you value neither of them as a gift, but see them only as an encumbrance. I'm afraid that you will choose your misery and your despair and your past rather than a future with me."

She'd never seen a person's face close off the way his did. It was as if he made an effort to block every single one of his thoughts from her. Even his gaze was fixed on the far wall as if he kept it there rather than look at her.

"I'm going, Marshall. I think it's the best, all things considered."

He nodded, just once, a gesture so easily accomplished that it broke her heart. She turned and walked toward the doorway, carefully avoiding looking at him. At the threshold she turned, again not glancing in his direction. She didn't want him to see the tears in her eyes. Instead she stared out the window behind him, at the faint shadow of Aidan's Needle.

"I suppose this is delicate, but it is a necessary topic."

Silence stretched between them.

Finally she spoke again, her composure once more restored. "I shall send you word, Marshall, if I'm with child. If I am, then I'll return to Ambrose for the birth, of course. If I am not, then there is the matter of an heir to consider. Perhaps you might visit me once a month. We can consider your visits like a stallion covering a mare. Strictly to produce a foal."

He didn't respond to her goad, and she turned fully in the doorway, her temper rising. "Have you nothing to say? Your wife is leaving you, and you remain silent as if it's the good and decent thing to do. Have you nothing to say to me, Your Lordship? Have you no words to convince me to stay? Are you not insulted or irritated or even angry? Do you not allow yourself to feel anything, Marshall?"

"You don't want to hear what I'm thinking, Davina. It's better if I remain silent."

She welcomed the surge of anger.

"You've made a prisoner of yourself, Marshall. It's not the Chinese who are doing it to you this time."

His gaze fixed on her.

"What would you have me do, Davina? Inflict myself on the world? Run howling through the streets of Edinburgh, a madman for all to point at?"

"I don't know how to answer that," she said, giving him the whole truth. "In all actuality, Marshall, I don't know how to answer most of your inquiries. All I know is that—"

She halted. He was not in the mood for undying avowals of affection.

"You haven't left China at all," she said gently. "Oh, the location of the prison might be different, but you're still there."

He stared at her unblinking. She couldn't help but wonder if, at this moment, he hated her. Sometimes, messengers of the truth were reviled.

In the end, however, she stepped back, knowing there was nothing between her and the door. Nothing between her and Edinburgh.

She left before he could see her cry.

Chapter 22

"It's all very well, Nora, but you needn't glower at me that way. I'm quite aware of your sentiments in the matter."

"No, Your Ladyship," Nora said meekly, but Davina wasn't fooled. The maid was obviously annoyed.

"I would prefer it, once we reach Edinburgh, if you did not tell anyone what transpired at Ambrose," Davina said.

"No, Your Ladyship."

"After all it's no one's concern but mine."

"No, Your Ladyship."

She sent an irritated look toward Nora, but Nora only smiled in response. A particularly annoying smile, as it turned out.

Davina stifled her sigh and looked out the window, wishing that the journey was done. On the other hand, she was in no hurry to explain to her aunt why she'd returned to Edinburgh barely a month after her marriage. With her husband's blessing, no less. No, with his encouragement. Perhaps that wasn't altogether correct, but Marshall certainly hadn't done anything to prevent her departure. She'd waited for him to appear in the doorway to her room, but he never came.

How very odd that the carriage wheels replicated those words, as if taunting her about Marshall's inattentiveness. *He never came . . . he never came . . . he never came.*

She closed her eyes before the tears began to fall.

Please—and she addressed her imploration to a higher power with more sympathy than He'd advanced over the last several weeks. *Please, do not let Nora tell tales.* It was one thing to be a scandal because of her own actions. Quite another for scandal to be attached to Marshall. Nor did she want to be known as an unwanted bride. That was another refrain the wheels echoed. *No one wants you . . . no one wants you . . . no one wants you.*

If she didn't do something quickly, she'd lapse into a decidedly morose period. She'd begin to feel sorry for herself, an attitude that never accomplished anything. She'd become a pitiful creature, not unlike Mary Beth Cahil, a woman of advancing years who would stop anyone on the street and regale him with tales of her once handsome and attentive suitor. The man had proven false, however, a fact that Mary Beth reminded anyone who wasn't quick enough to avoid her. She was a lone, pitiful creature, with unkempt hair and her dress often askew, dragging her shawl behind her.

Davina's world had crumbled as well, but her husband hadn't proven false. Instead, Marshall was imbued with too much nobility, perhaps.

She wanted the world back the way it was a day ago. She wanted the time back so that she could hold herself a little more in reserve, not be as silly or revelatory. How foolish she was to speak everything in her heart. She most especially wanted those times when she'd held him close and thought about how much she was coming to love him.

"If anyone asks, Nora," she said, keeping her eyes shut, "I am here for some shopping. Nothing more."

"Yes, Your Ladyship."

She sent another irritated glance in Nora's direction, but just as earlier, the maid didn't appear the least bit discomfited by her growing annoyance. If anything, Nora seemed almost pleased to have elicited some reaction from Davina.

"You know, Nora, that an aggressive female is not attractive. This time apart might be an asset. Perhaps Michael will begin to miss you."

"I haven't an interest in Michael, Your Ladyship. But thank you for your counsel." She glanced at Davina and smiled. "Is that what this is, Your Ladyship? A chance to make the earl miss you?"

"Don't be spiteful, Nora. Or too familiar."

Nora didn't bother to respond this time, but she raised one eyebrow rather imperiously, as if she were not a maid at all but some sort of regal creature. How very odd that the gesture reminded Davina instantly of her aunt.

Davina closed her eyes and pretended to sleep. It didn't make the journey go faster, especially since she was reminded of Marshall with each passing moment.

She'd never before considered that love might render her an absolute idiot. She was no longer a creature of reason or logic or curiosity. She was simply a woman who was thoroughly, completely, and absolutely miserable.

Perhaps it wasn't exactly true to say that her logic had departed; the fact was, rational thinking simply didn't matter. Her curiosity, her restless mind, brought her nothing in return—no satisfaction, no joy at learning something new, no answer when curiosity was satisfied.

Yet a smile from Marshall would ease her pain. The sight of him standing there, his hand outstretched, would have eliminated every dark corner of her soul.

Perhaps she truly was an idiot after all.

What if he was guilty of the hideous acts he'd confessed to doing? What if he indeed had been a coward, sacrificing his men for his own survival?

How did she stop loving him?

If it was true that a person could not be loved unless he was without sin, then the world would be a cold and loveless place. At what point was a man rendered unlovable? What deeds must he commit before he was deemed unworthy?

There were no answers, only questions, and the farther they traveled away from Ambrose, the less certain Davina was that she was making the right decision.

By the time their journey was over, Davina was ready for the confrontation with her aunt. Theresa was going to make her opinion known, simply because she had an opinion about everything. Most of those opinions would not allow for Davina's fallibility. She was always to be a little better, a little more learned, a little more charming, but not overtly so. Her father had been a well-respected scholar, and her family was related to a duke. They were not rabble.

However, Davina needed to find a tactful way to tell her aunt that her life and marriage was none of her concern. Her relationship with Marshall was not going to be muddied with the interference of another. There were enough people in her marriage—ghosts and goblins and demons; Davina was not about to willingly invite anyone else into the union.

"Good evening, Mrs. McAdams," she said to her aunt's housekeeper. The woman was as old as God, and she shuffled around with an old wooden cane, but Theresa would never have dismissed her—nor would Mrs. McAdams have willingly gone. No doubt one day they would find the poor dear dead in her bed with her cane beside her pillow, ready to answer a summons at a moment's warning.

"Would you send word to my aunt that I am here, please?"

The best thing to do was to simply address the issue immediately. Get the worst out of the way, although in this case the worst had already happened—leaving Marshall.

Mrs. McAdams, bless the old dear, just blinked at Davina, her surprise evident even though she didn't say a word.

"Mrs. McAdams," Davina gently reminded her.

Mrs. McAdams finally shook her head. "She's not

here. Off to London, she is. I don't expect her for a fortnight. She gave the staff a week off, she did. There's no one here but me."

"Well, we can certainly manage," Davina said, feeling relief seep through her that the confrontation wouldn't be coming today.

She gestured to the coachman and sent instructions via Nora that her trunks were to be brought to her room. Her unmarried room. Her room with its narrow little bed and its view of the square. The room she'd seen last on the day of her wedding.

Dear God, but she felt horrible.

She'd left him. Without a backward glance, she'd simply driven away. Her silhouette had been stony, determination aging her face.

Was this what he'd done to her? When she'd first arrived at Ambrose, surprise, concern, delight, and even fear had shown so quickly over her delicate features. Now, however, she looked as if she felt nothing. Either that or she was determined not to reveal her emotions to him.

What had he done?

He'd kept her safe from him, but the effort of doing so left him feeling almost bereft.

He wanted her back. As he watched the carriage descend into the wooded area surrounding Ambrose and out of his sight, he could nearly feel his heart being wrenched from his chest. Even his stomach lurched as if he knew what the next day, the following weeks and months without her would be like.

What utter rot.

He'd survived well enough without her; he would learn to do so now. Her incursion into his life had been a serendipitous miracle, something he'd not expected and a time he'd always remember. He'd learned in China to segregate the memories that were precious and keep them isolated lest they be tainted by the reality of the rest of his life. This month with her would remain just like that, a bubble within his memory, a special time never to be replicated but always to be cherished.

He turned and walked from the edge of the parapet down the circular stairs that led to the top floor of Ambrose. From there he turned to the left and headed for his suite. Right at this moment, he didn't want comfort of an intellectual sort. Instead he craved solitude, perhaps sleep. If that wouldn't come, he'd steep himself in wine, at least until the memories faded. Memories, not of China or his dead men, but of Davina, precious and rare, courageous and stubborn.

His wife. His love.

He pushed thoughts of her away in a gesture of self-preservation. He could not think of her now. He *would* not think of her now. He would banish all thoughts of her, and if they stole into his mind errantly, he would simply be disciplined enough to push them away.

The wound was still too raw.

Jacobs was in his chamber, and Marshall waved him away. Even the presence of his valet, normally unobtrusive, was an irritant right now.

Jacobs, however, refused to be banished. He followed Marshall into his study. When Marshall turned to reprimand the man, it was to witness the most surprising expression on the older man's face, an expression that Marshall had seen only once—when he'd told him about Daniel.

"You look as if you're about to cry, man," Marshall said.

"Your Lordship, I feel that way, begging your pardon."

Jacobs thrust something toward him, and Marshall was too surprised to do anything but react. He grabbed the package and stared down at it in confusion.

"What is this?"

"Something Her Ladyship wished me to give you, Your Lordship," Jacobs said, his round face appearing like that of a dejected chipmunk.

"And that is what has you nearly in tears?"

"No, Your Lordship. It's what's inside the package. I knew your mother well, you see. I came to know her in the last days. A more warmhearted and kind person I could not hope to meet. She inspired great loyalty, Your Lordship, and great love."

"My mother?"

Jacob nodded. "Your mother's journals, I believe. That's what Her Ladyship said. She wanted you to read them, especially the last one."

Marshall didn't respond, merely turned and walked toward his chair. He dropped the package on the seat, and without looking at Jacobs, addressed his valet.

"That will be all," he said, and waited for the sound of the man leaving the room. He braced himself for some sort of confrontation, more poignant comments about his long-dead mother, but Jacobs left the room without speaking again.

Marshall glanced over his shoulder to see the door being slowly shut. He suddenly felt as if he'd been walled into this room. He looked down at the seat cushion, and the books wrapped in brown paper and twine. She'd not written his name anywhere. She had not left him a last message. Or perhaps she had somehow, by providing his mother's journals.

He hadn't even known his mother had written in a journal. She'd never mentioned that fact to him.

What the hell. The day had been melancholy enough—he might as well suffuse himself in emotion.

He broke the string and pulled the paper off the journals and then sat on the chair holding the books in his arms. There were ten of them, and they stretched from before his birth to the year of her death.

As a boy, he'd adored his mother. As an adolescent, he'd been confused about his parents' estrangement. It was nothing they ever spoke about, and he did not doubt that they would have corrected him had he ever mentioned it.

His father was simply allowed to pursue his ambitions and his dreams, even if they led him to a country thousands of miles away. His mother, in turn, had been patient and waiting, never complaining, simply remaining in Scotland, the perfect wife.

He pulled open the last book. There were at least

two-thirds of the pages untouched. As if daring himself, he scanned the last few written pages.

I have thought about life a great deal lately. I have wondered at it, tenuous, fleeting, and such a blessing. Why is it that we never realize what a true blessing life is until such time as it is nearly taken from us? Wouldn't it be better if we knew the exact moment of our deaths? If we knew how many more months or weeks or days we had on this earth? Would we be tempted to waste them, then? Or would we spend each one in joyful contemplation of the sight of a sunset, a butterfly, or marvel at the sweet lilting laugh of those whom we cherish?

My companion is finding it hard to write these words. I don't wish to make her sad, so I will stop for a while. She has readied my medicine, and I, the grateful patient, will dutifully take what she offers. Death should not be so painful, I think.

His mother's words were a knife slicing through his composure. He flipped a couple of pages, and settled on a less painful paragraph, one that surprisingly mentioned him.

I worry about Marshall. He has learned lessons from his father and me, lessons that I am not proud of teaching. He has learned to be independent, and that is a fine thing, in moderation. He

*has learned to need no one, and that disturbs me.
He will be a fine earl, this I know, even though
he has had little training at it. He has a well-
developed sense of propriety and responsibility,
and those traits will serve him well.*

Marshall skipped ahead a few pages.

*My life has been like sand, dry and arid. It could
have been so much more. I could have had so
much more joy. I like laughter, and there was
never enough of it. I like to smile and please
people, and there were never enough people in
my life to make happy. I love the touch of another's hand on mine or a kind hand upon my
shoulder, and there were never enough people in
my life to touch me or for me to touch.*

*I would have Marshall's life be different. I
would have him live completely, not as his father
did. Nor as I did, but wholly, fully.*

*Leanne is looking at me with some concern.
I do believe that it is a sign that I must rest. I
wonder if my journals shall ever be read? I hope
in one sense that they are. Someone will know
who I was, and perhaps remember me. I shall
have no obelisk to mark my presence in the world.
Only the gardens, and my journals.*

Marshall put down the book and poured himself a
glass of wine. Oblivion was a fine goal. Oblivion, and
forgetfulness, and nothingness, perhaps.

A knock on the door preceded Jacobs's entrance. His valet carried a tray on which sat a full carafe of wine. What a perfect servant Jacobs was—prescient and perceptive. He was once more composed, a genial chipmunk again.

"Mrs. Murray sent this, Your Lordship."

Marshall nodded, watching as the man transferred the full vessel for the one he'd just emptied.

Had he made arrangements for Jacobs? The man was aging, and couldn't continue with his duties that much longer. There was gray in his brown hair, and lines around his eyes that hadn't been there a year ago. In the event of his death, Jacobs must be compensated for his years of loyalty to the Ross family.

If only he could remember that thought in the morning.

He had the odd and unwelcome sensation of being poised upon the brink of madness, so feathery light and without substance that a gust of wind could decide his fate. The time since China had only illuminated the acute aloneness of his existence. Now he found himself even more conscious of his hermitage. Because of his mother's words or because Davina had left him?

"Do you know the Wisdom of Hamenup, Jacobs?"

"I do not believe so, Your Lordship."

"In Egypt, it was the tradition that an experienced scribe wrote down instructions on life, what you might call the literature of wisdom for the younger scribes. Hamenup was considered one of the wisest of the old men. One of his passages read:

'The heart is not hardened by using it
For it is a vessel meant to be filled.
It is only the pot left empty
That cracks in the heat of the sun.'"

Jacobs only bowed low and left the room without a
word. What, after all, could he have said?

Chapter 23

"**Y**ou need to eat something, Your Ladyship."

Nora stood at the entrance of the room, holding a tray. Davina waved her to a nearby table. "Go ahead and put it there, Nora."

"Will you eat, Your Ladyship?"

It hardly seemed proper to be called Your Ladyship, especially since she had left His Lordship, but that was not a comment she'd make to Nora. Or to anyone else, for that matter.

As the years passed, she'd no doubt grow adept at this communion with herself, but for right now she desperately wished she had a friend with whom to talk. The friend, whoever it might be, would refuse to believe the worst of her. Instead, this friend would insist that she not judge herself so harshly. He would call her curious and stubborn and obstinate and brave. He would be her dearest companion and her lover.

But he would not be Marshall.

She poured herself a cup of tea and slowly finished it before replacing the cup on the tray. She folded her hands on her lap and reminded herself that this was where she wanted to be, in Edinburgh, in her aunt's home, in her room, alone, without her husband.

Dear God, had she lost her mind?

Was the day as chilly and damp as it felt? Was there snow on the ground despite the fact that it was summer? In the silence of the room, with only the rattle of the curtain rings and the wind as company, she felt like the hag of winter. Was Mrs. Murray acting as Spring?

Davina abruptly stood. She'd not sit and mope about Marshall Ross. Instead, she had other things on her mind. More important things, such as how to live the rest of her life without him.

God, give me the strength to live without him. Give me the strength not to think of him. Not even to pray for him.

She clasped her hands together, pressing the tips of her fingers against her lips. God would not think such a prayer was evil, would He? If she prayed for Marshall, which necessitated that she think of him, she'd have to worry about him. Worry would keep her restless and awake. If she were awake, she'd long for him, and longing led to yearning, which led to loneliness, and she didn't think she could bear any more loneliness because of Marshall.

"Very well, God," she said somewhat crossly. "If I must pray for him, let me do so like a woman of good works. Who sees a soul in need of assistance. Let me pray for him dispassionately, but kindly, knowing that he can never be more for me than a worn and troubled soul."

Let her not worry about whether his visions had

come to him again. She had left him to face his demons alone. Worse than that, God, she had created her own demons. They sat upon her headboard and dresser, little imps of angels, shaking their heads at her.

When she dreamed, it was of him. Marshall, smiling, the few times he'd laughed with such abandon that she'd been charmed. Marshall, riding his great black horse in the fog. Marshall, intent upon his hieroglyphs. Marshall, uncaring of his role in life, unaware that people thought him brilliant and troubled. Marshall, the Devil of Ambrose. How horrid that he'd grown into his soubriquet.

Days passed, one after the other, inexorably. Each day she awoke at dawn, knowing instantly that she was back in Edinburgh, in her solitary bed. She didn't bother stretching out her hand as she surfaced from her dreams, knowing that Marshall wasn't there.

Perhaps, however, he would come today. Perhaps today was the day he would venture to Edinburgh to rescue her from the folly of her own choosing.

She'd not wanted the life his mother had endured, and yet what she'd gotten was so much worse.

Salvation could not be found within a woman's smile. Absolution could not be brought to him by Davina's touch. Yet she'd been his talisman for a brief second of time. Somehow, almost miraculously, she'd kept him sane.

Perhaps he'd been so fascinated with her mind and her wit and the ineffable charm that was hers alone that he'd not spared much thought to himself.

Had he imagined it all? Not the visions. Not the visitations. But had he dreamed her? For a few blessed weeks, she'd been his wife. Yet he'd not spent a month with her, had he? His time had been equally divided between Egypt and his madness, with only pockets of time for her.

What woman would tolerate such behavior? Not a woman with spirit, intelligence, and curiosity.

She had the oddest habits—blinking at him when she didn't understand something. A look came on her face at the same time, almost as if she were angry about her confusion. She pleated the fabric of her dresses between her fingers, and then patted her skirts.

She'd left Ambrose without a backward glance.

Marshall took another sip of the wine and told himself that time would ease her departure. Soon he would be unable to remember her face, or the surprising color of her eyes. There would come a time in the next few weeks when she was erased slowly, yet completely, from his memory. He would soon be hard-pressed to recall his bride.

She would be relegated only to memory.

What was his life going to be like then? Would it fall into the same predictable pattern as before his wedding? Or would there come a day when he simply couldn't bear the loneliness anymore? When there was nothing left of him but regret, remorse, and the bitter dregs of his anger?

She might be with child. She might not be, necessitating that he visit her. Either consequence added complication to his life.

What if his madness was inherited and not the result of the massive amounts of opium he'd been forced to take? What if he'd doomed a child of his to the same fate?

Sunlight spilled over his elbow, dancing up his sleeve. If he turned, he would see a perfect Scottish sky, blue skies, white fluffy clouds, and perhaps, far off in the distance, the approaching signs of a storm.

Or perhaps the storm would dissipate before it reached him, and a clear moonlit sky would be the accompaniment to his troubled dreams. Whichever it was, fair and temperate, or stormy, he might not be aware of any of it. Perhaps he'd be too occupied with his memories of Davina, or too mired in his madness to even note the weather.

If she were not with child, he'd have to make a choice, wouldn't he? Never to see her again or summon her to Ambrose as he would a doxy, bed her, and send her away once more.

Or he might venture to Edinburgh, and take his madness to her.

He leaned his head against the back of the chair and closed his eyes. Could he bear that? To see her and to leave her again?

"Marshall?"

He opened his eyes to see her standing in front of him covered in blood, her hands outstretched, her expression one of confused horror.

"No. Please, no."

The sound of his denial was absorbed into the walls, the carpet, and the ceiling itself. Some force he could not see reached out and tore the sound of her name from his throat, until there was nothing left but a whisper.

"I didn't hurt her."

Yet fate or nature or God laughed, the sound so loud that he clamped his hand over his ears.

I did not harm her! he shouted in the silence of his mind. Mocking laughter was his only response.

She'd not been in China. She was not one of the ones he'd had to choose.

He heard her voice, soft and sweet, but with an edge to it that he'd come to expect.

"Marshall," she said softly. "Why?"

The blood dripped from her hands onto the carpet as she advanced on him. Her bare feet trailed in it, gory footprints that led to his chair beside the window.

She was not shy with her tears now. Until now she'd not cried freely in front of him, even though he suspected she'd wept on more than one occasion. Her pride would not allow her tears, but now pride was gone, and in its place a sorrow so vast, he felt as if he were drowning in it.

"Go away," he said gently. "You mustn't be here."

"I believed in you," she countered sweetly, her tears falling freely. "I did. I believed in you."

"That was your fallacy, Davina. I warned you."

Moans from his victims, multiple screams in the background mixed with the blue and white air to create his own magical world of hell. He might remain here for the rest of his life, his mind tortured, his spirit nullified until it was nothing more substantial than chilled air.

But Davina was possessed of a stubborn nature. She was a champion of lost causes, and as she stretched out her bloody hands to him, he wanted to warn her that proximity to him would only taint her more. She'd become the most grisly of his visions.   •

"I believed in you," she said yet again. Should he add her disillusionment to his litany of horrors?

He knew, in some far-off part of his mind that still functioned like Marshall Ross, that what he was seeing was not truly real. His shadow visitors in all their gore and despair were simply his memories given motion and impermanent substance. Peter, Matthew, Richard, Paul, Rogers, Thomas, all of them had once looked exactly as he saw them now. He'd seen the blood and the pain, heard their screams, and witnessed their agony. He'd been privy to the moment of their deaths.

Each time one of them died, he'd felt the loss, his soul turning blacker, his spirit sagging in defeat. He'd saluted their courage as he'd condemned his own cowardice. And still they came for him and tested him, and laughed when he begged, and when he cried, and when he pleaded for them to kill *him* instead.

But he'd never seen Davina this way, never witnessed her bleeding, and never seen her cry.

"Go away, Davina."

But the specter refused to budge. Instead she walked slowly closer to him, and he realized her skin was marred by a thousand tiny pinpricks, and she bled freely from each one.

"Did I do that to you?" he asked helplessly, reaching out both hands to brush against hers. How delicate a hand it was, how fine. He could barely feel her on his fingertips, and yet the memory of her was there, soft and warm and alive. "I'm killing you."

She knelt beside him and placed one hand on his knee. He could feel the heat of her touch through his clothing, as if she attempted to warm him somehow with her spirit, with the essence of her.

"Leave me," he commanded, but despite the nature of the order, his words were gently said, his tone tender. Despite the harm he'd already done to her, he wanted no further pain to come to Davina.

She shook her head from side to side, a soft smile lifting her lips.

"If I could only cause you to smile for more than a moment," he said.

She began to laugh, and then her skin suddenly melted, simply slid from her body to pool on the floor. In seconds, Davina was gone, and in her place was a hideous creature that bore no resemblance to her. Pieces of flesh dripped from the bones, stretched and elongated until they filled his entire field of vision. Her smile turned feral, sharp-toothed, and cruel. This creature dressed in Davina's clothing stood and waved its arms at him. He could hear the clank of the bones rubbing against each other.

He could not survive this.

Daniel was there. Daniel, with his smile and his habit of saluting smartly whenever Marshall looked in his direction. Daniel, who'd been his boyhood friend, and with whom he'd gotten inebriated on heather ale on more than one occasion. Jacobs had said good-bye to

Daniel at the front steps of Ambrose, reluctant to let his only grandchild leave for the Queen's duty.

What had Marshall said to the valet then? Something reassuring, no doubt. He was good with parents and grandparents. He'd probably said something idiotic about Daniel looking back on this adventure as the beginning of a long and distinguished career.

Daniel had died in agony, and Marshall had been powerless to do anything but listen to his screams. Now Daniel the ghost, the specter, and, in an odd way, Marshall's protector, raised his scimitar and sliced off the ghoul's head, leaving only a body. For long moments its blood continued to flow from the gaping wound in the neck until the monster fell to its knees and then to its back, dead.

Marshall was going to be violently sick.

But it was not done, as it was never done. It was never done until he was insensate, until he was unconscious.

Let it be over soon. Let him simply not draw breath anymore. He was in the throes of it now. Feeling all the things he should not be feeling, experiencing every single infinitesimal moment of it. His feet were damp with blood. His cheeks marked with smears of it. There was a handprint on his knee where Davina had knelt. His stomach was sour, and he prevented himself from becoming sick only by will. There was a pain in the middle of his forehead as sharp as a spear, and he flattened his hand against the skin there to ensure that a weapon did not, in fact, protrude from his skull.

He shouldn't be able to hear the voices, but he heard all the tongues clacking together like finger bones, whispers like insects jostling together in a dark closet. He could see and feel and hear, until this was real and the other, that life at Ambrose, his marriage to Davina, and his besottedness, all of that was only a dream.

Garrow Ross accepted the letter from the footman with some impatience. He opened it and stood smiling as he read the contents. His factor had received a very large sum of money from the man waiting to see him.

"Show the captain in," he commanded the young man.

As Captain Mallory of the *Nanking* entered his office, Garrow strode across the room with his hand outstretched.

"I am delighted to see you, Captain," he said. "I trust you had no difficulties on your voyage?"

The captain removed his hat and stood, feet braced apart as if the floor of Garrow's library was the rolling deck of a ship. "No difficulty at all, sir."

"I see that it was a very profitable voyage," Garrow said. His share alone had been equal to six months of opium production.

"Very profitable, and so easy that none of our preparations was needed."

"It never hurts to be prepared, however," Garrow said. "The cannon are necessary in case the British become even more intrusive."

He moved to the desk, extracted his journal, and retrieved his pen. Glancing up at the captain, he asked, "How many on this voyage?"

"Four hundred thirty. Only lost fifty in the crossing. Mostly women. The men are always heartier."

"But the women command a greater price," Garrow said. "At least the virgins."

Garrow carefully wrote the number in his journal and then placed it on the desk. Later he would tuck it back into its hiding place.

"It's time we moved to another port," he said, handing the captain a sheet of instructions. "You'll find a list of names there of men who are suitably interested in our venture."

Captain Mallory smiled. "Pretty soon coolies will be all over the world. Not a place you can go and not find one."

"Then perhaps I should consider what we're doing to be a benefit of sorts," Garrow said. "We're spreading Chinese culture."

Captain Mallory began to laugh, a great, booming laugh that, no doubt, carried through his house. Garrow didn't bother to quiet the man. Instead he rang for his majordomo, who would escort the captain from his house.

Garrow had another, more pressing, appointment with Theresa, snug and content, for the moment, in his bed upstairs.

Chapter 24

Nora stood at the entrance to Davina's chamber staring at her.

After a moment, Davina frowned.

"What is it, Nora?"

For nearly three weeks, Nora had been careful to be obsequious. She rarely spoke unless addressed, and Davina no longer confided in the maid. Yet, for all their distance from each other, they still had a bond—that time at Ambrose.

Now the girl didn't answer, merely stepped aside, revealing Jim.

Davina placed her book on the table, removed her spectacles, and stared at the young man as if he were one of Marshall's visions.

"Jim? What are you doing here?"

For one bright and shining moment, she thought he might have accompanied Marshall. Or had come on Marshall's behalf. But the young man looked so agitated that any hope was immediately dashed, only to be replaced by dread.

"What is it, Jim?" she asked, more sharply than she intended.

"Your Ladyship," Jim began, and then hurriedly pulled off his soft woolen cap, clutching it between both of his hands. "Your Ladyship, there is trouble at Ambrose. The earl, he's being taken away."

"Taken away?" A hand reached in and squeezed her heart. Davina stood, as if standing better prepared her for bad news.

Jim squeezed his hat and then pulled at it with both hands. The young man stood with his head downcast, his shoulders slumped, almost as if he feared she'd take a whip to him for such bad news.

"He hasn't been the same since you left, Your Ladyship," he said, his words so soft that she had to strain to hear him. "He stopped talking, and he never comes out of that room. Jacobs says the earl doesn't even blink, just keeps staring at the wall."

Her heart was not beating now. The pain in her chest made it difficult to breathe. Or was that simply grief she felt, so sudden and torturous that she didn't think she could speak?

"Jacobs says that sometimes days go by before he eats anything. It's just like China."

Marshall. There, a cogent thought. Dearest Marshall. Dear God, Marshall.

Jim looked at her, finally, his eyes troubled.

"He won't see me, Your Ladyship. He won't see anyone."

He shook his head, his gaze once more fixed on the floor.

"What do you mean, taken away?" Words were possible, after all.

"I overheard the housekeeper, Your Ladyship. She has orders to send him away. To where they put crazy people."

"Whose orders?" Her hands clutched at her skirts, and for once she didn't care. Let the fabric become hopelessly wrinkled. Let her be slovenly and unkempt, unladylike and scandalous.

Did it matter?

"It was Mrs. Murray who sent word to the earl's uncle. Said the earl wasn't fit to be around normal people no more."

"Did she?" How odd that she was cold. The day was a temperate one, but she felt like ice invaded her veins, coated her eyelashes, and turned her lips blue. She was the hag of winter.

"I heard what she planned to do, and I knew I couldn't let them send him away."

He looked at her, his blue eyes troubled. "I know there's something not quite right with the earl, Your Ladyship. But he's a good man, all the same."

Once more he looked down at the floor when he spoke, and shuffled in place. At another time, she'd have taken the time to reassure him, or to ease his discomfort. But she was too afraid for Marshall to help someone else.

"How did you get here?" she asked.

He looked surprised at the sharpness of her tone, and when he didn't answer her quickly enough, she repeated the question. "How did you get here, Jim?"

"I didn't think anyone would mind, Your Ladyship," he said. "I borrowed a coach from Ambrose."

"Where is it now?" she asked, moving toward the door.

"I left it in your stable. I'll be sure and take it back."

She didn't for a moment care that he'd taken one of the expensive coaches from Ambrose. Davina gathered up her skirts in her hands, and ignoring the rules about behavior and decorum, held them high above her ankles as she went through the doorway and down the corridor to the stairs. Once there, she began to run.

Her feet pounded against the steps, reminding her that she wore only her slippers, but she didn't take the time to change into her shoes.

Instead she raced down the two flights of stairs to the first floor. She ran as fast as she could down the hall, across the foyer floor, and into the back of the house. Turn left, then right, then right again, and she was through the bustling kitchen and out the back door, past the maids hanging up the linen in the small yard.

She didn't look back to see if Jim was catching up with her. If he wasn't ready to leave when she drove out of the courtyard, he'd have to find another way back to Ambrose.

The coachman was nowhere about, but she began shouting for him, and quickly enough, he appeared in the shadows of one of the stalls. He and her stable master were evidently sharing a convivial jot of whisky, but right at this moment, Davina didn't care if the man was drunk as a stoat. She'd drive the carriage back to Ambrose herself, if she must.

She turned to see Jim racing around the corner of the building followed closely by Nora. Both of their faces were flushed, but they weren't a bit hesitant about leaping into the carriage. She joined them a moment later after shouting the order to the coachman.

Davina hadn't brought her shawl or her bonnet, and her reticule was in her room. Her soft kid slippers were proper enough for home but not for public. She'd dispensed with her hoops for only two petticoats. Her aunt would think her disreputable. The matrons of Edinburgh would think her twice scandalous.

At the moment, however, nothing mattered but getting to Marshall.

Several long moments passed when none of them spoke. Nora sat beside Jim with their backs to the driver. Occasionally they'd share a glance, but neither Nora nor Jim questioned her actions or her haste. Perhaps they knew how dire the situation was, or perhaps they were simply being loyal. For whatever reason, she was grateful for their silence.

She took the time to compose herself, speaking to herself in the silence of her mind. *I cannot help him if I'm overwhelmed with panic. I must be sensible and logical. And courageous.*

How dare Mrs. Murray send word to Garrow Ross! Why not to her if things were so dire? Why did she not send word that Marshall was harming his health?

Because Davina had left him, and in doing so had abdicated—at least to the world—any responsibility, any sense of caring, any love.

Garrow Ross had told Mrs. Murray to send Marshall away. Davina wouldn't have done so. Instead she'd have returned to Ambrose and cared for her husband. She wasn't given the chance, however, and she didn't honestly know if she deserved one.

I cannot help him if I'm overwhelmed with panic. I must be sensible and logical. And courageous. Dear God, she must be as courageous as Marshall had been.

When she finally composed herself, she glanced at Jim.

"What happened in China?" she asked. "Is it true that Marshall gave up his men to save himself?"

The young man looked shocked. When Jim finally did speak, his voice quavered.

"He told you that?"

She nodded.

"It was a terrible thing, Your Ladyship." He looked toward Nora, and Davina knew he wished the girl wasn't there.

"Tell me, Jim," she said, uncaring if the entire world heard. The time in China was at the root of Marshall's agony. Somehow she must find a way to help him forgive himself.

Jim glanced once more at Nora and then nodded, his decision evidently made.

"The Chinese, they didn't care if they killed all of us, and they took a liking to it, making everybody die in a different way."

Silence stretched between them, during which Nora reached over and placed her hand on Jim's arm in a wordless gesture of encouragement. He looked up at her, and Nora smiled.

"I never saw them do to anybody what they did to the earl, though. It was like they wanted him to suffer the most. They fed him opium, day after day, until all he could do was sit in the corner with his eyes closed. Nobody could tell if he was alive or dead." He scrunched up his hat in his hands, and then sat smoothing out the wrinkles. His hands were old, older than his age, brown and scarred, with large calluses earned, no doubt, from being a sailor.

"Then when he was good and sotted with the stuff, they'd stop giving it to him for three or four days. Once they made him wait a week. He'd start shivering and seeing things, and then get sick. Then he'd just lie there and curl into a little ball. He used to beg them to let him die, but they had other things in mind."

"What happened then?" Davina asked.

Jim looked out the window, and she suspected that he didn't see the passing scenery as much as he did the inside of that prison in China.

"They'd give him a choice. Opium or one of his men. Then they'd give him a taste of it. He tried to hold out. His body would be shaking and he'd be screaming at them, and I know that he tried."

"And he chose the opium? Over his men?"

Jim stared down at his hat. "Twice. At the beginning. But never again. I don't know what he did, but he never gave up one of his men again."

"I do," she said, suddenly certain.

He looked at her curiously, but she didn't tell him

about the scars on Marshall's palm. Had he found a nail, gouging it into his own flesh until pain had eased the cravings? She closed her eyes and leaned her head back against the cushions.

Jim wasn't finished, however. "He never gave in after that, but I don't think he's ever forgiven himself for it, neither. I think those are the ghosts he sees the most."

"Thank you, Jim," she said, opening her eyes.

She leaned forward, opened the small metal window, and called out to the driver. "Is there nothing you can do to speed up the horses?"

The man was a stranger to her, but deferential, as were all of Ambrose's employees. He bowed his head and touched his fingers to the rim of his hat.

"Your Ladyship, it's growing dark, and these roads are not the best. If one of our horses breaks a leg, we won't reach Ambrose at all."

There was nothing she could do in the face of such prudence. She leaned back against the seat and wished that she could be magically transported in the air to Ambrose.

She glanced at herself in the small mirror attached to the carriage case. There was a look of fear on her face and panic in her eyes.

Opening the case, she pushed aside the visiting cards and reached for the carriage clock. Barely twenty minutes had passed since they'd left Edinburgh, but it seemed like an eternity.

Ambrose was a lifetime away.

Please let him be all right. What a paltry prayer to offer God. What else could she say? *Forgive me, God, for leaving him. Forgive me for my pride in staying away.*

When they reached Ambrose, she'd run to Marshall's library, kneel by his side, and hold his hands in both of hers. She'd keep him rooted in reality by her will alone, if necessary.

Davina wanted to consign Mrs. Murray to hell. Why was the woman so eager to send Marshall away? Because there was no relationship between them as there had been in the past? Had Mrs. Murray been as jealous of her as Davina had been of the housekeeper?

What was she to do? How did she stop them? Her thoughts raced from one answer to another until she calmed herself again. She was the Countess of Lorne; she'd find a way. Garrow Ross had no more power than she had. In fact, he had a great deal less. It was up to her to assert her authority.

It was up to her to save Marshall.

Chapter 25

It took four burly men to get him into the coach. Even in his delirium, Marshall realized that something was wrong. In the past, whenever he encountered that feeling, he paid attention to it, and this moment was no different.

As Marshall struggled, he thought he heard Jacobs shouting, but other than his valet's voice, no one else came to his aid. In due time, he was subdued and placed on one of the seats in the coach.

He didn't know where he was going. Not since China had he been forced to do something against his will. As if to remind him, Peter appeared, sitting opposite him in the coach. Next to him was Matthew.

The palm of Marshall's left hand began to throb, and he wished the pain were greater, ample punishment for their deaths.

He leaned his head back against the seat, and in a flash of lucidity realized that it wasn't Peter and Matthew sitting there but two very wary-looking men. One of them had a gash across his cheek. Another held his hand to his nose.

No doubt wondering how they came to be in this position, steward to the mad Earl of Lorne, trussed up like a Christmas goose.

If he were capable of speech, Marshall would have told them that he held no rancor for their actions. They had no idea, after all, what a horror it was for him to be imprisoned.

The jostling of the carriage made him feel sick. Or perhaps it was simply the fact that he had not eaten in a day or so. How long had it been? That was the last lucid thought he had until the carriage stopped and disgorged him like a black lacquered beast giving birth.

In front of him was a structure he'd never before seen, but on the tail of that thought he lost consciousness again. A moment later he roused to find himself being half carried, half dragged inside.

Strange, echoing voices surrounded him as he was being transported up a set of stairs. A door opened as another man with a deep, soft voice spoke. He heard the word *Ambrose*, and his title, and then someone addressed him, but the message was lost in his confusion.

He was placed on a bed, and then surrounded by silence. The only thing he heard was his heartbeat and the sound of a key scraping in a lock. He was a prisoner again.

Dear God, let him die first.

Davina. He conjured up her name, and her image followed. She stood beside him, bending down to brush her hand tenderly against his forehead. He'd loved her.

With the greatest part of his soul, with the most generous part of his heart, he'd loved her.

Suddenly everything was blue and white again, settling into a purple mist. And then there was nothing.

An interminable time passed until they arrived at Ambrose; the journey was even longer than the one to Edinburgh three weeks earlier.

Davina descended from the carriage before the footman could assist her, running up the steps to the great front door of Ambrose, up the stairs, and down the corridor to Marshall's suite.

The double doors didn't open. Frustrated, she beat both fists on them repeatedly until a footman came to her assistance.

"The door is locked, Your Ladyship," he said. "Shall I fetch a key?"

"Yes," she said, glancing at him. "And while you're about it, ask Mrs. Murray why she dares to imprison my husband in his room." She took a deep breath. "Never mind, fetch Mrs. Murray herself, and I'll ask her."

The footman looked as if he were being torn in two. Finally he spoke.

"I'm sorry, Your Ladyship, but Mrs. Murray isn't here. Neither is the earl."

"Where are they?"

How strange that her voice sounded so pleasant, almost calm.

She pressed both hands flat against the wood of one door, wondering why it felt so warm. Or was it simply because her hands were so cold?

"I don't know where Mrs. Murray is, Your Ladyship. She left in a carriage right after they came and took the earl away."

"Who came? When? Where is he?"

When the footman didn't speak, she turned to him angrily.

"Where have they taken him?" she asked. Her voice no longer sounded so calm. Inside, she wanted to scream, or to dismember Mrs. Murray slowly and with great relish.

"I don't know, Your Ladyship," the footman said, taking one precautionary step away from her.

"I do."

She turned to find that Jim had followed her up the stairs. Following him was Nora, her arm around a trembling young maid.

"Tell her," Nora commanded the young maid. The girl sent a fearful look toward Davina, and then in Jim's direction.

"Tell her," he said.

Evidently Jim's irritation frightened the young girl more than Davina's presence, because she began to speak.

"Your Ladyship," she said, bobbing an awkward curtsy. "They took the earl away, they did. Not more than an hour ago. I heard the coachman say they were going to the Black Castle."

Davina had heard about the Black Castle all her life. The structure was isolated, a private hospital, a place to house those patients whose families could no longer care for them in their homes, or whose maladies were so severe that they needed to be treated away from others. Known as the Black Castle but more properly named Brannock Castle, the facility was rumored to cater to those families with more money than patience. Still, the very name induced shivers.

"What shall we do now, Your Ladyship?" Jim asked.

"Go to the Black Castle, of course," she said, forcing a smile to her lips. Perhaps the expression looked odd, because the four of them—footman, maid, Nora, and Jim—looked at her as if she, too, needed to be incarcerated.

"Meet me at the carriage in ten minutes' time," she said to Jim. "There is something I must do first."

Without further explanation, she walked away from the group.

If Garrow spent the same time with a woman as he did with his hair, he'd be a very skilled lover.

But the hair always took longer.

Perhaps if she'd had more liking for him, Theresa might have gently hinted at his deficiencies. The fact that he was a ghastly lover was a fortunate occurrence. She hadn't had to worry about acting the part of seductress in the last month.

Garrow believed that a true lady did not become excessively agitated in bed.

So she lay stiff as a board, enduring his pumping while staring at the ceiling, a fixed smile on her face. Thanks to Garrow's wealth, it was not entirely a wasted experience. The man responsible for carving the beautiful plaster angels was remarkably talented. She quite enjoyed the sight of those angels.

Despite the fact that she was not to moan or groan, or evince any type of pleasure, she managed to convey to Garrow that he was the most delightful of lovers.

The damn fool preened whenever he left her bed.

Now he disappeared into the lavatory, and she heard the sound of water splashing. At least he was fastidious in his personal hygiene.

She sat up on the edge of the bed, reaching for her wrapper.

"I'm returning to Edinburgh," she said, when he came back into the room. "I'm worried about Davina."

He finished drying his face on the towel, uncaring that he was naked. In his current flaccid state, he really should have taken the time to don a dressing gown. He was not attractive at all, putting her in mind of shriveled berries hanging from a sagging twig.

"She's a grown woman, Theresa."

With some difficulty she clung to her smile.

"I have heard from my staff, Garrow," she said. Was it the wisest course to tell him? She decided to continue since the woman he thought she was—besotted and somewhat lacking in wits—would have done so. "Davina has left Ambrose. She's been in Edinburgh these past weeks."

Garrow didn't look surprised by the news.

"Did you know?" she asked him.

"The housekeeper has informed me." He turned, facing the mirror, and in the reflection gave her a tight-lipped little smile. "I am kept apprised of changes at Ambrose."

"Why didn't you tell me?" she asked. The lines between her duty and her true life were beginning to blur, and she felt a little panicky.

"Was it important that you know?"

What the hell did she tell him? That Davina had been more like a daughter to her than a niece in the past two years? That she was the only relative Theresa had left in the world? To reveal anything to Garrow Ross was to grant him a weapon over her.

"I need you more than Davina needs you, Theresa. I would not like it if you left me now."

She'd done what she could to help the Crown in the past two decades, and she'd done so with her whole heart. Her work was her life, the very soul of her life. It had taken the place of the young, idyllic man who'd been her husband. But the Crown had never asked more of her than now, as she fixed a submissive smile on her face.

"If you think it best," she said softly.

"I do, my dear."

She stretched indolently, allowing the wrapper to fall open. "Must you leave?" she asked.

"I must," he said. "I must meet with some people. You're welcome to remain, of course. In fact, I insist upon it. It would not do for you to be seen leaving the house at this hour."

Was he trying to regain a certain respectability? Did he think Victoria's court would tolerate him after word spread of his activities? If she could not prove what he'd done, she could at least ruin his reputation. Of course, hers would be tarnished as well, but it was a price she'd gladly pay to ensure that Garrow Ross was punished.

"Of course, Garrow," she said. Perhaps Lord Martinsdale was right and she had other talents not yet used. She'd never before known that she was such a skilled actress, or that she could bury her disgust so deeply.

He laughed, a smug, self-congratulatory laugh that grated on her nerves. Still, she managed a small moue of discontent.

"Your business doesn't involve a woman, I trust?"

As if any woman in her right mind would willingly involve herself with Garrow Ross.

Garrow turned to his mirror again and smiled at her in the reflection. He really did need to watch his intake of food. He was getting downright portly, and his derriere was vastly unattractive, what with all those dimples.

"Do not concern yourself with my business, Theresa. A woman grows masculine when she's too occupied in a man's concerns. I would hate that to happen to you."

"You think me masculine, Garrow?"

She threaded her fingers through her hair, letting it tumble over her shoulders, and artfully parted the wrapper further, allowing him a sight of one breast. He returned to the bed and stroked his knuckles across one nipple.

She tilted her head back and smiled up at him. Sweet little kitten, grateful to be petted. Dear heavens, she really should think of a career in the theater.

"You'll remain in London, then?" he asked.

"If you wish it, Garrow." Was that enough idiocy for him?

"I wish it," he said. His thumb tweaked a nipple.

"But what shall I do about Davina?"

"Evidently my nephew has become unruly. Since your niece left him, he's become more and more unstable."

A chill raced down her back, and Theresa had the sudden, unwelcome feeling that Marshall was in danger. From the tone of Garrow's voice, he didn't care whether Marshall was ill or healthy. She should alert someone, possibly Lord Martinsdale. He would know how to protect the Earl of Lorne.

"A missive from your housekeeper? What is it she expects you to do?"

He looked annoyed at her curiosity, and she smiled sweetly at him. He dropped his hand and returned to the mirror.

"I think the time has come to make arrangements for the poor boy. He's become a danger to himself and an embarrassment to the family."

Since there were only two people in Garrow's family, and one of them was Marshall and the other his wife, grieving, from all accounts, over their separation, then the only person who was embarrassed was Garrow.

What utter rubbish.

Garrow sold people by the shipload. He traded in Chinese peasants the way other men traded in spices. He used the port of Macao as a source for his inventory, selling his wares in Cuba and Peru, anywhere slaves were traded for gold, and he was embarrassed by Marshall?

She focused on her bare feet, trying to regain her composure.

"But that is none of your concern," he said.

"Of course not, Garrow. Forgive me for asking."

By the time she looked up, she knew her expression revealed nothing of the hatred she felt for him.

"Kiss me good-bye, darling," she said, stretching out her arms.

He bent over her and kissed her on the forehead. "You must cure yourself of this lamentable habit of being too direct, my dear," he said. "It's not an appealing trait."

She only smiled. What a pity the Crown had agreed to turn him over to the Chinese. She would have loved to have seen him hang.

Less than twenty minutes later, Davina was ready.

"Go as quickly as you can," she told the driver, looking up at him in his perch.

Night was full upon them, and the journey would be slower due to the darkness. Still, she would not wait until morning.

Jim, already seated in the coach, opened the door and leaned out, offering his hand. She took it and pulled herself up into the carriage.

He sat opposite her, Nora beside him. Davina didn't have the heart to tell her to remain behind at Ambrose.

She said nothing to either Nora or Jim, choosing instead a calm and resolute silence. There was nothing she could accomplish with words. Nor could she make the situation better or easier to comprehend by complaining about it. Instead she chose to marshal her energies, and wait until the moment of confrontation. She fingered the objects she'd placed in her pocket, hoping that it would be enough to gain Marshall's freedom.

Greed would have to feed justice.

After a few moments, Davina leaned back against the cushions and closed her eyes, fighting back tears. Now was not the time to surrender to her emotions. However, she was perilously close to weeping.

She'd known pain in her life. The pain of being a strange, bookish girl who didn't quite fit in with groups of her fellow students, who was giggled at and whispered about when time came for her introduction to society. That pain was like a pinprick, multiplied a hundred times. It captured her attention, but it didn't wound her all that deeply.

The pain of her mother's death was from long ago but still with her. That loss left her with a curious feeling of emptiness, as if there was an echo in her heart.

There was the pain of her own awkwardness—of being unsure about her body, how it would work and where her legs would take her. She'd been coltish for too long and without any discernible grace. Her eyes were not strong, necessitating spectacles, which only added to the ungainly nature of the whole. She was simply different, and while she claimed to be proud of being unique, the secret was she longed to be just like everyone else.

When she'd finally emerged from her own chrysalis,

life was not easier. Nor was it painless. Beauty did not exempt her from loss and grief.

Her father's death had been an agonizing red-tinged mist covering her entire world. She could hardly breathe for the pain of it. But over the last eighteen months, the sharp and tensile grief had muted to become only a dull and constant reminder of his absence.

What she was feeling now was unlike any pain she'd ever experienced. This was a spear to the heart. This pain traveled outward to numb the tips of her fingers and chill the whole of her body. This pain was so monumental that it surrounded her, merged into her, and became who she was. She was no more separate from it than a bright spring day was devoid of sunlight or a storm was without thunder.

How naïve she'd been only a few short weeks ago, concerned for things that were foolish, unnecessary, or simply inane. She'd been worried that someone else would ordain her life. She'd wanted complete autonomy, never truly realizing that autonomy was simply another word for loneliness. Nor had she known that being part of something was more enjoyable than being separate and free.

She'd been part of Marshall's life. Disjointed, odd, confusing, and sometimes frightening, that life was better than the existence she'd created in Edinburgh for herself.

Marshall was her partner, her lover, and her friend. He hadn't demanded her capitulation. He hadn't wanted to rule her. Instead it was almost as if with one hand he bid her join him in this great adventure of life and with the other he pushed her away.

Exactly as she had done.

The revelation so startled her that Davina sat up. Had she, too, invited people to come closer and pushed them away at the same time? Had she used her curiosity as an excuse to play at love, knowing full well that her heart was not involved and she could pull back and away if caught? Had she used knowledge as a shield to keep her from making friendships with the girls in school? Had she done the same with the women in her circle at Edinburgh?

She'd protected herself so completely that it was no wonder she and Marshall each had an affinity for the other. Perhaps he'd seen in her a little of himself, just as she was beginning to recognize that she, too, had been in prison. A prison created by her own fears.

He hadn't repudiated her at all, only stood by the door she'd opened and refused to keep her there. He'd made Ambrose a haven, and if she'd wanted to leave it, he wouldn't stop her. Prison had been an anathema to him—he wouldn't make Ambrose a prison for her.

Nor would he keep her there by force of his will. She must want to stay. All along she'd not recognized that. She'd not realized that he'd wanted her to come to him as a woman, not a little girl. A woman with the knowledge that she could walk away any time she wished, but that she wished, most of all, to be with him.

He'd known what was happening to him. He'd known and he'd wanted comfort in the way that all creatures need to be consoled. What had she done? She'd run away. She'd been a selfish creature who'd thought only of her own pain.

He'd thought himself beyond redemption and unlovable, and she had validated his fears by leaving him.

"Your Ladyship?" Nora reached forward, handing Davina a handkerchief. "You're crying."

"Am I?" Davina said, taking the handkerchief and blotting her cheeks.

Nora and Jim both looked at her with concern, but she didn't comment further.

Had Marshall realized that his sanity was slipping from his grasp?

She needed to find a way to save Marshall and, if possible, salvage his sanity.

Please God, don't let it be too late for that.

Chapter 26

A massive structure hunkered against the night sky. The building, its edges blurring into the shadows, looked almost like a crouching monster guarding the top of the mountain. A creature called up from myth and legend to defend this piece of the Highlands.

Scotland was all the rage, made popular by the Queen's fondness for the country. Davina had become accustomed to English tourists as well as English neighbors, and it was only occasionally that she reminded herself that she was a Scot and not English after all. It had been more than a century since the last battle had been fought between the two countries. The Empire stretched around the world, encompassing Scotland easily within its net.

At this moment, however, staring up at the towering building, a brick structure that looked as if it had been crafted in defiance, she felt the stirrings of pride in Scotland's past. She didn't feel civilized at all, but a woman who might've taken up the tartan not because it was favored by the Queen, but because it was a most convenient and familiar garment. She would have fought beside her husband, or behind him. His cause would have been hers.

She could do no less for Marshall now.

If madness overwhelmed him, she was determined to keep him at Ambrose and care for him with all the gentleness and love of which she was capable. But no one, no one, was going to imprison the Earl of Lorne again.

"It's a fierce-looking place," Jim said.

Davina nodded.

"What are you going to do, Your Ladyship?" The question came from Nora, but Jim looked as interested in her answer. All of them were not that far apart in age, but at the moment, she felt older and wiser.

"I am going to take Marshall home," she said.

"Can you do that?" Nora asked.

Davina only smiled, as confidently as she was able. "I am the Countess of Lorne. Of course I can."

Tears peppered her eyes, and she turned her head away so that no one else could see. She could not be weak, not now. The timing was simply not right to faint, give in to the vapors or the dozen or so other ways to avoid difficult situations sometimes chosen by her Edinburgh acquaintances.

Marshall needed her.

She pulled on the gloves she'd grabbed from her dressing room at Ambrose, as well as her bonnet. When she'd left Ambrose three weeks ago, she'd deliberately left some clothing behind, only packing a modest amount of her belongings. In the beginning, she'd thought that the separation from Marshall would be a short one. Marshall was going to come after her and demand that she remain with him. But of course he hadn't, and now it was a blessing in disguise. At Ambrose there were duplicates for all those items she'd left behind in Edinburgh.

She was now a properly dressed countess, and not a hoyden. She'd replaced her slippers with shoes and was now tying the bow of her bonnet beneath her chin. Her reticule sat on the coach seat beside her.

No one would find her appearance the least bit startling, especially not the authorities who ran Brannock Castle.

"Can they do that?" Nora asked, staring up at the structure. "Can they simply take you away from your life and put you somewhere?"

Unfortunately, Davina's curiosity had never extended to the care of lunatics. Granted, the Royal Edinburgh Asylum had been operating for many years, but it was never mentioned in polite company. She fell back on the only answer she could give, one couched in truth and determination.

"They cannot do it to Marshall," she said.

The approach to Brannock Castle was a serpentine road, lit only by the carriage lamps and much too dangerous for Davina's peace of mind. Her imagination furnished countless scenes of people being brought here without explanation in closed coaches. Would they be terrified and unable to understand why their relatives were consigning them to a strange and isolated place?

What had Marshall felt?

How very odd to think of Julianna at this moment. What an even stranger time to realize that Marshall's mother could have easily gone to Egypt if she wished. Or she could have demanded that her husband stay at Ambrose and act the part of earl. Instead, Julianna had simply been accepting of her fate. Was it her very placidity that had spurred Aidan to live in Egypt?

Wasn't that the true lesson of Julianna's journals? Life was a great gift that should not be thrown away without recognizing its true value. Love was the second most prized possession belonging to any person, and it should not be traded for a paltry thing like pride.

Julianna had lived the life she'd chosen for herself, never realizing that she could have made a different choice until the very end, when it was too late.

Davina would not sit at Ambrose and wring her hands in despair. Nor would she remain in Edinburgh mired in grief. Instead, she'd scour the length and breadth of Scotland for experts who studied melancholia, be it in Glasgow or Paris or America.

The wheels echoed, a hollow sound indicating to Davina that they were crossing over a wooden bridge. She smoothed her hands over her skirts, wishing she'd donned one more petticoat. Her palms felt damp and her pulse was racing. Her mouth was suddenly dry, but there was nothing she could do about that, or about the fear spreading through her.

She wanted to curl up in the corner, cover herself with a blanket, and pretend that none of this was happening. But that would make her a child, not a wife.

The carriage slowed, and she heard the driver shout

to someone. The coach finally stopped, the wheels rolling back several feet as it did so.

The castle sat atop a promontory of rock, and looked to be accessible only through a narrow archway carved into the black-streaked stone.

"It's not exactly welcoming," Nora said.

Jim didn't comment at all, but the glance he gave to Davina was not reassuring. He evidently doubted their mission or their possibility of success.

Davina focused on the castle. Lanterns had been lit around the structure and swayed from tall poles stuck in the ground. Up close the brick was red, but from the base of the mountain the structure had appeared as black as its soubriquet.

For the longest moment, none of them said a word. Nor did any of them clamber to be the first to depart the carriage. The coachman was under no such restraint, however, and she watched him disappear through the portcullis, followed a few moments later by the echoes of pounding blows against wood.

"What is Chambers doing?" Jim asked.

"What I should be doing," Davina said.

Did she follow him or remain where she was?

Before she could compose herself enough to follow Chambers, the door to the carriage suddenly opened. The coachman stood there accompanied by another man, dressed all in black except for a tiny bit of white at his collar. A Puritan?

"Your Ladyship, this is Dominic Ahern," he said. "A proper Irishman, I think. He says he's the warder of this place."

"I am not a warder, Your Ladyship," Ahern said. "I am the custodian of Brannock Castle."

The man was shorter than the coachman and about half his weight, with a narrow pinched face and a thin mustache that unfortunately curled differently on either side of the man's nose, as if one side was pointing toward his chin, and the other toward an ear. Davina found herself oddly fascinated by the sight of it. His face, otherwise, was young, deceptively so because he could not be that young to have assumed such a position of trust and responsibility.

Private asylums like the Black Castle were run for profit, and the owners would hire neither a neophyte nor a fool.

"I understand that my husband is here," she said as a greeting. "Marshall Ross, Earl of Lorne. I've come to take him home."

"I'm afraid that is impossible, Your Ladyship," he said, bowing before her. Since she had not yet descended from the carriage, it was tantamount to the obeisance given the Queen. "An emergency certificate was issued in the matter of your husband. In such cases, I am required to observe the patient for three days. I cannot release the earl before that time. However, if I deem it necessary to keep him longer, I will inform you of my decision."

She pushed open the door all the way and descended without the aid of either the coachman or Jim behind her. He followed her, as did Nora, the two of them standing close behind her.

"Who issued this certificate?" she demanded

"Dr. Marsh," he said, making another little bow.

"I am not familiar with the name, and I don't believe my husband is, either. Can anyone simply decree him mad and sign a certificate to that fact?"

"We are a private institution, Your Ladyship. We follow all the laws established for the health of our patients."

She understood immediately. "In addition, you've been paid."

He inclined his head in a gesture of assent.

"By whom?"

"I guard the privacy of those who employ me, Your Ladyship."

She stared at him for a long moment. She'd been wise to go to the Egypt House.

"I would think, Your Ladyship, that you would welcome a respite from his violent behavior."

"My husband has never been violent to me," she said.

"Yet the earl was quite combative when he was brought to us."

"What have you done to him in return?" she asked.

"As bad as the Chinese," Jim whispered behind her. "Making prisoners of people."

Ahern looked offended. "He is not imprisoned, Your Ladyship. Every care has been taken for his comfort. Our physician looked in on him at his arrival; he has been cared for with as much compassion as any of our other patients."

"If you had any true compassion, Mr. Ahern, you would take me to my husband."

"That I cannot do, Your Ladyship. He is under mandate to remain with us for at least three days. Without visitors."

He bowed to her once again.

"Human kindness would appeal to me more than servility, Mr. Ahern."

The little man looked annoyed, an expression that did not fit well on his rat-like face.

"Why is he not allowed visitors?" she asked.

"We wish our patients to be calm, Your Ladyship. We've found that visitors, especially family, are a detriment. Until his condition is ascertained, Your Ladyship, he is better alone."

Should he have looked so pleased after making that announcement?

"Then we shall remain here as well," she said, fixing him a look that dared him to argue.

"We have no accommodations for visitors," he said, bowing once more.

"Then I will sleep in my coach," she said, smiling. "Unless, of course, you object?"

"I do not control the roads, Your Ladyship."

"Quite," Davina said. How very much like her aunt she sounded.

She waited until Mr. Ahern walked back to the castle and disappeared through the portcullis. Only then did she look up at Chambers.

"I have an errand for you," she said.

"Whatever I can do, Your Ladyship, you have but to ask."

Davina gave him the instructions, and he looked surprised at first, and then vastly pleased.

"I'll do as you ask, Your Ladyship, but I don't like to leave you alone. You can't remain here. It's not safe."

"Jim will be with us," she said, "and we'll be safe enough until you return."

"By the time I get to Ambrose and back again, it'll be morning."

"Until then," she told him, "we'll occupy ourselves finding the most comfortable rock we can for a bed."

"Your Ladyship—"

"Do not fuss, Chambers. We shall do well enough. Get one of your stable lads to drive the carriage back— you, too, need some sleep."

"I'll not shirk my duties, Your Ladyship."

What was it about Ambrose that made the staff so responsible? Or was it Marshall who inspired such loyalty? All his life he'd been an example of duty and sacrifice. His time in China was no different.

"I'll take one of these all the same," Jim said, reaching up and releasing the catch on one of the lanterns. "She's right, man, we'll be fine. Sooner gone, sooner returned."

Chambers still did not look convinced, but when she, Nora, and Jim stepped away from the coach, he allowed his shoulders to slump, climbed up to his seat, and gave the command to the horses, cracking the whip in the air above their backsides. He turned the coach and began the descent down the mountain.

"The least the fool could do would be to offer us a meal," Jim said, staring up at the Black Castle.

"I'm afraid it's a night without dinner,"

Davina said, smiling ruefully at him. "I was in such a hurry that it never occurred to me."

"We didn't think he'd refuse to let us see the earl," Nora said, coming to her side.

Davina looked around her at the barren landscape. The outcropping of rock did not offer many comfortable places to spend the night. Near the road was a scraggly-looking tree and several areas of parched grass—it would be better than the dusty ground. She determinedly headed in that direction, lifting her skirts up to keep them as clean as possible.

"Jim," she said gently as she removed her bonnet, "will you turn around for a moment?"

He looked confused, but at Nora's nod did as Davina bid. Only then did she enlist her maid's assistance in unlacing her stays, enough that she could be more comfortable as she propped herself up against the trunk of the tree.

When they were done, she thanked Nora and arranged herself on the gorse, staring off into the darkness. The only illumination was the steady glow of the lamp Jim had taken from the coach. The lanterns near the castle had sputtered out, and were not replenished.

Nora was grumbling about something as she prepared her bower, but Davina didn't bother to either lecture or silence her. Ahern really could have offered them some kind of comfort. Did he look down on them from his lofty perch in the castle? Or was some poor madman looking at them and wondering why he was imprisoned when it was obvious that they were the lunatics?

Not ten feet away, the ground fell away, the only sight the blackness of an impenetrable void. How very frightening that was. Almost as frightening as Marshall being imprisoned in the Black Castle.

At least it wasn't raining.

Chapter 27

Davina had had enough experience with sleepless nights lately that it wasn't difficult to gauge that it was close to midnight. Both Nora and Jim slept on the ground beside her, far enough to retain some sense of propriety, but still close enough that she used some caution as she stood and walked toward the Black Castle.

The portcullis was lit by a single lantern, and her knock was answered by a tall, hulking man dressed neatly in white shirt and brown trousers. He opened the door without a word, and she stepped inside the asylum.

She'd expected something different, perhaps. Some sights or sounds that would repulse her, but the interior of the Black Castle was surprisingly ordinary-looking, with rough, whitewashed walls and arched doorways. Nor was the furniture a surprise, being thick oak, scarred, and obviously old. Still, it looked as if it had been oiled and polished on a regular basis. There were no gas lamps on the walls, only oil lamps and a few candles scattered here and there, protected from passing drafts by glass shields.

He was waiting for her, just as she suspected he would be. Dominic Ahern, with his little rat face. She could almost see his whiskers twitching. He was sitting in a chair in front of a table, a sheaf of papers in front of him. More certificates? More poor souls destined for this place?

She forced a smile to her face and drew her shawl tighter around her shoulders.

"Who is Dr. Marsh?" she asked.

Ahern evidently did not expect the question, because he blinked at her in surprise.

"I confess that I have had few dealings with him myself. His name is not very familiar to me, but he has followed the letter of the law, Your Ladyship."

"Is it the law or money that concerns you most, Mr. Ahern?"

His only answer was to incline his head. At least he didn't bow to her.

"Is my husband's imprisonment here paid for by his uncle, Garrow Ross?"

"We do not imprison our patients, Your Ladyship. On the contrary, we offer them a respite from a world that is often cruel, harsh, and judgmental."

"And is that respite paid for by my husband's uncle?"

"Were I to divulge the identity of our many benefactors, Your Ladyship, then we would have no patients. We strive to offer a certain—"

"Anonymity?" she asked.

He smiled. "Just so. Most of the families of our patients do not want it bandied about that their loved ones have difficulties. We offer that service."

She reached into her pocket and pulled free one of the objects she'd retrieved from the Egypt House. The queen's necklace dangled from her fingers, the rectangular green stones glinting in the candlelight.

His mustache twitched.

"What is that?"

"An inducement," she said softly. "A payment."

"I've been paid already."

"I would pay you more, Mr. Ahern. I would pay you the whole of my husband's fortune if necessary."

"It will not buy his freedom, Your Ladyship. I am bound by the law. He must remain here at least three days."

"Then if it will not buy his freedom," she said, "will it buy some comfort for him?"

"We treat all of our patients as if they were guests, Your Ladyship. There is no need for extra bartering. Your husband is being well treated."

"Then will it shorten your evaluation time? Instead of three days, would one suffice?"

He seemed to consider it. She placed the necklace on the table and stepped back.

"Consider it, Mr. Ahern. There are many more just like that. I will reward you for every day you release my husband early."

"How do I know he is not a danger to society, Your Ladyship? I could not live with myself if I turned a madman out into the world. Your husband might be an earl, Your Ladyship, but in this matter he is just like any other person. His rank will not protect him."

His rank had never protected Marshall, but it was not a comment she chose to make to Ahern.

She continued as if she'd not heard him. "A change of clothes, then? Would you allow me that?"

He drew the necklace closer.

"Consider it," she said again, and left the castle before he could refuse.

The minute she was certain Garrow had left the house, Theresa was out of bed. She threaded her fingers through her hair, tightened her wrapper, and donned her shoes. After listening at the door for several long moments and hearing only silence, she opened the door cautiously.

Garrow's staff was well-paid, but not necessarily loyal. She'd taken the precaution of slipping several five-pound coins into her pocket, just in case she was interrupted by a diligent servant.

She took the stairs slowly, prepared to explain her presence there in the middle of the night. Or perhaps any maid she'd encounter would have enough tact to simply not ask. But she didn't see anyone prior to entering Garrow's library, nor was the room occupied even though a lamp was still lit on the desk.

Had Garrow left it lit in preparation for his return? Or had the servants simply forgotten to check? She decided that it wasn't bright enough for her to be seen through the ceiling-to-floor window facing the street, and just enough illumination to aid in her search.

Garrow's library as a work of art, tall mahogany shelves with dentil molding lining the long side of the room. The shelves glittered with the sheer number of gilt-etched leather bindings. The man did know how to collect books. A pity that she'd never seen him actually read one. But the room gave him the aura of being a studious gentleman.

She made her way to the other side of his desk. In the weeks since they'd become lovers, he'd never before left her alone. She might never get this chance again.

There was nothing incriminating on the surface of the desk or beneath the blotter, but she'd already suspected that what she needed to find would be carefully hidden. Garrow wasn't a fool. She moved behind the desk. All the drawers on the right-hand side opened smoothly, an indication that there was nothing valuable inside.

The middle drawer on the left pedestal, however, was locked, capturing her attention. She opened it with practiced ease, using a tool she'd been given years ago. The drawer slid out slowly, revealing a sheaf of papers. She didn't bother to examine them. Instead she dropped to her knees and pressed her hand all the way to the end of the drawer.

Slowly and methodically, she fingered the area between where the drawer ended and the back of the desk. There was nothing there. But there was something affixed to the bottom of the drawer just above. She found the end of a string and followed it, her fingers tracing the pattern of a net tied to the underside of the drawer. A hammock. How inventive of Garrow. But what did it hold?

A book. Dear God, let it be what she needed.

She extracted the journal from its hiding place and, still on her hands and knees, began to read. The numbers on the right-hand side of the page seemed to be quantities. The number of humans shipped from Macao to ports all over the world? The figures on the left-hand side evidently represented his profit from these sales.

The names at the back of the book, however, made her smile. London would be ecstatic to contact these men. Some of the names were Chinese, but there were enough Dutch and English surnames to shame each country equally.

There was something so satisfying about holding this proof as she rose to her feet. There was something so eternally right about the moment that she almost wanted to share it.

"In the future when you're stealing from someone, Theresa, you might take the precaution of dousing the light. You can be seen quite clearly in the window."

Theresa looked up to find Garrow standing on the other side of the desk, a pleasant expression on his face, his smile firmly anchored on his lips. But the look in his eyes cautioned her that he was not nearly as affable as he appeared on the surface.

"I regret to say, my dear, that you had me completely fooled."

She slipped the journal into the left-hand pocket of her wrapper.

"That will never do, Theresa. Give me my book, please."

He extended his hand, palm up. She debated whether

she could escape from the room and the house before he caught her.

Probably not.

"I wasn't exactly stealing, Garrow," she said just as pleasantly. "But I will admit that it was foolish to leave the lamp lit. But I try to learn from my mistakes. Next time, I'll be more cautious. As for your book, I have absolutely no intention of giving it back to you. I've sacrificed a great deal to find it. My dignity, actually, if not my reputation."

She smiled. Would he consider the truth an insult? Evidently so, because his face darkened, his eyes narrowed, and he dropped his hand to his side.

"Just who are you?"

"A woman who believes in justice. Regrettably, I do not always obtain it. In your case, however, I've made your punishment my singular goal. You're an evil man, Garrow, and a thoroughly unlikable one as well."

Without any warning, he threw himself across the surface of the desk, intent on reaching her. She quickly stepped back, but he managed to grip her arm and pull her closer. She tried to get away, but his arm was suddenly around her neck.

She had absolutely no intention of being murdered by Garrow Ross.

She pulled the derringer out of her right pocket and pressed it hard against his chest as she turned and pushed herself against him.

He was so surprised that his grip lessened, enough that she could breathe again.

"Don't be foolish, Garrow," she whispered. "While

it would be an imposition to explain exactly why I was forced to shoot you, I'm willing to endure it."

His grip around her neck lessened still further, but he didn't release her.

"Rest assured that before I die, I'll see to it that you have a nice little hole in your chest. Right where your heart might be. That is, if you had one."

She'd never had to use the weapon before but she knew how to do so well enough. Also, she was fully prepared to kill him. Garrow must have seen the resolution in her eyes, because she was suddenly free.

She took a precautionary step away from him, keeping the gun leveled at his chest.

"Being with you has been interesting, Theresa," he said, as she began moving backward toward the door.

She'd send a messenger to Lord Martinsdale tonight. His men could pick up Garrow now that she had the proof they needed. Hopefully, those poor souls already trapped in the holds of countless ships could be freed.

She walked backward to the door, still watching him.

"I can honestly say that while it has been interesting, Garrow, it hasn't been exceptionally enjoyable. You are the very worst lover, Garrow; it's only fair that you should know. Is that too direct?"

She smiled brightly at him, closed the door, and made her escape.

Marshall awoke to screams.

For a long moment, he kept his eyes shut. His captors would expect him to protest, but he'd learned that it was better to keep them unbalanced, uncertain of his mood or his actions.

He expected to hear his name being called—his men were always compelled, somehow, to shout his name. He wondered if that was part of the torture. Or perhaps he was simply imagining that part of it: his guilty conscience being given voice.

The screams subsided but the sound of running feet increased. That was different. Perhaps his captors had learned his little trick and were keeping him unbalanced as well. He slitted open one eye and looked for Jim in his corner, but the boy was gone.

Vanished. Taken? Was he the man screaming?

God, please. His morning prayer, nothing more substantial than that: God, please. Please let him endure and be courageous. Please let him not shame himself, his family, or his country. Please don't let his men suffer. All were equally and fervently and devoutly wanted.

Jim. He was barely more than a boy, and of all the men in his command, Marshall felt a particular duty toward Jim. He barely had a past, being out of childhood by only a few years. God, grant him a future, at least.

Marshall closed his eyes and willed himself into oblivion.

Davina.

He wasn't in China. He'd come home to Ambrose by way of London. He'd seen the Queen, who'd expressed the gratitude of a nation, of the Empire, to him. He'd not mentioned the twenty-two men who'd died in agony so that she might be proud. They were the ones deserving of respect. Instead he'd bowed, always deferential to his monarch, but in the back of his mind was the thought that she'd known, all along, about the bargain with the devil England had made.

Now he slitted open one eye and looked around him. The room in which he lay was small, nondescript, and completely unfamiliar. He tried to sit up, but dizziness pushed him back against the bed. Nor was his stomach all that steady.

He wasn't in China and he most assuredly wasn't at Ambrose. Where the hell was he? The screaming had faded. There were no footsteps outside his room, and the mattress on which he'd slept—for how long?—was surprisingly comfortable.

He stared at the door. Was it locked? The small window in the top indicated to him that it would be. Where was he? He vaguely remembered being in a coach. Had he lost his mind completely? If he were insane, would he be able to reason out that he was somewhere different?

He tried to sit up again, but the dizziness that overwhelmed him was suddenly too much to fight.

Ahern still had not answered her, but in the morning he sent out water for their washing and offered them breakfast. Davina graciously accepted, and the three of them ate relatively well, considering that they were perched on a rock that served as both table and chair.

"Can he keep the earl there, Your Ladyship?" Jim asked.

She was very much afraid Ahern had a great deal

of power at the moment, but she smiled reassuringly at Jim.

"I tried bribing him last night," she said to their obvious surprise. "Ahern is either a very honest man, or not at all interested in Egyptian jewelry."

"Then are we going to stay here for the three days, Your Ladyship?" Nora asked.

"It isn't simply the three days, Nora," Jim said. "It's what the man said later. He could keep the earl here as long as he likes. All he needs is to think that the earl is mad." He glanced over at Davina. "Isn't that true, Your Ladyship?"

She'd come to the same conclusion, so there was no sense in adopting a positive face about the situation. She sighed. "I do believe it is, Jim."

"Then what are we to do?"

Davina didn't answer him, only stood and walked some distance to the edge of the clearing where it dropped off into the air. Across the way was a misted hill. To her left was a craggy outcrop of shale, to her right, a meandering brook silver in the morning light.

This land was once defended by Kenneth I when it was still known as Dalriada. Beneath their feet were probably the bones of men who longed for freedom long before the English learned to stand upright.

A lesson they needed to remember, didn't they? A reminder, perhaps, of the greatness beneath their boot heels. History was all around them, and history was the answer.

By afternoon, the coach returned, with Chambers stubbornly driving. He'd taken the precaution, though, of installing one of the stable boys beside him on the seat.

Behind him came a phalanx of vehicles, all from Ambrose: three carriages, six wagons, and, incredibly, a pony cart. The wagons were filled with men, all from Ambrose, and none attired in his livery.

Her eyes widened when she recognized Jacobs in the first wagon.

"It's every man from Ambrose," Nora said when Chambers halted the coach and six men climbed out.

"The carpenter couldn't come," Chambers said, climbing down from the seat. "Fool injured his leg falling from the roof. So I put him in charge of protecting the place while we were gone."

"Did you bring the other items I wanted, Chambers?" Davina asked.

The man nodded. "What you wanted from the Egypt House is in the carriage, Your Ladyship. I put what I could collect from the Great Hall in the second wagon. But I've a surprise as well, Your Ladyship," he said, smiling. "I found bolts of the stuff in the attic." He withdrew a length of tartan. "I'm thinking kilts."

She smiled at him. "Very good, Chambers. Thank you, for everything." She opened the carriage door and slipped inside.

Marshall awoke knowing exactly who he was. He didn't bother to look to the left or to the right, realizing where he was immediately. The same little room he'd awakened in earlier.

He knew, without looking, that there were no signs

of a madman's destruction the night before. He'd seen no specters, or ghosts. No hellish voices interrupted his rest.

The door suddenly opened and an enormous man appeared in the doorway. His jailer? When he asked the question, the man only smiled. "Your Lordship," he said. But that was all.

When Marshall glanced at the other man, he was surprised to see the light of intelligence in his eyes.

"Where am I?"

The giant smiled again, but he wasn't forthcoming with information. Instead he left the room, closing and locking the door behind him. A moment later he was back with a pitcher filled with hot water and a basin. After his second trip, he placed a tray at the end of Marshall's cot.

Marshall sat up cautiously, but his equilibrium was perfect, and he wasn't dizzy. He took a deep breath and realized that he didn't hurt anywhere.

"How long have I been here?" he asked, not expecting the man to answer.

The giant smiled again. "Two days."

"Two days?" He could remember only fragments of time, bits of consciousness. Two days? No wonder his body was making its needs known.

The man nodded and then stood with his back to the door surveying the room, as if questioning himself what was still needed. Evidently satisfied, he left, turning the key in the lock.

The sound grated on Marshall's nerves, but thoughts of being imprisoned were soon dismissed for more pressing needs. Those taken care of, he returned to the table beside the cot and washed his hands and face. Only then did he regard the tray the giant had brought him.

In China he'd not realized, until it was too late, that his food had been laced with opium. That fact made him a little wary of sampling this meal. But for once his stomach didn't feel as if it had been turned inside out, and now he was actually hungry. He settled for taking a few bites and then pushing down his hunger.

He looked around the room. There were no furnishings other than his cot and a small table beside the bed, an earth closet, and a chamber pot.

The air didn't waver, and there wasn't a hint of a vision or a nightmare. Now if he could only determine exactly where he was and how he could get out of here, life would be almost perfect.

Davina held out the garment to Dominic Ahern. He eyed it suspiciously.

"A clean shirt. My husband is fastidious. He will want to change."

"It will need to be inspected," Ahern said.

"I expected no less, Mr. Ahern. I understand your position very well. Are you prepared to release my husband?"

"You said there were more necklaces?"

Was that to be the price of Marshall's freedom? If so, she'd pay it gladly.

"Two of them to be precise. Shall I fetch them for your inspection as well?"

He gave a slight nod, squeezed the shirt between his hands, and then thrust a hand through each of the sleeves in turn. Finally he waved toward one of the men standing beside the stairs. "Take this to His Lordship," he said, before turning to Davina. "Is that good enough?"

"When will my husband be released, Mr. Ahern?"

"Another day is necessary by law to examine him, Your Ladyship."

"After that?"

"I haven't decided whether or not he poses a threat, Your Ladyship. I will need a physician to examine him."

"The same man who signed the first certificate? You and I both know that he would probably sign another for enough of a payment."

Ahern only smiled.

She wondered if he would be smiling if he was aware of the preparations taking place just outside his door. Two more wagons had just arrived from Ambrose filled with supplies.

"Then you give me no choice," Davina said. When had she become so bloodthirsty? She was actually looking forward to this.

"You're returning to your home, Your Ladyship? A wise decision."

"Actually, we're not. Look outside your window, Mr. Ahern. We're laying siege to Brannock Castle."

She smiled brightly at him before turning and leaving.

* * *

The door opened, and the giant entered, placing something at the end of the bed.

"Clean clothes," the man said.

Marshall looked at the shirt without interest.

"At least you keep your prisoners well fed and well clothed," he said.

The giant didn't respond.

"Tell them I changed," Marshall said. "Tell them I refused. Or tell them anything you damn well please."

The giant took a step toward him, and Marshall almost welcomed the confrontation. A punishing brawl might just be exactly what he needed. No, what he needed was to get out of this place, and drawing attention to himself would not be the best course of action.

He pushed down his temper and reached for the shirt, surprised to find that it was one of his own. He began to unbutton the one he wore, but just before he donned the clean shirt, he caught sight of something written on the inside seam.

He threw the dirty shirt at the other man and then dressed in the clean garment.

"There, you can tell your masters that I've dutifully changed."

The giant studied him for a long, uncomfortable moment and then nodded once.

He finally left, giving Marshall the opportunity to take off the clean shirt and examine what he'd seen. There, in writing almost too small to be so precise, was a cartouche. He closed his eyes for a moment, and in that brief span of seconds, hope nearly overwhelmed him. Davina had sent him a message. His beautiful, confusing, fascinating, intelligent, more-clever-than-all-the-females-in-the-world wife had crafted a hieroglyph to him. He studied the cartouche and read the symbols she'd written.

Freedom. She was planning on war, and the men of Ambrose would be her army.

He began to laugh.

"Your Ladyship?"

Davina turned at the portcullis to find that Ahern had followed her.

"Your Ladyship, are you not being precipitous? You cannot lay siege to Brannock Castle!"

"You cannot keep my husband here without my permission, Mr. Ahern."

"I will have to summon the authorities," he said, his voice rising.

"By all means, Mr. Ahern. If you can get them through my men."

She stepped aside to give him a view of the courtyard. Yesterday there had been only a few sparse trees and scraggly bushes. Now the space was filled with a sea of men. Victoria had made tartans popular, and the kilt acceptable. But the men of Ambrose made it a garment of war.

At the lift of her hand, each man raised his right hand in salute. The Great Hall had been emptied of its claymores and dirks, and each man was equipped with some type of weapon.

She glanced over to find Mr. Ahern staring at the assembled men in wide-eyed horror.

"You cannot be serious, Your Ladyship."

"As serious as war, Mr. Ahern."

"This is not seemly, Your Ladyship."

"Did you never hear of Lady Anne Macintosh, Lady Margaret Oglivy, Margaret Murray, or Lady Lude? Did you know that the Countess of Ross led her own troops in 1297? Or that the Countess of Buchan fought for Robert de Bruce? So did Lady Agnes Randolph, and she was known as Black Agnes. She held her castle against the Earl of Salisbury for five months. I am in good company, Mr. Ahern."

"I must protest, Your Ladyship."

"Protest all you will, Mr. Ahern, but the fact remains, we are here until you release my husband."

She smiled as she left him, feeling absurdly like laughing.

Chapter 28

Two more days passed. Two more endless days during which Ahern did not relent. Two more horrible days in which Davina worried about Marshall endlessly.

She slept because exhaustion took away her choice. She ate because she didn't want to faint. But she rarely spoke to her companions, and her attention was directed to the windows of the Black Castle as if she could see Marshall there.

On the morning of the fifth day, she was sitting where she normally did, on the outcropping of rock near the courtyard, Jim and Nora beside her. The men were staging mock battles, lunging at one another with spears and knives. If she'd any concern to spare for anyone other than Marshall, it would have been for the more zealous of them, too ready for warfare but lacking in training.

She herself was sorely lacking in patience as the hours creaked by, and when the coachman came to her, an uncharacteristic smile on his face, she felt the first stirrings of hope.

"Your Ladyship, it has arrived."

Davina began to smile. "Thank God," she said.

"What are your orders, Your Ladyship?"

"Intercept it," she told the coachman.

Both Jim and Nora looked at her in surprise.

"We've well and truly gone to war," she said. "With Ahern's supply wagon." Her smile grew broader. "And now I shall let Mr. Ahern know exactly how serious I am."

Without another word, she left them and strode toward the Black Castle.

A few minutes later she was standing in front of Ahern and he was looking nearly apoplectic.

"Your supply wagon for my husband," she said calmly.

"You imperil your own husband, madam, if you engage in such recklessness."

"My husband would rather die than be a prisoner again, Mr. Ahern," she said. "Can the families of your other patients say the same?"

"These men are ill. They need care."

"Then give it to them," she said. "Their families are not here to care for them. I am. I will care for my husband. Give him to me, and I'll give you your supply wagon."

He looked at her, his little rat face squinched up. "You are not going away, are you, Your Ladyship?"

She only smiled.

Ahern turned and walked away, leaving her standing in what must have once been the Great Hall of Brannock Castle. After a moment, she realized he wasn't coming back. Disappointed, she began to walk toward the portcullis.

A footstep on the stairs made her turn. She looked up at the head of the stairs where a shadowy figure stood. He descended a few steps, coming into the light streaming in through an archer's slit.

"Davina?"

Even if she couldn't see him, she'd know that voice anywhere. She blinked again, but the vision didn't disappear. In fact, he solidified behind a waterfall of tears.

"Marshall?"

He was dressed in the shirt she'd bribed Ahern to give him, but it was now wrinkled. His trousers, too, looked as if he'd slept in them. He was unshaven, his hair was unkempt, and he was barefoot. He'd never looked so disreputable and so utterly wonderful.

But the greatest blessing was evident when she grew closer. His eyes were clear, and there was no confusion in their depths. There was no uncertainty in his glance, and a small smile played around his mouth.

When he reached the base of the steps, she flung herself into his arms. She held tight, her arms linked around his neck. She kept shaking her head as if to negate all that had happened from the last time she'd seen him until this moment.

"Davina." Had his voice ever sounded so deep or so warm? "Davina." Her name was no more than a breath, a gentle summons, a wisp of sound.

She buried her face against his chest, allowing herself to feel for the first time since she'd come to Brannock Castle. When he tightened his arms around her, she took another step closer, the fabric of her skirt mating with the cloth of his trousers.

One of her hands fluttered to his neck, trailed around it. A thumb brushed his skin while four fingers danced along his nape, feeling the growth of his hair.

She was used to reserving herself, but no longer. She wanted to know him, in the way that friends truly knew and accepted each other. She wanted to be able to sense his presence in a crowded room, speak to him of her wishes and wants, and share herself with him in a way that she could finish his sentences, anticipate his thoughts, and empathize in a wordless communication.

Instead of telling him this, instead of explaining that she'd never be parted from him again, she kissed him.

When his lips touched hers, hers pillowed them in a comforting, gentle way of long standing. There was no hesitation when she opened her lips, no reservation. It was a kiss of longtime lovers, companionable in their passion, well acquainted with each nook and crevice, curve and angle of body. It was a gesture of welcoming, of satisfaction, of bodies remembering rapture.

Her left hand brushed against his chest, felt the cloth encasing his skin, envied it. His two hands were pressed against her back. She felt him, hard and angled where she was smooth and curved.

It was such perfect joining, even clothed, that Davina felt the spiking of tears in her eyes.

She pulled back and stared at him, placing her palms on either side of his face, feeling the abrasiveness of his beard against her skin. Proof that he was there, that she was touching him.

"Are you well?" she asked tremulously, nearly desperate for the affirmation of his answer.

"I am well," he answered, extending his arms around her waist once more.

"They didn't harm you?"

"They did not."

His voice was the most soothing thing she'd known, calming her as if she were a fractious cat. As she stood so close to him now, with her hands pressed against his face, it was inconceivable to her that she'd not been as close to him for endless days and weeks. He should have known her as a child, would know her as an old woman, and would be by her side for all the events of her life from this moment onward.

Slowly, tenderly, she placed her fingers against his temples, her thumbs brushing his cheeks.

"And your visions?" She held her breath for his answer.

"Gone," he said, still smiling.

That word encapsulated all that was right and wonderful about the world.

"Vanished," he said, "as if they'd never been."

"Which is a state of affairs I dearly wish, Your Ladyship. Now will you retreat from Brannock Castle?" Mr. Ahern stepped out from the shadows, his rat face twisted into an expression of annoyance.

"Yes," she said simply, smiling at the little man. How very tolerable he appeared at the moment. But then the world was a wondrous place, was it not?

Marshall was beside her.

* * *

They walked out into the courtyard, and every single one of the men from Ambrose began to cheer.

Marshall stopped, stunned.

"Is it the number of men that amazes you?" she asked, putting her hand on his sleeve. "Or is it their loyalty?"

He turned to her. "You *were* prepared to go to war, weren't you?"

"I still am."

He frowned. "Against whom?"

"First, Dominic Ahern. Now you, I think," she said agreeably.

She turned and placed both her hands flat against his chest.

He looked intently at her face, as if he wanted to memorize it, keep it in his mind for all time. She was so beautiful and so fierce. Her loyalty made him feel humble in a way he'd never before felt.

"Why me?"

"I'm a very intelligent woman, Marshall, one blessed with a questioning mind. I knew that there were secrets that shamed you. You are, after all, not a god but a human man. A human man," she repeated. "But does that mean that you're unworthy to love?"

He didn't answer.

"There may come a time in the future when I shame myself again, when I harm someone else, when I commit an act of extreme stupidity. I would hope that you'd forgive me, knowing that I'm fallible. Isn't that what love is all about? Seeing the flaws of others and discounting them?"

She was oblivious to the men of Ambrose watching them.

"Do you love me?"

He silently saluted her bravery. He didn't know if he would have had the courage to ask that question.

"I once thought love was for foolish boys. Those who think themselves immortal. Or those who have no sins for which to atone. I've believed that I've had too many sins to be worthy of love."

She grabbed his hands, holding them imprisoned between hers.

"Why do you punish yourself so much? Why are you, of all people, subject to a different set of rules? Why do you have to be better than anyone else? Stronger? Braver?"

He looked out at the landscape, focusing on it rather than her. Words came so much more easily when the object of them wasn't standing right beside him.

He didn't care for the ache that resided somewhere in his chest, an indication that emotions too long buried had been reluctantly jarred open like a trunk with a rusty hinge.

Davina didn't move, but he could feel her tension, as if she drew herself up in a small ball to be less of a target.

"I said that I once thought myself unworthy of love. But since you came into my life with your stubbornness—may I call it obstinacy?—I've become accustomed to the idea of it."

She stared down at her clenched hands, and if he could have, without revealing that his own hand trembled, he would have tilted her chin up so that he could stare into those luminous eyes of hers.

"Come back to Ambrose with me. Come and live there and keep me sane. Come and love me, and I will love you with all the power and the strength of which I'm capable. To refuse you, to refuse love would be the true definition of madness, I think."

She stepped closer, lifted both his hands to her lips, cupping the backs of his hands within her palms as if in offering. Then she bent her head and kissed the center of his scarred palm, a kiss so soft and sweet that it speared his heart. It was not an act of passion as much as one of benediction.

If they were in a different place, he would have pulled her into his arms and kissed her again. But the men of Ambrose surrounded him, dressed in kilts and holding spears, claymores, and dirks.

"It's a stirring sight to see us all outfitted for war. You've stripped Ambrose of its weapons."

She smiled and nodded.

"I confess there's a great deal missing from Ambrose. As well as Mrs. Murray," she added. "She seems to have departed with some alacrity. Not that I mind. I'm rather happy about the event."

He stared down at her, a dozen pictures flashing into his mind. Mrs. Murray with the ubiquitous decanter of wine. Mrs. Murray with her soft-eyed glances, reminding him of earlier days. Mrs. Murray with her excessive servility.

"It was the wine," he said, all the pieces suddenly fitting into place.

"The wine?"

"Something was in the wine. I haven't had any

since I've been here, and I've no hallucinations of any kind."

The thought struck him as loud as thunder.

Before his marriage, he'd taken to sitting in his library, musing upon his inability to sleep. A glass or two of wine was his habit. He'd never associated the wine with the visions he'd experienced, but then he'd never read his mother's journal, either.

"She used to give my mother her medicine. It would have been easy enough to do the same to me."

"Mrs. Murray? She's Leanne?" Her eyebrow arched upward. "She was your mother's companion?"

He nodded.

"Why did she become the housekeeper at Ambrose, Marshall? Because you felt guilty about seducing her?"

There was enough truth in the accusation that he felt uncomfortable.

"She didn't want to go back to Edinburgh."

"Of course she didn't," Davina said. "She was in love with you."

He glanced at her. "I doubt that was the case."

"For a well-respected diplomat, you're incredibly obtuse, Marshall."

He would have taken umbrage at that comment but for the fact that she had just brought an army to rescue him.

"I never experienced the hallucinations around you," he said slowly. "Only once, when I went back to my room and had a glass of wine. But I'd eaten prior to that, which is probably why the visions weren't as bad."

Once he'd been married, he'd spent fewer nights in his library dreading sleep. Instead he'd been with Davina, allowing himself to be thoroughly charmed by her wit, mind, and passion. When Davina had returned to Edinburgh, he'd resorted to his previous habits. Only then had the ghosts returned in earnest, exhorting him to join them.

He bloody well wasn't going mad.

She stared at him in wonder. "Why did we never think of that before?"

"But you did," he said, gently reminding her.

"I think I would have said anything at the time," she admitted. "I was desperate for answers. I didn't want you to be mad."

"But why would Leanne do that?" At her look, he said, "So she poisoned me out of love? That hardly makes sense."

"What better way to keep you dependent on her than to render you insane?" She eyed him with an irritated glance. "Or she could have been poisoning you from spite. Did you ruin her, Marshall?"

He hadn't the slightest idea, but he wasn't about to make that remark.

"Why did she send me off to an asylum? Or was it her decision?"

They shared a look.

"I think it's time to have a talk with my uncle as well," he said.

"Well, I sincerely hope that Mrs. Murray has gone a very long distance," Davina said.

"Or else you would be tempted to go after her?"

"I've been deprived of a war," she said. "But surely a small battle would not be amiss. And I would very much like to engage in battle with Mrs. Murray. Was she ever truly married, or did she simply take the title to become more respectable?"

He shook his head. "I don't know," he said.

He held out his hand, and she took it without comment. But she was smiling, and her eyes were sparkling.

He wanted to kiss her softly and tuck her under his arm and keep her there for the next millennium or so, just until he grew accustomed to her presence.

He led her across the courtyard. A few men pushed their way to the front of the crowd. Marshall stopped and greeted the men individually. From time to time he'd clamp a man on his shoulder, expressing his thanks.

One man, however, startled him so much that he could do nothing but stare.

"Jacobs?"

"Your Lordship."

His valet was attired in a kilt and gray shirt, and holding a dirk, all the world like a warlike chipmunk.

"It's good to see you, Jacobs."

Jacobs smiled. "And you, Your Lordship." In the next second, he raised the dirk and rushed forward.

Marshall threw up his arm to block the knife and felt the blade slice through his shirt and the skin beneath.

He feinted left, and when his valet struck out in that direction, Marshall dove for Jacobs, his shoulder a battering ram into the man's stomach. In seconds, Jacobs was on the ground, the knife skittering across the dirt.

"What the hell is going on?" Marshall asked, pinning Jacobs to the ground. His arm was bleeding, but not badly. A little deeper, however, and Jacobs could have done real damage.

"You killed him," Jacobs said. "I know you did. I heard you."

There was no reason to ask the question. Marshall knew that the only person Jacobs would kill for was Daniel.

"I sent him to China with you, and you killed him."

Marshall reared back and looked at the man he'd known all his life. "I didn't kill him, Jacobs."

"You promised to keep him safe."

How many times had he made that banal comment? How many reassurances had he given, how many platitudes had he uttered in his life of diplomacy? Too many. Words always meant something, if not to the speaker, then to the listener. Jacobs had somehow believed that Marshall had the power of life and death, that being the Earl of Lorne also gave him the ability to spare Daniel from torture, and ultimately death.

If he could have saved Daniel, Marshall would have.

"I'm sorry, Jacobs. He was under my command, and I should have protected him. That I didn't, that I couldn't, will be a regret I shall have to live with all my days."

"I'm supposed to be content with that? Regret?" Jacobs stared up at him, his face twisted into a mask of hatred. "You should have died along with him," Jacobs said.

"And you tried to ensure I did, didn't you?" He stood, looking down at the valet. "Leanne wasn't the only one who knew my mother took Chinese herbs to help her pain, was she?"

Jacobs looked up at him. Two men reached down and hauled the valet to his feet. "You should suffer for what you did."

"I have, even without your intervention, Jacobs."

Marshall turned and began to walk away, intent on reaching Davina. The look on her face, however, changed from concern to alarm as she stared behind him.

"Marshall!"

One moment the solid ground was beneath his feet, and the next, he was flying over the end of the promontory, the dizzying vista of the valley below him. The earth sloped just before it ended, and it was that fact that saved him. He fell, hard, began to slip, feet and hands clawing for something to hold on to. Davina's screams echoed his own panic.

A chunk of slate, chipped and broken from centuries of exposure to the elements, jutted from the promontory, and he gripped it like a lifeline, his feet swinging free.

Evidently Jacobs had wrestled free of the men who'd held him, and pushed Marshall off the edge of the cliff. The momentum had carried Jacobs over as well, because he was only a few feet above Marshall, his arms around a boulder, his legs kicking at Marshall's hands.

Marshall heard his name, knew Davina was calling to him, but he could spare her only a glance. Her face was stark white, her beautiful eyes wide with terror.

Not now. Not when he'd just begun to believe in the future. If death hadn't taken him in China or in the last year, Marshall wasn't about to die now. Not here. Not now.

A rope was tossed in his direction, slapped against his face, and hung beside him. Marshall heard his men above him shouting encouragement, but above all he heard Davina's voice.

The earth began to move, a low creaking sound the only warning. The boulder Jacobs was using to hold on to started to pull free of the earth. Jacobs didn't scream; he didn't make a sound as he fell. He was simply gone, vanished into the air.

Marshall looked up at the sea of faces above him. He gripped the rope with first one hand and then the other, and hooked a foot in the trailing length of it. The cut that Jacobs had inflicted was bleeding profusely, but Marshall shut out the pain, and the protests in the muscles in his arms and chest. An inch at a time, he made his way to the top. Arms reached out to pull him to safety. Seconds later, he was flat on his back on the ground, Davina holding him, rocking him back and forth with his face pressed into her bodice.

Not an altogether unpleasant place to be.

He lay there for a moment, and then sat up, wrapping his uninjured arm around her as he surveyed his rescuers.

"It seems you've saved me not once but twice," he said to the men of Ambrose.

More than one man looked in Davina's direction, and he knew what they didn't say. He stood, his legs still a little shaky, and held out his hand to her.

* * *

There were some things that should be marked on a summer day: the purity of morning light, the gentle breeze whirling among the rocks and weeds, the emerald green of leaves and grasses, the brown of the tree trunks, the brilliant blue of the sky, and white, fluffy clouds being pulled apart by upward winds.

Davina could smell dust, and a hint of rain, and flowers as sweet as a child's prayer. She felt the warmth of the sun on her face, and the usual discomfort of her shoes. The breeze tickled her nose and made her want to sneeze.

Her footsteps were measured and calm. No one could tell that she could barely walk for the trembling in her legs. Her heart was racing frantically, and her hands still shook.

She'd almost lost him again.

Once they were in the carriage, however, she ceased being circumspect. She didn't care if Nora or Jim witnessed her tears, or if they thought she was too demonstrative with Marshall. She simply didn't care. The two of them would simply have to get used to the idea of her being excessively cordial around her husband. Her husband. Was there ever a better title for anyone? Love. Perhaps that was better.

Well. Her aunt certainly wouldn't like this. Her husband was sliding her onto his lap. Instead of correcting him, however, she wrapped her arms around his neck and wept against his neck.

"Davina. It's all right."

"I almost lost you again," she said, clutching his shirt

with both hands. When he flinched, she sat back and stared at his bloody shirt in horror. "Twice. I almost lost you twice."

"You'll never lose me, I promise."

"Your arm needs treating," she said.

"You can be my physician once we reach Ambrose."

She nodded, separating the cloth to look at the wound more closely. Normally she didn't mind the sight of blood, but his injury made her shiver as if it had been done to her. No, it was worse than if it had been done to her. He was hurt.

He wrapped his uninjured arm around her, and held her close.

"It's all right, my love. Truly it is."

She nodded. "I know. You've suffered worse. You've endured so much more. But I don't want you hurt," she said fiercely. "You should never be hurt again."

She truly didn't care that Nora and Jim were no doubt listening with great interest.

"I shall promise to be very careful from this moment on," he said, smiling.

Before she could answer, he wrapped his arms around her and pulled her head down for a series of very, very passionate kisses.

All in front of the servants.

Oh my.

Epilogue

"**A**re you very certain that Mrs. Murray isn't guilty of something?" Davina asked, looking from Marshall to her aunt.

Theresa looked amused, as did Marshall. She really should have been irritated at their response, but she was still basking in the relief that Marshall was alive and well.

Two weeks had passed since the siege of the Black Castle, and Marshall had been healthy ever since. They'd found a supply of a brownish-looking powder in Jacobs's room and could only guess that it was the source of Marshall's dreams and hallucinations.

As to Mrs. Murray, she hadn't disappeared entirely. She'd taken a coach to Edinburgh and from there a train to London.

"Mrs. Murray's only sin was in accepting a post from one of your wedding guests," Theresa said. "Without giving proper notice."

"I still think we should count the silver," Davina said, unconvinced.

"However, if she hadn't sent word to Garrow," Theresa said, "there's every possibility that Jacobs might have succeeded in poisoning Marshall. As it was, taking him away from Ambrose truly saved Marshall's life."

Davina considered that for a moment. As much as she wanted to refute Theresa's words, there was something in what she said.

"Very well, she did something correct, but only accidentally."

Marshall reached out and squeezed her hand. They were seated in Theresa's home, the parlor warm against the stormy day. She and Marshall sat on the sofa together, with Theresa opposite them.

Her aunt looked tired, but then she'd just recently returned from London.

Davina didn't know quite what to say to the news she'd brought. Garrow obviously needed to be punished for the hideousness of his deeds, but he was still Marshall's uncle.

She glanced at him. In the last two weeks they'd truly become wed. She slept in his room every night, the mattresses having been taken from the walls. She'd learned that Marshall had a deliciously wicked sense of humor, an appreciation for the most aromatic of cheeses, and an intellectual curiosity that she could only admire.

Marshall had arranged for Jacobs's body to be returned to Ambrose, and the man was buried in the small churchyard in the neighboring village. They had attended the short service, and when it was done, Marshall had spoken with the cleric and paid for a grave marker to be erected.

Not once had he commented on Jacobs's actions. It was not until she had broached the subject that he spoke of his valet.

"He was grieving. Sometimes pain can make a man do stupid things. If he'd talked to me about Daniel, I would have known how much he blamed me, but he rarely mentioned him."

Could she have been as understanding, or as empathetic? Probably not, because Jacobs had almost succeeded in his undertaking—to kill Marshall.

"Garrow should be punished for giving the order to send Marshall to an asylum," Davina said.

"I think his fate is decided," Marshall said. "The Chinese will see to it that Garrow is punished for his crimes."

"How can you say that? You were their prisoner; you know what they'll do to him."

He looked away, staring off into the distance as if to see the past. "I do," he finally said. "But I also know that when a man chooses an action, he chooses the result as well."

"Spoken like a true diplomat," Theresa said, smiling. "And a wise man."

"I doubt Garrow chose to be surrendered to the Chinese," Davina said. "I doubt he saw that far ahead."

"Then who should be blamed?" Theresa asked. "The British for believing that slavery is abhorrent? Or Garrow for being too narrow-minded to see the consequences of his actions?"

"Garrow," Davina said. "For selling people as if they were vases and boxes." She sighed. "But we are a family, aren't we? I've a reputation for shocking behavior. Marshall is mad, and Garrow is the worst of us all."

"You don't include me," Theresa said.

Davina eyed her aunt with some amusement. "I think, perhaps, you are the most surprising. You tell a lovely tale about how Garrow was caught, but I think there is more to the story than we'll ever know."

Theresa only smiled.

Author's Notes

The Earl of Lorne's adventures in China were mirrored after real historical events in which representatives of the Crown were imprisoned, tortured, and killed. The remaining prisoners were freed only after the Summer Palace in Peking was burned to the ground.

Opium is highly addictive, inducing passivity in the smoker. Heavy smokers have an average life expectancy of five years from the time they become addicted. It is estimated that there were almost forty million opium addicts in China by 1880.

Many Chinese herbs have hallucinogenic properties—among them Yang Jin Hua, Nao Yang Hua, Gan Di Huang, and Hong Hua. What Julianna Ross took for pain, and what made Marshall so ill, was probably corydalis, which has both analgesic qualities and can produce hallucinations.

In the nineteenth century a flourishing trade known as the Coolie Trade existed that was tantamount to slavery. Chinese peasants were kidnapped and sold for the sex trade. Or they were offered a five-year indenture, during which they were overworked and treated abysmally.

In Egypt an experienced scribe often wrote down instructions on life for the younger scribes. However, Hamenup was my invention, as well as his poetry.

In nineteenth-century Scotland, an emergency certificate could be issued by one doctor to keep a mental patient under observation for three days. After that time, a certificate signed by two physicians was required. Private asylums were created to treat patients who could not—or weren't wished to be—cared for at home. Brannock Castle is modeled after one such private asylum.

Unforgettable, enthralling love stories,
sparkling with passion and adventure
from Romance's bestselling authors